A
Forbidden
Romance

IN
Desperate
RUIN

G. ELENA

Copyright © 2023 by G. Elena

All rights reserved.

No part of this book may be reproduced in any form or by any electronic or mechanical means, including information storage and retrieval systems, without written permission from the author, except for the use of brief quotations in a book review.

Edited by Jenni Brady

Proofread by Cassidy Hudspeth

Cover Design by Covers by Jules coversbyjules.crd.co

For a complete list of content warnings, please check out:

www.graceelenaauthor.com

❦ Created with Vellum

For those who never felt enough or worthy of love.
You are enough.
You are worthy of love.
Never doubt it for a second.

Playlist

Someone's Love Song by Peytan Porter
False God by Taylor Swift
pov by Ariana Grande
Delicate by Taylor Swift
BLENDER by 5 Seconds of Summer
Mayores by Becky G, Bad Bunny
Call It What You Want by Taylor Swift
Bitch Back by Olivia O'Brien, FLETCHER
Meddle About by Chase Atlantic
Write Your Name by Selena Gomez
Wherever I May Roam by J. Balvin, Metallica
Sugar by alayna
Volví by Aventura, Bad Bunny
Cool for the Summer by Demi Lovato
Dusk Till Dawn by ZAYN, Sia
Dress by Taylor Swift

Author's Note

Clementine is a sexual assault survivor. Her trauma is discussed in this novel as well as her attempts to cope in not only healthy ways, but damaging habits as well. Although the assault is not on page, it is embedded into the way Clementine is written.

She is a warrior, despite her scars—visible and invisible.

I hope you, as the reader, are able to take this time to acknowledge if this book is right for you. It is my duty as an author to offer you the warning that this book might be difficult if you've been through what Clementine has.

Please take care of your mental health and your heart. Always.

Love,
Grace Elena

Resources

National Sexual Assault Hotline
1-800-656-4673

National Sexual Violence Resource Center
https://www.nsvrc.org/

National Resources for Sexual Assault Survivors and Their Loved Ones
https://www.rainn.org/national-resources-sexual-assault-survivors-and-their-loved-ones

Content Warnings

In Desperate Ruin has content for a mature audience over the age of 18.

Warnings include: explicit sexual scenes, slow burn, insta-lust, mental health topics such as anxiety and ptsd, mention of sexual assault, mention of separation, minimal self harm on page, mention of past self harm, drinking, cursing, jealousy, and kinks such as praise, size, spit, belly bulge, daddy, and breeding.

Chapter One

CLEMENTINE

TEARS BRIM MY EYES, cascading slowly down my cheeks. I want to believe that the world *isn't* crashing down on me.

It feels worse. Much worse.

How would anyone feel about their one shot at getting out of this damn town, this damn *country*, being pulled from their reach? It's anxiety-inducing, and I hate that it's become my reality.

"Honey, are you there?" my mom's voice comes through the phone that's still clutched tightly in my hand. I blink a few times before taking a deep breath and bringing it back to my ear.

"Yeah, I'm here."

She sighs on the other end. "I'm sorry."

It's not her fault; it's not really anyone's fault. I want to scream at her, sure, but she doesn't deserve it.

"I can't stay home?" I ask again, knowing the answer.

She's quiet for a moment. "No, honey. I already told your Tía that she can stay there with her family."

My eyes shut tightly, and I find myself latching my free hand onto my bare thigh. My nails *dig* into the skin, leaving marks–

soon to draw blood. She's still talking, but I've tuned her out. The pain distracts me for as long as I can take before I need to clean an open wound.

Feeding into this vice is the only way to stop my thoughts from spiraling. I have nowhere to stay—that's my predicament.

The study abroad program at my university canceled at the last minute with their plans to go to Greece. It was going to be *three* months of sunshine, beautiful landscapes, all the food, and the best time with my best friend, Rosa. That was rare at Frontier University, and I got accepted. I'd be able to finish quite a few credits while there, which was the main appeal for me.

Going to Greece was just the cherry on top.

My mom has been to Greece four times now that she's remarried after Dad died. She loved it so much that she wanted to make another trip out to see me while she and my stepdad traveled Europe this summer. It would be nice to also see him again, I won't lie. I've only seen him on holidays when I travel back home to Maryland. He moved us into this nice lake house once he married my mom when I was fifteen.

College kept me busy to the point where I didn't even have time to go home for the summer. The first summer, I volunteered at an animal shelter, and they gladly paid for summer campus housing. The second summer, I worked at the University for their new student orientation program, and it allowed me to stay on campus for free. Now, this third and final summer before senior year, I don't have *anywhere* to go.

With Tía Selene taking over the lake house with her husband and *four* kids, there would be no room for me. Even if I wanted to go there, I'd be sleeping on the damn floor instead of the room that's reserved for me. I didn't have the fight in me to call my Tía and ask if she could change her plans. Their house flooded in Florida, and since she's my dad's only sibling, she reached out to us. My stepdad, Declan, didn't hesitate at all to open his house to them, which was very kind of him to do.

It didn't make sense for him to say no since they were going to travel all summer in Europe, and I was supposed to be in Greece. So, I *really* couldn't be mad at them. This was just the reality of how much my life sucked.

"Clem!" my mom's voice breaks my thoughts. I pull the phone away, tapping the screen softly to see that we've been on the phone for a solid thirty minutes.

"Sorry, I'm just stressed," I confess.

"Did they refund you yet? You can see if they can use that check for campus housing, *mija*."

I roll my eyes at her attempt to call me her daughter in Spanish. After my dad died, she stopped trying to talk to me in Spanish unless it was to scold me or comfort me in not-so-comforting times. Although I've got her blonde hair, I've got my dad's dark brown eyes and tan skin matched with tons of freckles that I used to get made fun of for growing up.

I love my mom, I really do, but there are times when she does things that make me miss my dad so much. Like talking to me in Spanish. It felt like an *us* thing she was trying to insert herself into. My dad only spoke to me in Spanish. I miss our conversations.

"*Todavía no. No es suficiente dinero, necesitaré más*," I tell her.

She's silent for a moment, and I crack a smile. She doesn't remember Spanish because she doesn't keep up with it.

"Translate, Clem, this is serious," she scolds.

"*Okay*," I sigh dramatically. "I said, 'not yet. It's not enough money, and I'll need more'."

"Did it increase from last summer?"

"No, but remember, since it's a study abroad program during the summer term, it's much cheaper than a regular semester. Still expensive, but not as much as it could've been. It wouldn't cover the cost of summer housing."

"Shit, baby, I'm sorry."

"It's fine. I'll figure something out. I'll just find a motel—"

"Absolutely not. I can ask Declan."

"No!" I shuffle to grab the phone. "Please don't. You guys already paid for my study abroad. It's not fair to ask for more. I'll just see if there's a friend around town and ask if I can use the check to pay for some kind of rent if a motel is too expensive."

"What about…" My mom's voice trails off as she tries to remember how many friends I have.

I don't have many. After sophomore year, I secluded myself a lot. I dropped out of the sorority I was in and contemplated changing my major or even *transferring*.

I stuck it out, though, and am really enjoying being a marketing major. It's got fun classes, and I'm set to start an internship in the Fall.

"Rosalía!" My mom's voice finally screams through the phone, and I have to move it slightly away from my ear before I lose my hearing.

"Mom…"

"What? She lives in town, doesn't she?"

"She does." I smooth my hand over my thigh. I take a few deep breaths and think about it.

Frontier University is nestled in the tight-knit town of Sunny Cove, Alabama, near one of the massive lakes. We're close to Birmingham, which is the only big city nearby. We take trips there sometimes for birthday dinners or shopping, but this small town has enough to keep us entertained, especially with it being a University town. Rosa just happens to be a Sunny Cove native, but I haven't been able to reach out to see if she'll stay in town after our trip was canceled.

"Well?" My mom breaks my thoughts once again.

I clear my throat.

"I'll have to see if she's decided to stay after everything that happened. She was going to join me too, remember?"

"Oh, right," she replies.

"I'll figure it out," I reassure her. But my voice cracks, and I know she hears it. Her motherly instinct kicks in.

"Do you want to join us in Europe?"

"No! God no. I don't want to be a third wheel the entire summer. You guys planned this for months, and we all thought I'd be in Greece."

"Yeah, but we also planned to visit you there. We can buy your ticket. It's not a big deal."

"No," I argue.

"Are you sure, Clem?" Her voice is softer now.

"Yes. Please go have your fun with Declan. I'm going to ask for the check today and see what Rosa has planned."

"Alright, baby. Call me if there are any hiccups. We leave in two days."

"I know, I will. Love you."

She says it back and hangs up. I place the phone on the table and glance around the dorm room. I'm supposed to be out already. All of my things, except for a suitcase full of summer clothes, have been shipped back to Maryland. Declan and Mom didn't want to waste any time with me stressing about moving out of the dorm room before my trip. It was a thoughtful gesture, but now I feel like I'm going to have a panic attack without my things.

I get up from the chair and pace the empty room, save for the standard dorm room essentials. The bed is stripped, and my lip quivers. Fuck.

They're expecting my dorm key in the lobby downstairs any second now.

What am I going to do?

My legs shake, and I can't help myself with the dramatics and lean against a wall near the dresser and sink to the floor. I clutch my knees to my chest and press my forehead against them. My heart is already racing, my palms are starting to sweat immensely, and all irrational fears come to the forefront of my mind.

I try to complete the five senses grounding technique I learned in therapy a while ago, but this room is too suffocating to focus. My hands go to my bare thighs again, and this time, they draw blood.

MY HANDS SHAKE as I pat them against my thighs, stomach, chest, and then my cheeks. Why am I nervous? It's just my best friend.

I've got the check in my pocket. What I don't have? Courage. It was fleeting the moment I got news from the admissions office that I could only take *one* of the four courses on campus this summer. The other three were offered solely to the study abroad program. Everything is ruined, and now I'm standing like a beggar in front of my best friend's house.

To make matters worse, I've shown up unannounced.

I couldn't muster the confidence to call or text her about my situation. I felt like a fool and there was no doubt in my head that she'd give me those brown eyes of pity that she does so well for the animals in the shelter.

It wasn't far off from how I felt–a lost puppy. Kicked to the curb with a check in my pocket that might not even be enough for what I was asking for.

I try to shake the nerves before I press the doorbell once. The chime travels through the two-story house, and my feet shuffle in place. I wait a few moments before I start to panic and take a step back. I turn on my heels and walk down the pathway that connects to their driveway. There isn't a car parked, so I know her dad isn't home.

There's the sound of a door creaking open behind me, and I

halt in my steps. I turn slightly and see Rosa with her dark brunette hair in rollers. Her brows raise, and I take a deep breath.

"Clementine? I thought you'd be on your way to the airport?" She takes a step toward me, and I close our distance so she doesn't have to walk barefoot on the pavement.

Her brown eyes follow mine, and I try to steady my breathing. "My Tía is staying at the house with her whole family. House flooded or something."

She studies me for a moment before taking another step closer. She slowly grabs my hand that's planted to my side. With gentle hands, she pulls my fingers and rubs them in a reassuring manner.

"That's stressful. Want to come inside? My dad's not home, working on a huge project this week. He'll be here for dinner, though."

I nod my head. "S-sure. You don't mind?"

She smiles. "Of course not, Clem. *Mi casa es tu casa.*" Without another word, she pulls me into her home and I forget how beautiful the Santos house is. The foyer is bright, with tons of light peeking through windows around the door. I haven't been in this house much to remember it since we have the dorms so close, but I've seen enough with random movie nights and while FaceTiming her during holidays. She invited me once for Thanksgiving, but that was when Declan had big plans to surprise my mom and me with a trip elsewhere.

We navigate ourselves to her kitchen, and it's quite a spacious one. It's got a marble island in the middle with four bar stools on one side. She heads to the large fridge to the left and pulls out a pitcher of cold water. She then grabs two glasses from a nearby cabinet. I thank her as she pushes a glass toward me.

"I forgot how nice it is in here," I mumble, looking around to where the kitchen connects with the living room. There's an expensive speaker system there. We tried watching a scary movie last semester on Halloween weekend, but it was so loud and eerie that we had to shut it off. Her dad never seemed to be home whenever I got the chance to come over, so I've yet to meet him.

"Yeah, my dad is proud of his work. He plans to renovate the basement so I can have it to myself once I graduate. That's if I don't run away to LA or New York."

I widen my eyes. "That's so nice of him."

She nods. "He's great. Though he is a little pissed that I'll be home for the summer. Not the fact that I'll be around, but that I'll have to retake those classes somehow. Who knows."

"Rosa..." I start, feeling my heart rate increase with each passing second. "I have to ask you something."

"Sure, *nena*. What's up?" She leans her elbows on the marble island and peers at me with expectant eyes. I shift on the barstool uncomfortably as I rack my brain for the right way to break the news to her.

"I—uh. I need your help. I have this." I pull out the check from the front pocket of my shorts.

The check almost burns in my hands as I drop it on the counter and let her grab it. Her eyes widen as she reads the amount of zeros on it. *Okay,* it's not a lot. But it is to us, at least.

"Woah, I forgot how much it costs to study abroad."

"It's not as much compared to a normal semester, but yes. It's not mine to keep, though."

"So, why are you showing it to me?" she asks, placing the check back down. Without another thought, my left hand moves to go under the counter and latch onto my thigh, fingers already knowing where to go. I know I have to stop and let the earlier marks heal, but today's been too stressful to even bother with the thought.

This is the only coping method that keeps me from doing anything worse. My therapist would be upset if she heard I still self-harm, but what else can I do in such a stressful time?

"I—uh..."

"Clementine? What's wrong?" She straightens her posture, and her brows raise. I feel like throwing up. I have to spit out the words before I change my mind and run out.

"It's way too expensive to stay in the dorms this summer and now it's too late to apply to any campus jobs, and I really don't know where to stay. Yes, I have this check, but it wouldn't be enough to get a hotel for three months. There's no room back in the lake house for me, even if I tried to go back. My parents offered to let me join them in Europe, but that's just too much to ask of them. I have nowhere else to go, and you know I wouldn't be asking you or your father if it wasn't urgent." My words come out a mile a minute, and Rosa focuses her eyes on my lips to catch everything.

She's quiet as she takes in my final sentence. "So, what are you asking? Clementine, you know I'll always help you out. You and your family were there for me when I needed it the most."

I think back to when her parents separated right when college started. It was a dark time for Rosa. She was still living at home at the time before she moved on campus that Spring and roomed with me. My mom and Declan offered to take us all to California for spring break, and as much as Rosalía fought not to waste their money on her, they wouldn't take no for an answer.

It was a good way for her to stay away from her home, which was going through ruin. Even though her parents weren't married, they were together her whole life. Her mother moved out in haste, leaving her dad in an empty house. That's when he started renovating the place the summer after freshman year.

He did what he could, in Rosa's words, to have her come back home and be with him. It didn't work, though, as much as he'd like. She decided that living on campus was the best for her relationship with her parents. She barely speaks to her mother now, who whisked herself away to some town in Montana and is now in a relationship with a dude who owns a ranch.

"Can I give your dad this check and possibly stay here for the summer? I'll help with chores, mow the lawn, anything."

Rosalía's lips twitch before she barks out a laugh. "Mow the lawn?"

I nod.

"I'm serious, Rosa!"

"I'll ask him, but don't mention the lawn part. He doesn't like anyone messing with his lawn care, apparently. He got into a heated argument with his neighbor, who has a lawn mowing business."

I can't help but laugh too. "Your dad seems funnier than I remember."

"He's annoying, that's what he is." She rolls her eyes, but her face stays amicable. "Why don't you come for dinner when he's back from work? Wait, where's your stuff? Did it all get shipped back?"

I shake my head. "No, they're letting me keep my one suitcase in the lobby. I almost begged them to let me stay for as long as I could, but they seemed stressed. I overheard one of them saying how there were other study abroad programs that flaked as well."

"I can't believe they let us go through all those meetings and sign up for classes just to pull the rug out from under us!" she wails.

It was stressful for all of us, but it could be even more stressful if tonight doesn't go well. If her dad doesn't let me stay, then what?

"It sucks, but thanks, Rosa. I'll go get my suitcase and meet you back here! Unless you want me back closer to dinner?"

She smiles with a hint of red on her cheeks. "Yeah, I actually have a date with Garrett from the program. Did I forget to tell you I hung out with him a few times after our study-abroad meetings?"

I gasp. "What! You forgot! No wonder you guys kept ogling each other during those meetings."

The blush turns more scarlet on her tan skin. "Don't mention it tonight, okay? Haven't really found a way to tell my *very* protective father about my dating life."

"My lips are sealed." I smile before I get up and place my empty glass in the sink. She gives me a side hug before I head out of her house and call an Uber back to campus. My stomach fills with flutters, but the nervous kind. I'm terrified to know what will happen to me this summer. It'll either be fun and free with my best friend, or I'm going to be a stressed-out mess.

I hope for the best as the Uber arrives and I get in.

Chapter Two

ARLO

MY FINGERS, palms, and wrists are caked in dirt and remnants of oil. Today was one of the more important days of a huge renovation project we have with a client that owns land about half an hour from Sunny Cove. They wanted the house to keep its 'farm' feel while creating a more modern touch inside.

It wasn't too big of a job for me and my men, but it was tough and prolonged work. We were there from six in the morning until almost seven at night. I had to call it quits the moment I realized the time. I promised Rosie I'd grill some steak and make her favorite salsa for dinner, and I can't let her down.

I try to remove the dirt from my hands with wipes I keep in my truck for this exact reason. It takes almost four wipes to get the grime and dirt off to a reasonable state where I can drive without my palms slipping off the wheel. The last thing I need is to crash and miss out on dinner with my daughter. I've spent too long trying to rebuild my relationship with her, I can't chance it.

She'd probably throw the salsa ingredients on top of my grave instead of flowers out of spite. Rosie used to love taco nights growing up, so I try to make it home whenever I promise her it.

It doesn't take me too long to get home and see that some lights are on. I park the truck before grabbing the cooler from the backseat and hopping out. I almost forget the baseball cap on the dash, slipping it on backward.

I slam the truck door before heading to the front door. I used to walk through the garage, but it's become such a hoarding mess after the separation that it's the last place I want to be. One day, I'll have the strength to go in there and clean it out. But not today. I've got steak to make.

The house is quiet in the foyer as I slip off my work boots. I don't miss the suitcase near the coat hanger and I pinch my brows. It might've been Rosie's suitcase she packed before hearing about the cancellation of her study abroad trip to Greece.

I head to the kitchen, hearing some giggles upstairs, and smile. Rosie was torn that her school canceled the trip, but I took it as a sign that it would be the perfect time to bond with her. Ever since the split, it felt like she pushed her mother and me away to cope. I didn't want to force her to communicate if that was her way of healing, so I gave her space. But it's been 3 years, and I want to repair things.

My feet are loud as I make my way down the hall from the kitchen, after cleaning the cooler, to the master bedroom to strip off my dirty clothes. The method is meticulous: there's a hamper right near the door so I can get inside, strip, and not leave any muddy prints or falling pieces of debris on the nice floor. I worked on them relentlessly last summer, so I'd be damned if a muddy print got on it. Beside the hamper, there are flip-flops so I can walk easily to the bathroom without making a mess.

I'm so busy during the week that I rarely want to spend my weekends cleaning this room because of the mess I make, so I stick to this system. I even have a specific body wash for the grime, oil, and mud that might still be on me while I shower.

The house is still quiet as I head to the kitchen after my

shower and whip out the prepared steak: arrachera. It's seasoned with salt, pepper, tons of lime, cilantro, onion, and even some orange slices. The longer you marinate it, the better it tastes, according to *Mamá Santos* recipe. As I chop more onion and cilantro for toppings, I start the salsa as well. There's music drifting from the living room of a playlist I'm not familiar with. It was already playing softly on the TV, so I just turned it up.

I hear footsteps heading into the kitchen, and I turn to see Rosie's small frame as she smiles widely, but her eyes tell me something different.

"*Mija*, I didn't forget about the steak," I rush to tell her as I continue to prep the salsa ingredients and take out a pot to boil the tomatillos in. She watches me for a moment before she clears her throat.

"I have something to talk to you about," she starts. I give her a small smile as I try to stay concentrated on the dinner. It's already nearing nine p.m. and I hate to know that she was probably looking forward to her favorite meal since six. There's a moment of slight worry that I'm focusing on the wrong thing right now, and I silently pray that it's just about the late dinner and nothing too serious. I hear her let out a heavy sigh.

"What's up, baby?" I ask, grabbing what I need for the grill that I forgot to start. Fuck, I need to get the charcoal from the garage.

"Dad, please," she says sternly. I stop in my tracks with the steak on a plate in one hand against my ribs and the other full of grilling tools. Her brown eyes sparkle like her mother's, and I look away briefly before gazing back at her.

"*Mande?*"

She nibbles on her lip for a moment before taking a deep breath. "My friend is here, in my room. She was supposed to go on that study abroad trip to Greece with me…"

"That's nice she's over. She's more than welcome to join us for dinner."

"That's not it…" Her voice fades, and I pinch my brows. She takes another deep breath. "Long story short, she can't go back home to Maryland, and she's kind of stuck here. Can she stay?"

"Like for the night? Of course." I smile.

Rosie huffs out a breath, and I wonder what the hell I'm doing wrong. I look down at the steak and then back at her.

"*No. Escúchame, por favor.*"

"I'm listening," I say with a deeper tone to my voice. I wait for her to gather her thoughts before she spits out whatever is getting her caught up in a web of nerves.

"Clementine, my friend, has a check. Since the program was meant for the entire summer, she wants to know if she can stay with us for a month or two, if not longer, based on her situation. She'll pay for it with the refund they gave her."

Now I'm the one biting my lip in nerves. That's a lot to ask for, but I can see how much this means to my daughter with the way she is looking at me with puppy dog eyes and nibbling on her own lip.

Rosie and I are slowly getting to a good start in our relationship, and I don't want to fuck anything up. Having her friend stay with us for a summer won't be *too* bad. I'm busy as hell during the week, and girls their age go out on weekends, so I'd have the place to myself…

"Ask me again once I've made the steak," I tell her with a warm smile. I don't want to make promises so quickly, plus my mind is on the dinner.

For a moment, I think she's annoyed by my response and will turn on her heels in anger, but instead, she smiles warmly before nodding. "Thanks, *papá*."

She hasn't called me that since she was little, and my heart almost lurches out of my chest. "Of course, *mija*."

Before she can say anything else, I retreat to the back of the house to the glass sliding doors until I'm in the backyard. It's vast, with a pool, hot tub, shed for tools, and a makeshift patio.

The grill sits atop the patio, and I place the tools and plate down on the table before assessing the grill to make sure it's clean. I try to clean it after every use so it stays pristine.

I enjoy keeping my expensive things looking nice.

Once I've got that situated, I drag my feet around the backyard, through the wooden gate, and find the extra garage key under a nearby potted plant. I open the garage door and flip on a switch. The walls are lined with boxes, and the center has even more piled in, plus some bikes, a treadmill I don't use anymore, and a small grilling section. I head there quickly, making sure not to look around for anything that might trigger me into a full-blown panic attack. I can already feel the air suffocate me, entering my lungs and wrapping around them, squeezing tightly. A cough slips out of me as I grab the bag of charcoal and I speed walk out of the garage. I slam the side door harshly and throw the key under the mat with force. I look up at the fading orange and pink sunset sky as I take a few deep breaths.

"You can do this, Arlo," I mumble to myself before I head to the grill.

"ROSALÍA!" I yell from the kitchen, rinsing my hands one last time. I've got the food all grilled and laid out on the island. I don't hear her loud steps down the stairs, so I call her again.

I wait patiently before giving up and leaving the kitchen to head upstairs. There isn't any other reason for me to be upstairs. There's Rosie's room, a guest room, and then a study that Rosie doesn't really use. There's a bathroom in the hallway as well.

Once I'm upstairs, I head to her closed door. I knock on it a few times before I wait. The door finally opens, but it's not Rosalía. It's a very short blonde. Her freckles against her tan skin are like stars in the sky. I try to keep my eyes off her frame as she assesses me.

Her brown eyes widen for a second before going back to normal. I study her for a moment before clearing my throat.

"She's in the bathroom taking off her makeup," the blonde says softly. She shifts in her place, and I look behind her to see Rosie's bathroom door shut. I nod curtly at the girl before turning on my heel. Before I make it to the staircase, I turn my head back and see her watching me still.

"Dinner's ready. It won't be out for long. Got an early wake-up call," I say briefly before heading downstairs.

Within ten minutes, I hear their footsteps down the stairs, as if they're running to the finish line. I'm already eating a taco on a barstool. I moved to the other side of the island to give the girls their space. They reach it, and the blonde is quiet as she takes in the spread of food.

"Wow, this smells amazing!" Rosie smiles before licking her lips and grabbing a plate. She hands one to her friend, who thanks her so softly that I almost miss it. Rosie is too busy filling her plate with tortillas, steak, and salsa to see me watch her friend. Under the bright kitchen light, she's even more breathtaking than what I saw upstairs.

She doesn't have a small frame like Rosie, but she is shorter. Rosie's got maybe five inches of height to her. Her shirt hugs her curves in a delicious way when she leans over for a tong to place some grilled onions on her plate. I shift in my seat from the sight, seeing her lips press together in concentration. She looks up briefly, catching my eyes, and I clear my throat before focusing back on my plate.

Nice going, Arlo.

"We can sit here." Rosie guides her friend to the barstool, and they both plop down.

"Drinks?" I ask, seeing they have nothing yet. Rosie looks up and nods with a smile. Her friend keeps her gaze on her plate. Rosie nudges her, and she looks up.

"Yes, please."

"We've got Sprite, ginger ale, Miller Lite, or Corona," I say as I get up and head to the fridge.

"Miller Lite for me!" Rosie calls behind me. I pull out a can and crack it open for her before I place it on the island, and she reaches for it.

"And you?" I ask, raising a brow at her friend. Her cheeks have a tint of mauve as she catches my gaze, and she shifts in her seat. I watch her for a moment, wondering if she can hear my erratic heart thrumming against my chest.

What the fuck is wrong with me? She's my daughter's friend. I fix my gaze back to the fridge, waiting for her to answer.

"Corona, please," she finally says behind me. I grab a bottle and decide to get two. It's my favorite beer.

I shut the fridge and pull a bottle opener magnet before popping off both caps. She smiles kindly as she grabs it, taking a small sip.

My heart is still thumping loudly as I take a seat. Rosie is making three tacos on her plate, something she's always done. She'd rather have the tacos all ready to eat instead of making one and eating it and then having to prep another one. Her friend, on the other hand, preps one, eats one, and then preps another.

"This salsa is the best," Rosie squeals with delight, and it warms my heart.

"I'm glad you like it. It's *the* recipe," I tell her, taking a bite of another taco I just made. My methods are like her friend's as I finish a taco and start prepping another one.

"You made it?" Her friend's angelical voice pipes up. I stop myself midway from biting into a taco to look at her and nod.

"Yeah, he cooks almost everything he eats. Unless it's for a special occasion and we go to a restaurant," Rosie states from her chair. Her friend whips her head from Rosie to me.

"I've got lots of recipes to try, not enough time," I confess. My mother taught me to cook at a young age, and all the recipes I have are from her. She passed away a few years ago but left me with a dingy binder full of her recipes that I have tucked into a drawer for safekeeping.

"It's delicious," her friend bubbles and takes another bite of her taco. The salsa drips from her lips, and she licks all around her mouth and *fuck*. The sight of her plump pink lips makes my cock go into a frenzy.

I stiffen in my chair and curse myself. *This isn't happening.*

"You okay, dad?" Rosie speaks up, and I finally notice I'm clenching my jaw, and my vacant hand that's not wrapped around the taco is in a fist. I relax my features before locking my eyes with my daughter and nodding.

"Yeah, baby, I am."

"So…" Rosie speaks up as she finishes her tacos. She washes it down with the beer before locking eyes with mine. I raise a brow, and I know she wants to revisit the topic from earlier.

"Mr. Santos," her friend says softly, causing my dick to twitch in my pants. *Jesus Christ, what the fuck?*

I give her a small smile before pressing my lips together. Rosie smiles brightly and looks at her friend with encouraging eyes.

"Clementine León, ask him!" Rosa mocks in a teasing tone. *Clementine León*–the name echoes in my mind, and it's the prettiest fucking name I've ever heard.

Clementine looks at me, a blush creeping up along her neck and then up her cheeks as she shifts in her seat. "I know Rosalía mentioned some of my situation. It would mean the *world* to me if I could pay rent for the guest bedroom. I'll do chores, make sure to even abide by any curfew, and I'll even mow the l–"

"Sure," I say without protest.

Clementine opens and closes her mouth a few times before looking at my daughter, who just shrugs.

"Wow, I expected more pleading," Clementine whispers, looking down at her plate.

"Any friend of my daughter's is welcome to stay. I don't need the money, but if your parents think that is best, then I'll accept it. Make sure they're aware of your decision. I'll give you my number for them to have."

"Thanks, *papá*," Rosalía pipes up, leaning over to squeeze my arm. I give her a smile before looking back at Clementine.

"Of course, sir," she nods quickly.

Sir. The way her mouth pours that word out makes me take a deep breath. I regret my choice immediately in agreeing to let her stay, but I've already told her she can. I can't back out now, and it seems to be the only other option the girl has. It would be cruel of me to kick her to the curb.

"Please, Mr. Santos is fine," I say almost too quickly, and the faintest of a smile hits her lips.

"Okay, *Mr. Santos.*"

I finish my beer before tossing the remnants of my plate in the trash, including the beer bottle. I place the dish in the sink, knowing I'll have to do it tomorrow.

Turning to the girls who are already in their own world, giggling about something, I clear my throat, and they both look up. "You guys don't wait up for me. I'm going to head to bed. Clean up after yourselves and leave any leftovers in the fridge."

"Yes, Dad. Goodnight, *te amo*," Rosie says with a two-finger salute to her temple. I walk over and wrap my arms around her from behind. She sinks into my chest, and I kiss the top of her head. She giggles before I release her, and it's awkward for a moment as I stare at Clementine, who twists her head.

"Goodnight, Mr. Santos. Thank you again for letting me stay. It means a lot, and I'll let my mom know before bed."

I nod before tailing it out of there and making it to my bedroom just in time to cover my prominent erection. My head hangs as I take a few deep breaths and think about what the hell I'm doing.

I need to get laid. That's what's wrong. It's been a while; I've been so busy planning this project at work that I haven't had the brain cells to even think about finding someone to hook up with. The dating apps aren't for me, and I'm no longer into the bar scene as much as I was during the beginning of the separation.

After stripping naked, I hop in bed. Sleep doesn't come easy, and I find myself dreaming about pink plump lips and a blonde-haired beauty saddling my waist and sinking herself onto my cock.

Chapter Three

CLEMENTINE

I CAN'T SLEEP. The room is too dark, but if I open a curtain, it's too bright. I twist and turn in the sheets, count sheep, and even attempt to count backward from 100. None of it works, and I contemplate going downstairs for a glass of water.

Rosa went to bed almost immediately after dinner, talking about needing beauty sleep for her next date tomorrow. So I was left alone in the kitchen, finishing up my beer and tacos. I didn't necessarily want to impose on Mr. Santos' lifestyle, but he asked us to clean up, and Rosa left in a hurry. I cleaned up as best as I could, found some containers in a random cabinet to put the leftovers in the fridge, and even did the dishes.

I didn't mind at all and hoped Mr. Santos would see it as a thank you when he woke up. Even if he thinks it was his daughter who did it, the gesture counts.

"Ugh!" I twist again in the bed and sit up. My chest feels hot, and I press my palm to my skin. The room isn't cold, but it isn't hot—it just feels suffocating and stuffy. The fan isn't on either, so I get up slowly and tiptoe to the door to flick on the switch. I tiptoe back to the bed and it creaks as I lay back down. But sleep *still* doesn't come.

I grab my phone from the side table, noticing I have a few unread messages from my mom and Declan. I answer them quickly, telling them goodnight and that I'm all settled in, including Mr. Santos' phone number so they can reach him if needed. It's a lie about being settled in since my suitcase is still downstairs in the foyer, but it was way too heavy to carry up the stairs.

As I lay my phone back on the table and nestle into the pillow, I feel a pang of loneliness and stare into the darkness of the ceiling. I thrum my fingers on my stomach, and I take a few deep breaths.

The next few weeks ahead of me will be hard. I don't start class for another two weeks, and it's only a month-long course. I really wish they'd let me take the other three classes as well, but it's not an option.

Bang!

I whip my head to the locked door, and my heart thuds against my chest. It sounded like something fell. I get out of the bed and slip on my pajama shorts. I creep to the doorway, cursing myself for not bringing up a sweater or borrowing one from Rosa.

My hands shake as I open the door. The hallway is dark, but there's a faint glow coming from under Rosa's door. I don't know why the hell I'm shaking, but the sound was rattling enough to scare me.

"Take deep breaths, Clem," I remind myself, thinking of all the grounding techniques my therapist taught me months back. Digging my nails into my skin apparently isn't a healthy one. Who knew?

As I tiptoe down the hall, I don't hear Mr. Santos, which is a good sign. If we need him, we'll scream. I knock softly on Rosa's door, but it's quiet on her end. I twist the knob and pray she's not passed out on the floor or something. I'm not sure how well I'd be able to work under that kind of stress—I'm a wuss.

"Rosa?" I ask, peeking my head into her room. The glow is coming from her bedside lamp, but she's not in bed. I press my body against the doorframe and enter completely before finally spotting her near the window. It's open, and her mirror that was up against the wall is face down on the ground.

She's not facing me, and I creep up toward her, placing my hand on her shoulder. She yelps before twisting around and sighing. "Clem! What are you doing in here?"

I take a step back and assess my friend. That's when I finally notice she's not in pajamas but a shirt and jeans with sneakers on. She's got a book bag near the window that's open.

"The mirror," I point to it. "I woke up from the sound."

"Shit, sorry. Didn't mean to be so loud." She laughs before turning back to the window and looking out.

"What are you doing? It's past midnight."

She cranes her neck back at me before answering. "Garrett is picking me up. I'm going to sneak out, and you're not going to tell a soul."

"Who would I tell?" I laugh, finally standing next to her to watch for Garrett. She smiles when I look at her.

"My dad, silly. He's so protective. If he knew I snuck out, even at our age, he'd ground me. That won't stop me from leaving the house, though, if he did."

"He just cares for your safety," I mumble, almost too low for her to catch. She raises a brow before shaking her head.

"You need to live a little, girl! Come with me! Garrett is taking me to a party his friends are hosting. It's at one of the frat houses."

I shake my head. "I'm good. Frats aren't really my thing anymore."

"Why? Didn't you date that one guy for a little bit? What was his name?"

And that's when I feel like the worst best friend. She doesn't know. She can never know.

She knows his name, Nathan, but I don't want to remind her about him. I've tried so hard to forget about him and that damn frat house.

"It's not important. I just don't really want to hang with frat dudes this summer, ya know?" I try to play it cool.

"What, you'd rather spend your days rotting inside this house? No thanks. I love my dad, but I can't be near him every weekend. I'd rather spend it with Garrett or anyone else that comes my way! It's my last summer to be *free*."

I press my lips together tightly before nodding. I don't want to turn this into an argument, so I don't respond. She grabs her bag and hitches it on her shoulder. There are faint headlights in the distance that finally make it to the front of the house. Garrett, I assume.

"That's my ride, *nena*. Remember, you saw nothing." She winks. I nod and step back as she slips out of the window, and I hear a thud as she finds her way to the ground and takes off running to the car. Before I can even blink, they're gone.

I shut the window, with just enough of a gap in case Rosa needs to get back in and close the curtains before picking up the fallen mirror. Thankfully it's not broken. I make my way to the bedside table and click the light off and head out of her room. The door clicks closed, and I turn around before screaming.

My hands instinctively go to my chest in a protective stance and the light flicks on to show the silhouette near the stairs is just Mr. Santos.

"Sorry, I didn't mean to scare you," he mumbles. I take a deep breath, leaning back against Rosa's door.

"It's okay, sorry for screaming. I don't do well in dark spaces," I tell him.

He takes the last step from the stairs and enters the hallway. That's when I *notice* him.

He's shirtless, with a golden necklace dangling elegantly over his tanned and *muscular* body. Boxers cover his lower half just enough to leave something to the imagination. The happy trail points like a neon sign to parts of him that I know I shouldn't be curious about. Not that I'm thinking about what's underneath... He stalks toward me, and I lay my hands back at my sides.

His eyes trail my body for a split second, but I catch it. That's when I look down and realize that my nipples are poking out against the fabric. I lift my arms and cross them over my chest, and my face feels hot.

"I heard a noise. Is Rosalía okay?" he asks gruffly. He sounds like he was in a deep sleep and was woken up. His voice is hoarse, and I swallow the cottony feeling that's taking over in my mouth.

"She's fine," I squeak out. He gets closer, and I press myself even more against the door. He's tall as he gets a few inches away from me and looks down. Very tall. Well over six feet. His brown eyes are magnetic, and my stomach flutters.

He's your best friend's dad, Clem! Stop looking at him!

But I can't. He's mesmerizing as he places his hands on his waist. I look down at his hands and notice how *manly* they look. Thick fingers, and veins prominent along his wrist and forearm. I swallow and look up at him to see that he's already watching me.

"Is she in her room?" he asks in a whisper. He raises his hand up to the door, inches from my ear. I shake my head and then nod, fucking up.

"Y-yeah, she's in there. She's asleep. Something fell, but I picked it up. She's out like a light in there. You shouldn't go inside." I'm rambling at this point, and he seems to enjoy it. I squirm underneath his stare, and he finally lowers his hand to his side and takes a step back.

My arms are still crossed, but I don't miss the way his eyes take their damn time to look at my chest and then my lower half. My fingers press against the back of my arms, and my nails dig into the skin, giving me some kind of distraction from his wandering eyes.

"Mr. Santos," I start, but he turns on his heel and heads to the staircase.

"Turn off the hallway light," he mutters before heading downstairs. My heart feels like it's exploding out of my chest, and I release my arms and smooth out the nail indents on my skin. I really need to stop that habit. I need to stop these *feelings*. It's not enough that I went to therapy, but I have to work these coping skills daily for them to be manageable?

How is that fair? I shouldn't have to live every day like this just because of someone's horrible decision to ruin my life. Why am I the one paying the price?

I sigh before flicking the hallway light off and heading back to the bedroom. If sleep doesn't come now, then I don't know how I'm ever going to survive an entire summer in this house.

THE BIRDS CHIRPING wake me up. My neck is sore, and I curse myself for falling asleep with two pillows instead of one. I sit up and stretch before heading out of the room to get my suitcase. It has all of my things.

But the moment I whip the door open, I halt. My suitcase is waiting right outside my door with a note attached to the handle. I look around the hallway and even step aside to open Rosa's door to see if she's home, but she isn't. I finally rip the note off the handle and read it.

Seemed too heavy to lug up the stairs. I hope it's okay that I did. Fridge is all yours to raid. Corona too. I'll be home at noon.

A smile surfaces, and I haul the suitcase inside the bedroom.

I take my time this morning to unpack the suitcase and take a shower to wash off the stress from yesterday before slipping on a bikini.

I grab a book, my headphones, and then strut downstairs to the kitchen to get a glass of water. The house is silent and eerie, but I try not to focus too much on it. Getting outside for a breather will help my running thoughts, and then I can make breakfast.

And that's what I do. I find a pool chair and lay on it, letting the morning sun hit me as I read my book. I then take a break to eat some breakfast and make a mental note to thank Mr. Santos for letting me raid his fridge.

I still have to give him the check, and I plan to once he's back.

I head back out where the sun is beaming more and plop myself onto the chair, laying on my belly this time so the tan is even. I don't have sunscreen, which is stupid for a day like this, but I'll worry about it later. Maybe Rosa has some, or her dad can tell me where he's got a bottle stashed.

Maybe he could make sure I cover every inch.

Shit. I shouldn't be thinking about Rosa's dad like that.

With the thought of my best friend, I whip out my phone from under the chair where it won't overheat from the sun's rays and open our text thread.

ME

Where are you??! Please tell me you're okay.

Within a moment, her response rolls through.

ROSA 🌺

I'm with Garrett 😊 We're headed to a pool party at his apartment complex!

> ME
>
> You have a pool at home! I'm literally here haha

ROSA

> My pool doesn't have hot boys. Just an overly protective grumpy father.

> ME
>
> It doesn't. Don't be mean, he can't be that bad.

ROSA

> Comeeeeee

I stare at our text thread for a moment and I want to go, but I'm comfortable and really didn't want to order an Uber to take me to another pool.

> ME
>
> Next time, okay? Already getting my tan on 😎

ROSA

> Garrett says hiii! Love you! 🥺

> ME
>
> be safe, love you 🖤

I click my phone off and place it under the chair. The water moves slowly with the slight wind that picks up overhead. I look around the yard and see that the wooden fence is pretty high, which makes me feel even more safe.

Just the thought of being at a pool party with tons of people, tons of drinking, and the possibilities of what could go wrong doesn't seem appealing.

I feel the safest in my company right now, as much as that goes against my therapist's advice. She wants me to go out more, test my boundaries, and even try dating again. Of course, it's not forceful. She's right. I *do* need to go out more and mingle.

Since summer started I haven't spoken to her, but I mentally make a note to set up a session soon. It would be good for me to update her on what's going on. Especially with the drastic change in plans.

Having to find a place so quickly after the last-minute cancellation of the study abroad program has gotten my mind into a frenzy, my stress levels to the point where I can't stop my old habits from coming back, and now slowly feeling like I'm pushing away my best friend's invitations.

I shiver from the sudden cloud that hangs above me, so I get up and cross the yard to where there's sun. I dip my toes in the pool before walking down the steps until I'm waist-deep. Taking a deep breath, I count to five and then plunge my whole body in. It's not too cold to shock me, but it feels just as effective.

Once I surface, my hands move to make waves in the water. It's obvious Mr. Santos takes care of it. He seems to care a lot about his things, including Rosa. But last night was weird.

He left so abruptly once I told him she was asleep. He wasn't dumb or clueless–he had to have known she wasn't home, right? He believed me *too* easily.

My back arches as I let myself float on the water as best as I can. I stare at the blue sky and count the clouds above while I think of Mr. Santos. The way his golden necklace glistened against his skin. The rippled muscles in his arms, his torso, his–

I cough as I almost inhale a gallon of chlorine water from sinking too much in deep thought of him. I wade my way back to the steps and get out of the pool.

I'm losing my mind, I think as I lay back on the chair and let the sun dry me off. I close my eyes for a moment as I try to calm my thoughts.

It's not long before I realize I'm drifting off, and I wake to the sound of sliding doors and footsteps. I jolt awake and feel like I just woke up in another timeline. I look around the pool and see that it's the same as it was before. My body is dry from the sun, but my skin is *red*. Not burnt, but almost to that stage. I hiss as I press my fingers against my stomach.

"Clementine?" A voice calls behind me, and I freeze. I look over my shoulder and see Mr. Santos, and that's when I swallow whatever thoughts I have of him, but it's no use.

He's wearing tight jeans with some mud stains on the knees. His thighs are *thick* as sin and almost popping out of the fabric. He's wearing a collared shirt, and even the sleeves are suffocating around his biceps. I see the hint of the golden necklace underneath the shirt peeking through. Flashbacks of last night fill my vision of how I got to see the whole necklace on display under the hallway light.

He's got one brow raised in curiosity as he reaches me. Once he gets close enough, his eyes widen as he takes in my state.

At first, I think he's noticing my red skin, but that's when he finally makes it in front of me. He swallows hard, and I feel the heat rush down south.

"What are you doing?" he asks, his brown eyes grazing over my body before locking on my face.

"Tanning, but I fell asleep," I whisper. I cover my chest as best as I can with my arms and hitch my knees up on the chair. It's an awkward movement, but it covers my body from his gaze. Not that I'm uncomfortable from the staring, but I don't want *him* to be uncomfortable.

"Tanning? You're red," he exclaims with a slight laugh, moving his hands to his hips in an authoritative stance. It makes my skin grow even more hot.

I wince. "I don't have sunscreen."

He looks up at the sky before sighing and looking back down at me.

"Come with me," he curls his finger at me before walking back toward the house. I don't know what to do with the sudden order, but my feet find the pavement and I head to the sliding doors. Once I'm inside, I shiver from the AC that's encased the house.

"Here," he says, tossing me a shirt out of nowhere. I catch it in time as I watch him walk to the kitchen. I pull the enormous shirt over my head and see that it's a Metallica band tee. It smells like faint cologne of blue cypress, bergamot, and something else. I gulp and immediately want to take this shirt off.

It's *his*.

"Come," he orders once more. My feet drag to the kitchen, and he's shutting the fridge door before placing a bottle on the island. "Use this before you go back out there."

I make it to the island and grab the bottle. It's aloe vera, and it's obviously for the creeping sunburn I'm inevitably going to get after this dumb stunt.

"Thanks," I murmur.

"Sunscreen is in the guest bathroom, third cabinet to the right," he says before crossing his arms again and leaning back against the counter behind him. His eyes stay on me as I flip the lid open and squirt the cool substance onto my palm. I place the bottle on the island before rubbing my hands together and smoothing the aloe vera on my arms. I let out a relieved moan at the cold sensation, and he clears his throat from his place. My cheeks burn from the sound that just came out of my mouth.

I can't believe he heard that.

"You don't work today?" I ask, busying myself from the utter embarrassment and grabbing the bottle, repeating the process before I rub it over my cheeks and neck.

"I'm done for the day," he grunts. I whip my head toward him, and he clears his throat again. His left foot is tapping meticulously against the floor. "Rosalía home yet?"

"No."

He hangs his head before looking up at me from beneath his

lashes. My stomach flutters, and heat rises between my legs.

"She wasn't here last night, was she?"

I gulp, not knowing what to say. I can't betray my best friend. But I know that he's just protective of her and cares for her safety. I wished I had someone like that at a time when I needed it the most.

"I didn't want to meddle," I finally say.

Grabbing the bottle, I head to Mr. Santos. He watches me, straightening his posture. I crane my neck to look up at him before pressing the bottle to his chest. His large hands go to it, wrapping around my wrists. His touch is warm, and it brings tingles to my body–the hairs on my neck stand in a heavenly way. A fleeting thought of his hands wrapped around my wrists and guiding my arms above my head while he's fucking me relentlessly fills my mind.

His lips twitch for a moment, and I panic, pulling my wrists back and stepping away. Fuck, he's a mind reader, for sure.

"I'm going to get sunscreen," I say before he mumbles something I don't pick up as I run down the hall and up the stairs.

That's the last time I see Mr. Santos today.

Even when Rosa comes home for dinner, he leaves us bags of takeout with a note for us to eat without him.

Chapter Four

ARLO

I'VE MANAGED to dodge Clementine for two days straight, and it's now Saturday. It's not like me to avoid someone in my house, but that's the circumstances I find myself under.

My mind is full of flashbacks of her in a tiny bikini that accentuated her curves *just right* on that pool chair. The things I'd do to her if she'd let me.

I'd make sure she screams my name for all the neighbors to hear. I want her voice hoarse by the time I'm finished with her.

"Jesus," I whisper.

I finish an order of supplies in my makeshift office at our renovation site. My erection is prominent, and I have to think of not-so-filthy thoughts to make it fade. There's a knock at the door, and I scramble to find some papers to push at the end of the desk to cover my bulge.

"Come in!" I holler, watching the door as the person finally walks in. It's just Francisco Flores, or Frankie, as I like to call him.

"Arlo, what the fuck are you doing here?" he asks as he makes his way to the small desk. There's a foldable metal chair already open, so he takes a seat. His jeans look cleaner than what

I'm used to seeing during the week, and he's got on a bright red shirt. He lifts one leg and balances his ankle on the other knee. He leans back in the chair, and he's chewing on a toothpick, flipping it this way and that with his tongue.

"Wanted to get a head start for Monday," I lie.

I couldn't tell him I wanted to be nowhere near the house where *someone* had been running rampant in my thoughts the past two days. Frankie doesn't know about Rosalía's friend staying with us.

"Bullshit." He sees right through me, and I fucking hate it.

He crosses his tan arms over his chest and stares at me dead on, but I don't budge. Without missing a beat, he takes a deep breath before taking out the toothpick and rolling it in between his fingers. His brown-eyed gaze flicks to mine once more, and he smiles.

"You had a one-night stand and didn't want her asking for breakfast in bed," he pipes up. He bellows out in laughter, clapping his hands, and I want to lean over and punch him square in the jaw. My own ticks as I clench my teeth in annoyance.

"*No,*" I quarrel.

"Come on, *hermano,*" Frankie puts the toothpick back in between his teeth and gives me a wink. "Tell me."

I sigh and spin a little in the swivel chair I'm in. It's not a nice chair by any means since we don't really try to fancy up this makeshift office that's really a trailer. We'd rather utilize the funds on other things.

"Frankie..." I warn.

"What? I deserve to know what's going on. You're never here on the weekends. Last time I checked, you try to stay home in case Rosita comes to visit. There's a reason you came to work today–I know you. *Órale.*"

Shit, he's got me there. I tell everything to Frankie. He really is like a brother to me, and it's not fair to lie to him. What I *won't* do is tell the truth about what has been going on lately with my *thoughts*.

"Rosie's home for the summer, so it has preoccupied me, and I just wanted some space from the house."

"*No mames*. You say you want to spend more time with her, yet you're here... What's really going on?"

"She's got a...friend," I pause, gathering my thoughts. "who can't go back home because of the trip cancellation, so I'm letting her stay with us until she can figure things out. So that'll be something."

Frankie's eyes light up, and he smiles widely. He almost laughs before I give him a stern look. "Arlo... You're playing with fire."

"What the fuck are you talking about?"

He looks around the room, even though it's just the two of us, before leaning closer to the desk. I lean closer too. He winks before answering. "You were never one who could keep his hands to himself."

"Jesus, Frankie! She's my daughter's age! I'm at least twenty years her senior. It's *wrong*." My chest tightens at the forbidden aspect of even having simple thoughts about her. And now she's under my roof? Fuck me.

"Woah, *cálmate*. Rosita is an adult, and so is her friend. But don't make me remind you how you let those college girls at the bars fawn over you whenever we went out! You're barely thirty-nine. You're not *that* old. The ladies *love* you, you old grump. How do you plan to keep your hands to yourself?"

"Don't bring Rosie into this kind of conversation," I plead, lifting my hands to rub my temples. I smooth a palm over my face and then look at Frankie, who is giving me a sour expression.

"Yeah, my bad man. No more Rosita talk. But she texted me to let me know that she's going to look for a summer job."

I raise a brow, thankful for the change of topic, but also

curious to what Rosie might've told him. "Oh? This is news to me. She's been gone every day this week and has been sneaking out of the house at night."

Frankie gasps. "Not Rosita! Wow, Arlo, really?" That's when I notice his sarcasm, and he laughs. "Arlo, she's an adult. She's going to meet a boy and sneak out to meet up with him. Don't tell me you didn't make a girl sneak out of her house to meet you in your twenties."

I roll my eyes and don't bother answering that. "I don't want to think about my baby growing up. She still looks five to me."

"May I remind you that she's twenty-one? She's not five. You gotta let her go one day. She's not gonna live with you forever, and she's gonna find someone and then run off with them for the rest of her life."

"Don't give me that visualization," I sigh, wishing we never started this conversation. I'm already trying to make up for lost time with Rosie, but to have her Uncle Frankie talk about her future like this? I don't like it. She's still my baby girl, and I don't like the inevitable thought of her finding someone to spend the rest of her life with. They better meet all expectations, or I'll break their neck.

"Back to Rosita's friend." Frankie tilts the conversation, and I shoot daggers at him.

"Absolutely *not*. I'm already keeping my distance. End of discussion."

He raises his hands in surrender before finally standing up. "You're the one that agreed to let her live with you. Gonna have to face her some time. Don't be a dick, Arlo. Be nice."

I huff out a breath and watch him as he winks before heading out of the trailer. I try to focus back on the paperwork in my hands and then the laptop for any more orders, but my mind is frazzled. Frankie's right. I need to go home and try to make that place a space of solidarity. Wave a white flag if I have to to make it a safe zone for my feelings. The last thing I want to do is make her feel uncomfortable under my roof.

It will be hard with how much I'm already being affected by that woman's presence in just 3 days, but I'll try my damnest.

·◦· ✦ ·◦·

THE HOUSE IS QUIET, and I know Rosie isn't home since she finally texted me, letting me know she had dinner plans. I slam the front door loudly just in case Clementine is home, not wanting to catch her in another bikini again and hoping she can put a cover-up on in time.

I take my time untying my boots, heading to the bedroom, and doing my routine, even though I didn't work outside the trailer today. It's lunchtime, and by the time I'm out of the shower and changed, the sunlight is filtering nicely into the kitchen.

I bring out ingredients to make a simple sandwich and go to grab a beer. I almost drop the can as I catch sight of Clementine out in the backyard wearing a different bikini. A much more revealing one.

The bikini top is practically getting eaten up by her breasts that spill over the sides. The bottoms are no better when she twirls around, showing her bare ass and barely any fabric that is not even a thong by definition. I curse under my breath and watch for a moment as she holds her phone up in the air and walks around the pool.

I'm not sure if she's taking videos, photos, or simply trying to get service. There's a loud sound as the beer can in my hand crushes from the grip I have on it and sprays everywhere. I curse under my breath and toss the can in the sink before grabbing a towel to wipe the beer from my hands.

"*Carajo, girasol,*" I spit out. I look up at Clementine once more and pinch my brows, in pure disbelief at the sight and what I just slipped out of my mouth.

Sunflower in Spanish. Where did that come from?

I turn back to the island to not be so obvious in my gawking while I finish preparing three sandwiches. It's out of habit to make two for me and one for Rosie. Might as well start the whole 'nice guy act' right now with a peace offering sandwich for Clementine.

I place the food on paper plates and even grab two Coronas with the bottle opener before sliding the glass door and stepping out into the backyard. Clementine whips her body towards me, and it doesn't help *at all* seeing her breasts bounce with the movement. Her eyes widen, and she heads to the pool chair and grabs a cover-up dress that barely goes over her ass.

"I made lunch, have an extra if you'd like." I place the plates on the table that's in-between two chairs and look up at her. Her phone is nestled in between her hands, which are practically turning white from the grasp.

"I'm not hungry," she mumbles before looking around the pool and not keeping eye contact with me.

"It'll go to waste," I say, hoping she can just take the friendly gesture, and I'll be out of her hair.

She finally looks at me, and her brown eyes wait for something… what? I don't know. There's softness now in her features before she nods and clears her throat.

"Thanks, Mr. Santos." She sits on the chair, picks up a plate, and sets it on her lap.

"Mind if I join?" I ask, gesturing to the vacant pool chair next to the table.

She shrugs. "It's your backyard."

"But it's your space right now," I state. She looks up at me with a swirl of questions in her eyes.

"What?"

"It's your space right now," I repeat. "It might be my backyard, but you were here first, and I don't want to impose on that."

"That's—" She takes a bite of the sandwich and chews on it for a moment before swallowing. "Really nice. I've never had someone…"

I give her a tender smile as she's in deep thought. It comes with the territory of having a daughter, to be honest. Teaching Rosie how to say no and reminding her that 'no' is *enough*. She doesn't have to fight with anyone about her decisions regarding her autonomy, her choices in life, and anything else for that matter.

Something in me tells me that Clementine hasn't really had anyone to enforce this mindset into her. Or someone violated her enough to lose that strength. It almost breaks my heart to think of the latter.

"It's okay. If you'd like me to go, I can. If you want me to stay, I can pull the chair all the way across the pool and even face the other way."

She laughs at this and shakes her head, blonde strands flying this way and that. "Thanks, Mr. Santos, but you can just sit there in that spot. That's fine with me."

I nod and take a seat, picking up the other plate and digging into the sandwich. The bottles of beer are on the ground, and I remember them briefly. Placing the plate on the chair, I grab the bottles and pop one open. I look at her, but she's staring at the sky.

"Beer?" I ask, lifting the unopened one.

She looks over, and a smile spreads across her face. "Yes! Thank you, Mr.–"

"Please, you don't have to say Mr. Santos after everything," I laugh. There's a tinge of mauve creeping on her cheeks as she nods, watching me pop off the top of the beer.

"Thanks," she says in a voice so hushed I almost miss it.

"Of course."

We eat in silence, the birds in the background filling our ears. It's nice, and I look up at the sky with her.

It's not until we're done with our plates and beers that I finally ask her, "So what do you do when you look at the sky?"

She seems lost in thought as she settles down on the chair and places a hand behind her head. "I like to count the clouds. When it's nighttime I count the stars too. It calms me."

Calms her? I turn to look at her, finding myself stuck on her pink plump lips. "I never thought of the sky as a calming vice."

She nods, continuing to look at the sky, but I can sense a shift in the space between us. She takes a deep breath and lets it out slowly. "It's very calming. Better than other methods."

That's when I see her other hand go down to her thigh and trace over her bare skin. It's not done in a sexual manner, but I find myself focused on the faintest scars on her skin that she's tracing over.

Is that a method of hers? Cutting her thigh? There are some that are longer in length than others, but those ones look like from long ago. The fresher ones are smaller and even have curves to them, obviously not done by a knife or blade of some kind. I can't help but wonder what else she might've used for those ones.

"You've got plenty of clouds and stars out here," I reply.

She turns to look at me and I quickly avert my gaze from her thigh. "Thank you again, Mr–," she stops herself. "For everything. It's been a pretty stressful week, but being here seems to calm my nerves." I glance at her thigh momentarily and she thankfully doesn't catch it.

"Stay as long as you need."

"I still have to give you the check."

"Right," I nod. "You can leave it on the fridge if you'd like. Your parents got my info?"

She nods. "They've got it. Don't worry if they don't reach

out. They're traveling around Europe all summer and enjoying themselves."

"Noted."

She's quiet for a moment as she keeps her brown eyes on mine. It's not awkward. And there's no tension within the stare. It's just *comfortable*. She smiles after a moment before turning back to look at the sky. I clear my throat and sit up, gathering the plates and empty beer bottles.

"Thank you again," she says as I head back to the house.

"Of course, Clementine," I respond before slipping inside. I toss the paper plates in the trash and the bottles into our small recycling bin I attempt to remember about. Sometimes I forget and toss recyclables in the trash, sue me.

I don't want to impose on her backyard time any more than I already have, so I wander to the vast living room. I settle into the comfy couch, letting my body sink into it. The sound system is one I've spent months collecting. It's one of my favorite places to be, immersed in the movie or song I'm listening to.

I flip the channels until I open up a streaming app and turn on an old favorite movie before the sounds basically rock me into a steady snooze.

"MR. SANTOS?" A soft voice calls, and I squint before focusing on the figure in front of me. My arm is asleep, and I groan as I twist my body and try to move it to get the blood back flowing.

Clementine is watching me from a few feet away, and she's still got her cover-up on. My eyes try not to focus too much on her curves or the way her thighs squeeze together. I finally settle my eyes on hers.

"Yeah? Sorry, I knocked out."

"It's okay," she says with a small smile spreading on the corners of her lips. "I wanted to let you know that Rosa called me. She's going to have dinner with–she won't be here for dinner."

I raise a brow and sit up on the couch, stretching my arms over my head before sighing and standing up. Her neck cranes up to look at me, and I give her a curt nod.

"Thanks, she texted me earlier about it. And you?"

She watches me for a moment before her forehead creases in confusion. "Me, what?"

"Dinner plans. Do you have any?"

Her eyes flutter for a moment, her cheeks turn rosy, and I raise my brow again.

"N-no, I don't," she stumbles out.

I had plans with Frankie tonight to grab beer and pizza at the nearby pub, but looking at how she is right now makes me want to cancel them. But I can't. It wouldn't look good on my part, and I need to keep my distance until Rosie can come home and start hanging out with Clementine. I'm not annoyed that she's been around the house all week, but I can't keep bumping into her in scenarios that don't play out well in my head.

A lot of them are full of fantasies that shouldn't ever escape my mind.

"I'll be at the pub tonight with a good friend, but raid the fridge if you're hungry. Our home is your home."

She's quiet as she mulls over my response. Her lips twitch as if she wants to say something, but she stays silent.

Before I can ask her if that's okay or that I'll cancel my plans and have dinner with her here, she nods and turns on her heels. She's quick to leave the living room before I hear her go up the stairs and then the sound of the guest bedroom door closing.

Fuck, why does it feel like I messed up? I try to clear my mind of those thoughts as I head to the kitchen to grab my phone and see that Frankie has already texted me to confirm dinner. I respond quickly that I'll be there. My nap didn't last long and I've got about three hours before I have to meet up with him.

Without a second thought, I head downstairs to the basement and measure shit and draw horrible sketches of how I want the renovations to go. I get lost in my work so easily, hoping to avoid Clementine as much as I can in the house, that the time comes fast for dinner, and I'm making my way to the pub.

Chapter Five

CLEMENTINE

MR. SANTOS IS GONE by the time I come downstairs for dinner. The house is quiet yet again, and I'm about to lose my mind. I need the next two weeks to end and classes to start so I can be busy.

I don't know how much longer I can last being in this house where Rosa is never around, and I bump into her father every so often. I don't mind bumping into him, per se, but it's how those moments happen.

Like today, I was in a skimpy little bikini that I forgot I had and really wanted to use to fix the uneven tan from the other days basking under the sun. But it wasn't exactly appropriate when Mr. Santos made his way into the backyard, so I had to run to grab the cover-up that barely covered my ass. I was embarrassed, to say the least.

The fridge is stocked, but my appetite isn't there. I grab my phone and contemplate calling my mom again, but she's sleeping by now. We talked while I was finishing my sunbathing earlier and when it was a more reasonable time to call her. They're in England right now, and she sent me some photos.

If homesick was a feeling to be with people, then I had it. I wanted to be with her and Declan, and as much as I hated to admit it, I wish I had taken her up on her offer to join their trip. But I know it's just the loneliness talking.

I scroll through my contacts, find Rosa's, and hit *call*. She picks up on the fifth ring.

"Clemmmmyyy! *Donde estás*?!" There's loud music in the background, and I look at the kitchen clock to see that it's only eight. Mr. Santos has been gone since around seven. At least, that's the time I think I heard the front door slam shut.

"About to raid your fridge," I tell her, looking at what's inside and willing for an appetite, but it still doesn't come.

"Wait, you're home? It's Saturday night! Is my dad there?"

"No," I sigh. "He's out with a 'good friend' at the pub."

"Oh, he's probably with *Tío* Frankie," she giggles. "They go there a lot. *Tío* Frankie told me sometimes dad would bring a woman home, so watch out for that." She pretends to gag over the line, and I press my lips tightly together.

Just the thought of *that* happening while I'm under his roof spoils my appetite even more. I don't even know why I'm so affected by this piece of information, but I wish she didn't just say that.

"I'll try to find a place to go then, so I don't have to witness that," I say coldly.

The music seems to get louder and then thins out for a moment as I hear more shuffling on her end. She sighs heavily. "Okay, I'm outside. Garrett's brothers are having another party, and it's *wild*. You should come!"

I chew my lip in thought for a moment before shutting the fridge and heading to the small pantry they have. It's got a few shelves, and that's where they have the good snacks I found out the other day. My eyes scan the area before spotting the Nutella and Oreos. I yank them out and set them on the island.

"I'd love to, but I'm just not in a party mood," I lie. I don't want to confess that being ground up against frat brothers that stayed on Greek row for the summer is not my ideal night out. Being twenty-one, I'll never understand the hype of still going to frat parties. I've also got my prejudice against them, but that's beside the point.

I twist the Nutella jar open before ripping the Oreo package and pulling one out. I almost dunk it into the jar before remembering guest etiquette and going to find a plate and knife.

"You say that all the time! Come on, *nena*," she pleads with a whiny voice. "It's summer! We might not be in Greece, but we could still get some *Greek* on frat row. Might as well make the most of it."

"I'll go when you go to the bar. How about that? I just don't want the frat houses right now," I kindly tell her.

"Deal, Clem. I'm going to tell Garrett that, and we'll make a night out of it!"

Before I can protest and tell her I'd rather have it as a girl's night out, she makes kissing sounds before hanging up. I place the phone on the counter, scoop a big wallop of Nutella onto the plate, and pile it high with Oreos. I head over to the couch and sink into the soft cushions.

Hmm, no wonder Mr. Santos looked like he woke up in another universe–this couch is *soft*. I feel myself start to really relax and sink into the cloud material before turning on the TV and finding my favorite regency-era show.

I swirl an Oreo in the Nutella before popping it in my mouth as the episode starts. It's an emotional rollercoaster as the Duke tries to swoon the woman, and she keeps running away. I cheer her on throughout the night, laughing as she makes the man relentlessly tired but still pining for her. Good for her, making the man do all the work.

It's not until three episodes later that I'm bawling my eyes out at their romantic confessions. He swears he's loved her since the moment he met her months ago. He gets on his *knees* and begs her to listen to him. She stands there strong, and I want to be *her*.

I want her strength to make a man work for it–make him so desperately ruined for her he can't think until she's there. He can't speak until he sees her. He can't do *anything* until he's got her.

I want that, as stupid as it sounds. Someone so wholeheartedly in love with me they can't contain it and must be on their knees begging for me to give them an ounce of love in return.

Because that's what it's supposed to be, right? I shouldn't have to give my all to someone who will strip me of everything and leave just as easily.

I want and *deserve* someone to stay.

Once the episode ends, I sniffle and bring my shirt up to my face to wipe the tears. The plate of Nutella and Oreos has been demolished and sits at the small coffee table in front of the couch. I don't even realize the time until I hear the front door opening and closing. I jump and quickly smooth my hair, attempting to make myself look less like a disastrous mess.

As much as it didn't feel pathetic to have these emotions while watching those episodes, it feels silly now that I'm back to reality.

Shuffling of feet makes its way to the kitchen, and I get up, grab the plate, and turn to see Mr. Santos opening the fridge. His back muscles are flexing underneath his navy shirt, and I swallow whatever thoughts that are churning.

My core flutters as his biceps twitch while pulling the freezer door open and shutting it. He finally grabs a beer, and pops it open with his *bare hands,* and it's the hottest thing I've ever seen.

He lifts it to his lips, shuts the fridge, and turns around before he jolts and almost drops the beer.

"*Dios,* you're like a mouse," he mutters, running his free hand through his dark brunette curls.

"Sorry," I meep, walking to the sink and putting the plate down. I turn the faucet on and begin washing the dish and then placing it on the drying rack. It's silent as I dry my hands on the towel nearby and then go find a glass before heading to the fridge. Mr. Santos doesn't move, so I have to squeeze between him and the island before I reach the fridge and pull out the milk carton.

"Uh, have a good dinner?" he asks softly.

I nod, pouring milk before putting it back in the fridge. I take a few big gulps of the milk, my mouth basically parched from all the chocolate I devoured. "Had Nutella and Oreos. Then cried to some regency show."

The truth comes out so much easier than I expect and I widen my eyes before looking at him. There's a faint smile on his lips before he takes a sip of beer and leans back on the counter.

"Regency show?"

"Like 18th-century love stories. Big poofy dresses, elegant hairstyles, British accents, and the best love confessions."

He quirks a brow. "Best love confessions?"

My cheeks burn, and I nod again. "The best. American shows don't do it like the men in that show. Makes us swoon with just a few words."

"Hmm," he responds before taking another sip of his beer. I watch him as his eyes stay on mine, slowly gliding down and then back up. I shift on my feet before I walk around the other side of the island, so I don't walk by him. I drain the glass before cleaning it.

"Did you have a good dinner with your friend?" I ask, drying my hands. He nods and sets the bottle down on the counter.

"Yes, there weren't any love confessions, but we made some pretty great jokes."

This makes me laugh, like *really* laugh, and he smiles widely. "Really?"

"Frankie is a funny soul. He gets it from his dad. The pizza was good. The beer sucked, hence the drinking now." He gestures to the bottle.

"Well, I'm glad you had a good time."

There's a brief span of silence as my words fall from my lips, and he smiles again, this time softer. He opens his mouth to say something, but then he shuts it just as quickly. I stand there waiting for him to talk, but he doesn't. The silence is starting to slowly turn into *awkward* silence, and that's just something I can't handle. I give him a small smile before making my way into the hallway. I hear a groan behind me before I make my way upstairs to get ready for bed.

I try not to overthink what he wanted to say at that moment, but it's stuck in my mind as I shower, get into pajamas, and then slip into bed. He's the last thing I think about before I fall into a blissful sleep.

THERE'S a loud knocking at the door that jolts me out of bed. The sheets are stuck to my skin, and I've sweat through the pajama top. I get up and peel off the sheets to the best of my ability. I can't remember a thing about my dream, but I know it must've induced this sweat.

I head to the door and open it slowly. Rosa wiggles her brows as she walks inside and puts her hands on her hips. "Get dressed, *nena*. We're going to the pool with Garrett!"

"Rosa, what time is it?" I ask, a perfectly timed yawn coming after.

She scrunches her brows and whips out her phone from her back pocket. She's dressed like she's ready for a photoshoot. Done hair, makeup, and pretty clothes. I have a feeling she doesn't go to these pool parties to swim, but to mingle around it. Envy seeps through me for a moment before I attempt to recenter myself.

"It's almost ten, which means the sun is about to be at its

peak! Do you want a gorgeous tan or not?" I contemplate answering her, but she beats me to it. "Of course you do! Plus, you promised, remember?"

Fuck, I did promise her. I curse myself for even promising such a thing, but I have no choice. I've already spent too much time in this damn house. I might as well be developing cabin fever.

"Okay, fine. But I'm taking my time getting ready," I joke.

She squeals before leaning in and kissing my forehead. She runs out of the room, salutes me with two fingers, and then shuts the door. I groan before going back to the bed and plopping back onto it. I close my eyes for a moment before finally pushing myself up to get ready.

I head to the bathroom to get ready before working on some basic makeup. I don't know if I'll go into the pool, so I skip out on the mascara.

Once I'm back in the bedroom, I slip on a less skimpy bikini and then grab the first pair of jean shorts and shirt I can find. There isn't a mirror in this bedroom, but I don't want to waste any more time up here, so I head downstairs after grabbing my phone and sunglasses.

My steps are loud as I get downstairs and into the kitchen. There's laughter as Rosa is talking with her dad, who has his back to me. She's pouring a glass of water before she looks up and smiles.

"Clem! You're *finally* ready." She pauses as she takes in my outfit, and I wait for her to chastise me for wearing an oversized shirt, but that's what I feel most comfortable in.

But that's not what she does, instead, she raises a brow and *laughs*. "Nice shirt, babe. Didn't know you were into Metallica."

That's when Mr. Santos whips his head around, and I notice he's in the middle of biting into a spoonful of cereal and almost chokes as he looks at my chest. I horrifically look down and notice that I am indeed wearing a Metallica shirt.

And it's the one *he* gave me the first time I used their pool.

"Oh my God," I say, cheeks flustering, and I cover my arms over it.

"What? Don't be ashamed if you do!" Rosa starts. "My dad actually loves the band. Right, *papá*?"

Mr. Santos still has his eyes on my chest as he finally nods and clears his throat. "Y-yeah. Looks a little big on you, though."

My cheeks burn at his words, but Rosa doesn't seem to notice as she takes a sip of water. I walk to the glass doors past them, reaching down for the small box of tanning supplies I've stashed there in the corner for my pool days. I hurriedly grab a bottle of sunscreen and walk back to them.

"I'm ready!" I yell, almost a little too enthusiastically. They both look at me. Rosa's staring as if I just told her I have secret powers and can fly, while Mr. Santos smiles *proudly* at the Metallica shirt.

He runs his tongue over his teeth. I swallow, hoping any embarrassment goes away. If I have to change out of this, I will, but before I can think about going upstairs, my best friend is already placing her cup in the sink and clapping.

"Let's go! Dad, get your keys. Your girls are going to a pool party!"

He shakes his head and looks exhausted already as he stands up and heads for the front of the house. Rosalía nears me and links her arm through my elbow. "Sorry, we have to be the embarrassing ones being dropped off by my dad. He's super against drinking and driving and won't let me take his truck. But, good news! You know who's going to be there?"

I snap my neck at her. "Who?"

"Boys. Tons of boys. We're going to have so much fun today, Clem. I can't wait!"

We're nearing the front door, and Mr. Santos holds it open for us. I brush past him, and my shoulder hits his torso. He exhales just loud enough for me to hear, and it makes my stomach flutter. Heat pools lower and lower, and I bite my lip, hoping to focus back on Rosa's conversation, but I already drowned it out.

As she pulls me along the walkway, I turn back to look at Mr. Santos. He's slipping on a baseball cap, *backward* I might add, and flipping the keyring along his middle finger, and I gulp. He catches me staring, and I look away quickly.

The doors unlock, and Rosa heads for the shotgun seat, and I sit behind her. Mr. Santos gets behind the wheel and turns on the engine. He leans back, placing his long arm behind Rosa's seat, and I stare at his rugged, *manly* thick hand. He backs the truck up, focused on the road behind him, but my eyes trail to his face, and he glances at me briefly before putting the truck into drive and gunning it.

Rosa screams happily, rolling down the windows and hooking up her phone to play a pop song. I take a deep breath and try to calm any nerves that are lingering at the thought of the pool party.

I can't back out now. It would be pathetic.

My hands move to the sides of my thighs. I dig my nails into them ever so slightly. They stay there, digging *more* and *more* to the point where the pain is the only thing I can feel.

That's until we go over a bump that brings me back to the moment. I look up and peek in the rearview mirror just as Mr. Santos does. His eyes are gentle as we stare at each other.

My body relaxes as I take a deep breath. I move my hands away from my sides, tightly lacing my fingers together over my lap.

Chapter Six

ARLO

SEEING her in my Metallica shirt did something to me.

Not only did I practically choke on the cereal I was eating, but it brought images to my mind that I would shamefully replay over and over again tonight. It took everything in me to not drag her upstairs and force her to take off that shirt and change.

She doesn't know the effect she's had on me since the moment she stepped foot into my house. I don't even know *why* she's having this monumental effect on me. I have to stop, I have to.

I can't give in.

Rosie aggressively pulls down the visor and slides the mirror open to check her makeup.

"Call me if you need me, baby," I tell her and she rolls her eyes before leaning in to kiss my cheek.

"Okayyyy, *papá*. Nothing will happen!" Right as she speaks, we see a group of guys her age carrying a *keg* to the pool. I look at her sternly and she gives me an apologetic smile.

I look back at Clementine and she's staring out the window, looking like she's taking deep breaths with the way her chest and shoulders are moving in big movements. I furrow my brows. "You got my number?"

She whips her head to me and shakes her head. I turn to my daughter and give her a look.

"I thought I gave it to her! Here, Clem," she says, whipping out her phone and pulling up my contact. She reaches her phone over to Clementine and she takes it, adding my number into hers. She's silent and was the whole car ride, so I wonder what's going on.

It's obvious that my daughter is the more outspoken and energetic one of the bunch, but the way Clementine is not even mumbling a word to us makes me believe there's something else going on.

I don't want to insert myself into anything, so I keep quiet as the girls hop out of the truck and slam the doors shut. I watch Rosie link arms with Clementine as they walk to the pool area. I assess the area and stay for a few more seconds as I take in the faces of the people that are within distance. More guys than girls and it makes my stomach churn.

I try to push any thoughts away. Rosie is a big girl and can handle her own. And if she can't, she'll do her best to reach me. I won't hesitate to shut down a party to save my daughter.

With that, I pull out of the parking lot and make my way back home to change quickly into gym clothes. Frankie used to go to the nearby gym before deciding to make his own in his garage. It's pretty nice, with what you can do to a garage. He's installed floor to ceiling mirrors on one wall with a squat rack and dumbbell rack. There's even a section of turf that I enjoy using.

Before leaving the house, I make sure to grab a banana and pre-workout in a shaker bottle. The drive isn't long, but my mind continues to swirl around inappropriate thoughts of my daughter's friend.

I need to keep my distance if I want to find some peace at

home. It's not fair either. What if she just thinks I'm some kind of creep who stares at her at the most inconvenient times?

Just the thought of that makes my stomach twist. The last thing I want to do is make her uncomfortable under my roof. So, keeping my distance will be the best thing I can do.

Frankie's got the garage door open, and I can see him curling dumbbells in front of the mirror. I park my truck in his driveway before hopping out and heading to him. He's got earbuds in but notices my entrance and gives me a nod.

I find my way to a corner of the garage to set my shaker bottle down and rip off my shirt. Seeing my muscles while working my upper body keeps me motivated. I head to where the squat rack is and adjust the safety bars to my torso before grabbing a few plates and loading them on. I secure the safety clips before taking a deep breath, leaning down to grasp the bar, and picking it up.

I start curling it with deep, even breaths. Frankie always makes fun of me for curling in the squat rack, but I prefer it. I can do as much weight as I want versus the limited supply of dumbbells he's got.

Once I finish a set, I set the bar down and turn to my friend, who is taking his earbuds out and heading my way. He gives me a smile before leaning in, and we do a side hug.

"You're not at work," he teases with a slap to my back.

"It's a Sunday," I remind him.

His smile is contagious and one splits my face before he starts looking at the mirror and flexing his arms. "Exactly," he finally says. "Got any plans tonight?"

"Nope," I shake my head while returning to my position behind the bar. I pick it up with ease and curl another set before dropping it obnoxiously.

"I have a date," Frankie spits out. He's heading for his dumbbells again and does a set as I watch him.

"You what, now?"

He grunts through his set before laying the dumbbells down again. He gives me a wink. "You heard me, *cabrón*."

"Since when do you date?" I ask, laughing.

He rolls his eyes.

"I *date*, Arlo. You've just never bothered to ask."

I give him a look and place a hand on my hip. "I never have to ask because you happily tell me all the details. Remember Beatrice?"

He picks up the dumbbells again and goes for another ten reps with deep breaths. "Yeah," he starts. "she wanted me to see her family on the second date. I might be old and single, but that doesn't mean I'm *that* desperate for commitment. I'm not even sure what type of commitment I want with someone."

"That's fair," I say. "So who is it?"

"No one," Frankie answers almost too quickly. I peer at him with narrowed eyes before turning to my own workout space and deciding to increase the weight. I add 45 more pounds and curl it while only breaking *minimal* sweat.

"Keep her a dirty little secret, fine."

Frankie laughs from his place.

I take off the weights from the barbell before adjusting the safety bars to my chest height. I then add some weights for warm-up squats. I focus on the necklace in the mirror as I take a deep breath and go down. It's easy, so I add much more for the next set.

"So, how's *you know*," Frankie coos. I take a deep breath and grunt through the squat before yelling and slamming the barbell on the rack.

I wipe sweat from my forehead before throwing daggers at him. "Frankie, shut the fuck up."

"What?! You know why I'm asking."

I shake my head. "There's nothing to tell. I'm trying to keep my distance. It's wrong. *Esta muy mal*."

"Hmm," is all he says.

"Come on," I continue. "She's too young, and she hasn't even graduated. She's under my supervision while her parents are in Europe. I can't think like that right now."

Frankie is silent as he takes in my response. I want to shout at him to say something back, but he doesn't. I take a deep breath and move on to my next set before upping the weight again. My thighs shake from the weight before I finish the last rep.

Sweat dribbles down my chest, and images of being a sweaty mess while fucking *her* fill my mind. I shut my eyes tightly and try to push those thoughts away.

"You seem like you're trying to convince yourself. I'm not buying it," Frankie finally answers. I snap my head toward him, and he's moving onto the bench and doing chest presses. I back out of the squat rack and get behind his head, being his spotter.

Frankie does ten reps before sitting up, looking in the mirror, and making eye contact with me. "Well, if you're not going to spill what's really going on... how's Rosita? Still sneaking out?"

This, I grunt at. I hang my head back, and Frankie chuckles. "Yeah, she is. Dropped her off at a pool party. Remember when we had those kinds of parties?"

"Kegs, drugs, lots of kissing. Lots of–"

"Frankie!" I swat the back of his head before he can say the last word. He yelps and covers his head.

"The fuck, Arlo!"

"*Pendejo*," I spit out.

Frankie shakes his head before grabbing the dumbbells again and leaning back, making eye contact with me for a moment before I nod. He does eight reps this time before sitting back up.

"Sorry, man."

"It's okay," I sigh. "I told Rosie to call me if anything shady goes down. But she can hold her own."

"And her friend?" Frankie smiles through the mirror. I raise my hand as if to swat him, and he scoots up on the bench.

"I don't know, Frankie. She has my number if anything

happens. I trust that either of the girls will reach out if they really need to."

"Good, because after this workout, I won't have the strength to fight off drunks."

I'm with him there. We tend to go overboard in our workouts, feeding off of each other's egos and energy. Whenever we get inside this garage, we hit PRs like no other and get the best pump in.

"The couch is calling my name already," I confess before heading back to the squat rack to set up a bench near it to do overhead presses.

"Maybe someone *else* will call you too," Frankie teases one last time before I flick him off and focus on the rest of my workout.

I DON'T GET any calls, but I hear the door open and footsteps. They're soft as if they don't want to be heard. I get up from the couch and walk to the hallway to see if it's Rosie, but it's not.

It's Clementine. She looks like she's been through a marathon. Her blonde hair is stuck together in thick strands and with a lazy attempt of a ponytail that's already halfway down the length of her head.

Her brown eyes flicker toward me as I get closer. She's still wearing the Metallica shirt, but I can see the strings of her bikini top peeking through the collar. The instant desire to rip off the damn shirt and that bikini top sparks through my veins like a wildfire.

I try to remove these thoughts, but she puckers her lips slightly before giving me a small smile.

"Have a good time at the party?" I ask coolly.

"Mhm," she whispers. Her eyes glide down me slowly, and they're half-lidded. She's inebriated. Fuck, she needs to get upstairs. Now.

"The keg you saw earlier was definitely for our group," she giggles, leaning forward, catching the railing in time. I step closer, grabbing under her arm. Her skin is delicate and *soft,* and I desperately push away the onslaught of thoughts rushing into my mind.

She gasps and cranes her neck to look up.

"I think that's your cue to get to bed."

She takes a deep breath and exhales, and I instantly smell the alcohol off her breath. Her eyes are a little glossy, too, from what I can tell, being this close. I don't miss the way her eyes flicker down to my lips when I press them tightly together.

"Sure is," she smiles, and I swear there's a fucking devious curl to them.

I'm playing with goddamn fire, and I need to get away. But I can't. The desire to take care of her overpowers the need to stay away from her alluring beauty. She's like a siren, and I'm a hopeless sailor, bound to get my soul wrapped around her pretty fingers by just one hum from her lips.

"Clementine," I whisper in an almost hiss. She smiles once more before stepping up the stairs, guiding herself with her hand on the railing. I let my hand fall when she gets high enough on the staircase.

"You're something, Mr. Santos," she giggles from the stairs. She hiccups, and it's the cutest thing ever. I fight back a smile.

Will she remember this when she's sober? Or will she pretend this never happened?

"Go to bed, Clementine," I order.

She halts on the steps, about ten away from the second level. She dramatically sighs and nods.

"Yes, *sir,*" she says before turning on her heel and making her way upstairs. Her hips swaying, and I can't take my eyes off the curve of her ass.

I'm left at the bottom of the staircase with a pounding heart, whirring thoughts, and an erection.

I have to take care of this now before all hell breaks loose. She did that on purpose. The last time she called me *sir* was at dinner, and I politely asked her not to. Does she know why I did?

It's a word that I fucking adore when I'm on top of a woman. I don't know why, but my mind goes into a frenzy when I've got a woman calling me that while I'm driving my cock into her.

If I really wanted to, I could go to the bar and find someone to bring home, but that would take too long. And going upstairs is off-limits.

Instead, I head back to the bedroom and will myself to the bed. There's only one way out of this, and it's an orgasm.

So, I lie down and strip my clothes. I lick my palm and lie my head on the pillow before wrapping my fist around my cock. A hiss leaves my lips as I pump my cock a few times. I spit on my palm to add more lubrication and close my eyes as I continue to pleasure myself.

But it's not enough. I try to picture any woman wrapping her lips around me, but it's no use. Everything veers toward a pretty blonde and her pink plump lips…

"*Fuck*," I hiss, pre-cum leaking out of my tip, and my fist moves faster. Just this once, I'll allow these thoughts to come to fruition. But that's it! If I'm able to do it this one time, then I will never again.

I think of her kneeling at the bottom of the bed, spitting on my cock, and then wrapping her lips around me. My hips tilt upwards with this fantasy, pretending I'm pushing myself deeper into her throat. I want her to choke, gag, whatever I have to do to make pretty sounds come out of her pretty mouth.

My hand moves faster and faster, imagining it's her mouth all over me. It doesn't take long for me to curse loudly before I cum in thick ribbons over my thighs and abdomen. I slowly stop my hand and open my eyes.

I stare at the ceiling as I gather my breathing, knowing what I did was so *wrong*. It felt so good at the moment to finally give in to the desire. But reality sets into what I just did. Masturbating to my daughter's best friend wasn't something I'd ever do, yet I did.

Fuck, I'm going to hell.

Chapter Seven

CLEMENTINE

MY HEAD IS POUNDING, and my tongue feels like the Sahara Desert. I pull my eyes open the best that I can without feeling like the sun is piercing through my vision.

Flashbacks of last night jolt me upright, and my vision is dizzy. I clasp my hand over my head and groan.

"What did you do, Clem? *En serio?*"

I'm naked in bed, and I have a little freak-out moment that I somehow was downstairs naked as well, but that's silly. I wouldn't do that. Drunk Clementine wouldn't do that to me, especially with Mr. Santos under this roof.

Mr. Santos.

Memories of him last night are still a bit fuzzy, but I remember what I said. I basically *flirted* with the man. I guess drunk Clementine has no shame. I bury my face in my hands and sigh.

Why, why, why? He's probably going to kick me out now for the stunt I pulled. He just looked so pretty last night, from what I remembered. He touched my arm, too, I think. I run my hand underneath my other arm, and my skin tingles. Yeah, he held me up when I basically fell up the stairs.

I have to play it cool tonight when he's home. Or I can be somewhere else… He doesn't need to witness any more embarrassing moments. I can't handle anymore, anyway.

Without another thought, I get up and grab my phone, peeking at the time. It's already eleven a.m. and I'm slightly frustrated that I'd let myself sleep in. I still have one week left until classes start, so I really wanted to get my sleeping schedule in check before then.

Rosa texted asking to meet up for brunch at one of our favorite spots: *Chismosas y Mimosas*. It's more or less a Mexican fine dining brunch spot that offers, you guessed it, mimosas. We love it, and so does the town. It's booked almost every weekend. Thankfully, it's a Monday, so it shouldn't be too bad.

Replying quickly to her that I can meet up in an hour, I get ready. I'm slow and have to pause a few times to stop myself from almost throwing up. I know it's really dumb to get back to drinking mimosas after day drinking yesterday, but I need it.

It's better than digging my nails into my skin 'til it bleeds, right? I saw Nathan at the pool party, and although we barely spoke, the hairs on the back of my neck were raised the whole time until I just kept chugging beer.

How silly, though. The one thing that helped him to get what he wanted was the one vice I could reach for at the moment. And I didn't stop drinking. I did the keg stand a few times and resorted to playing beer pong with a few of the guys that Garrett knew. Rosa and I won every game, which resulted in more shots.

It made me forget everything he did to me. His touch still burned my skin, even now. I want nothing to do with him, yet he plagues this town and my mind. It doesn't help my case that he's in the frat that's super close with Garrett. That means that the closer Rosa gets to him, the more I might see of Nathan whenever I hang with them.

My whole body shudders at the thought of seeing him even more than I want to. The only way to stop it... would be to tell Rosa the truth. I know she'd believe me, but it's just not something I can handle right now. I'm still slowly recovering from the aftermath.

And. He. Seems. *Fine.*

It infuriated me to see how well off he seemed. How does that happen? I'm burying myself with the grief of who I was before he ruined me meanwhile, he's having the time of his life, probably with a new girl too. I didn't see someone latched on to his hip yesterday, though.

I finish curling one last strand of hair before I set down the curler and assess my final look. I've opted for denim shorts and a cute flowy top that is open in the bottom half and flutters to the sides. It's bright green because I heard somewhere that green makes brown eyes pop more.

Not that I want any more attention on myself than I'd like, but the thought of maybe *someone* seeing me in this brings a simmering feeling to my core that rushes between my legs.

"No, Clem," I tell myself in the mirror before heading out of the bathroom. I can't think of him anymore. What I did was wrong, and I have to apologize. And I will.

I grab my purse from the bedroom and slip on some pretty beige sandals before heading downstairs. My steps are loud against the hardwood floor as I near the kitchen and head straight to the cabinet and pull out a big glass before filling it. I gulp it down in seconds before filling it up again. I really need to do better about staying hydrated if I drink, I think to myself.

I look around the kitchen, and it seems untouched. My eyes fix on a door a little ways down the hallway I just passed. It's ajar, and my heart races. Mr. Santos isn't home, but he left his door open. I glance around me as if to catch a camera watching my every move before I set the glass down on the island and make my way to the door. My hands rest on the door and doorframe, and I take a deep breath.

What am I doing? This is definitely pushing boundaries and invading his personal space. I push the door a little more, and it creaks, scaring the shit out of me. The fates are testing me, and they're warning me to stop. But I don't listen to them.

The door opens wider until I can take one step inside. I'm not sure what I was expecting, but a *clean* room wasn't it. The king-size bed is made with black sheets. The pillows are white and look fluffy. Images of Mr. Santos lying on that bed while I crawl to him fill my mind.

"No, no, Clem. Stop!" I whisper before taking a step back and slamming the door shut. My heart is thrumming erratically against my ribs, and I try to even my breathing. I can already feel the sweat start to form at the base of my neck.

I have to leave this house before my dirty thoughts of Mr. Santos take over. Quickly, I head to the kitchen to grab my things and pull open the Uber app. Within minutes my ride is here, and I head to the brunch spot to meet my best friend.

"AND I TOLD him that I can't go with him to LA!" Rosa pouts.

I raise my champagne glass and take a sip of the mimosa. It's practically 90% champagne with the slightest pour of orange juice. I look at my best friend before she raises a brow, waiting for a response.

Her black hair is curled perfectly, and it makes me wonder if she moved a lot of her things to Garrett's already... how else would she curl her hair if she didn't come back to the house today?

"Why not?" I ask before taking another sip.

IN DESPERATE RUIN

She widens her eyes and she looks like she's about to grab me and shake me. "Clem! *Mi papá! No puedo ir a ninguna parte con él alrededor.*"

"He doesn't seem like the helicopter parent type," I retort.

"He isn't," she concedes. "But! That doesn't mean he will let me go on a trip with a *boy*. He'd let *us* go."

I giggle at this. She wasn't wrong about that. My parents would do the same. I don't even know if I'd ever date again in college, but I know for sure they wouldn't let me go on a trip with another guy before they knew exactly the kind of guy he was. They're the only ones who know what happened with Nathan besides my therapist.

A pang of guilt flashes over me, and I try to gulp it down as I stare at my best friend.

"I really want to, though, Clem. I *need* to," she pleads, pouting her lips and giving me puppy dog eyes.

"Me? Why are you looking at *me* like that? That's reserved for your dad, he's the one you have to convince," I laugh. She huffs out a loud breath before waving her hand at me.

"I was going to ask you to cover for me, but I guess you don't want to."

I roll my eyes at this and hold back a laugh. "Don't guilt me into doing something that will probably get me in trouble with your dad."

Her eyes sparkle at this, and she smirks. "He wouldn't get mad at you. You're our guest. The least he'd do is hide the beers or something. He's harmless."

Instantly, thoughts of her father *punishing* me fill my vision. I lean into it, finding myself daydreaming of what he'd do to me if he did find out I was covering up a lie for his daughter. Would he tie me up on his bed? Wrap his huge hand around my throat like a necklace? Fuck me until I spill everything–

"Hello! Clem! What are you thinking about?!"

I blink a few times before I touch my cheeks and take a deep breath. She looks at me with a confused expression before I smile. "Nothing!"

"It was not *nothing*! You looked like you were… having a sex daydream. I know how those look, *nena*."

My eyes widen and I shake my head. "What? No, I wasn't."

"I swear the fact that you can go from a conversation about my dad to basically fucking someone in your daydream is wild to me. Don't be ashamed of it, babe. I would do it too if I had to keep this conversation about my dad."

"Hmm," I mumble, not wanting to say something that will get me caught. But the reverberating sound of his possible moans as he pins me down and sinks his cock into me, is all I hear.

And that's when I realize that as much as I want to lie to myself about my attraction to her father, I can't.

I want him. I *need* him. Every fiber of my being is burning for him. And I'll willingly walk into those flames.

"So, were you?" Her words break my thoughts, and I nod before widening my eyes and shaking my head.

"I wasn't."

"Okay, sure." She giggles. "Help me find a lie for my dad so I can go to LA, please! I need this, Clem."

"I'll be going to school next week, so I don't know how much help I'd be," I confess.

She pouts again and lifts the champagne glass to her lips. "I'm falling for him, Clem."

"*No, no lo estás.*"

"Okay, fine. Not really falling, but I am really starting to feel like a couple." Her cheeks turn rosy, and I smile at that. I like it when my best friend is happy. She deserves it.

"He's nice to you, and I saw how you two were yesterday," I agree. She smiles brightly before drinking the mimosa. We've already finished our food, so we're trying to drink the rest of this mimosa pitcher on the table. I grab it and fill our flutes once more.

"Clem, he really is. If you ever want me to introduce you to his friends, I can!" Before I can respond, she gasps. "Wait, I think Nathan was there yesterday. Wasn't he?"

My mood goes sour and I nod slowly, grabbing the flute and taking a big gulp. The bubbly liquid fills my body, and I try to focus on that feeling as I wait for Rosa to continue.

"I still don't understand why you guys broke up, but you don't have to tell me. Did you guys talk?"

I shake my head.

"No, we didn't." My words are sharp, and I don't intend them to be. He does this to me. Makes me put up a wall that I wish I never had. Especially toward my best friend.

"Well, the offer's still on the table if you'd like me to introduce you to Garrett's friends, okay?"

"Mhm," I murmur before finishing my glass. The tension is building in the air and I know she can sense it. Rosa hates conflict, and I can see it in her body language. She's touching her hair more, looking everywhere but me, and pulling her lip between her teeth.

We finish the pitcher before a waiter comes over and hands us the bill. She takes it and doesn't let me pay for my half.

"My dad's treat for his girls," she winks, all tension dissipating with her smile as she slaps a credit card down.

"Is that yours or his?" I laugh.

"His, I snuck it out of his wallet yesterday. Don't tell him, Clem. Now *that* is something he'd really get mad at me for."

"Wouldn't he see the charge on it though?"

She looks horrified for a moment. "Didn't think about that, but you know what? I still stand by what I said. His treat. For his girls."

His girls. Those two words make my stomach flutter. I busy my hands at my sides, but before I can dig my nails into them, the waiter comes back and takes the card. He's back within a few minutes, and Rosa signs the receipt.

We're outside in no time, and I give her a long hug. She sways our bodies, and she hums a song I don't know.

"I'm going to find a lie, and then I'll tell you," she whispers. "I really want to go to LA, and my dad isn't going to stop me."

We pull apart, and she grabs my face in her hands. I look at her soft eyes before I smile and nod. "Sure."

"You're the best, *nena.*"

But despite her words, I don't feel it. My emotions have been everywhere today, and I've been awake for barely five hours. We both call our prospective Ubers before hers comes first, and she gives me a kiss on the cheek.

"*Con cuidado,*" I tell her as she steps into the car. She looks back for a moment before giving me a smile and a wave.

My Uber comes almost ten seconds later, and I stumble in, resting my head against the headrest. My body is spent, like I ran an emotional marathon, and I know just the thing that will calm me.

My Regency show and that big, comfy couch.

THE LAST EPISODE of the season ends, and I'm blowing my nose. I go through all the emotions and feel silly once reality sets in, and I find myself in the living room surrounded by tissues.

It's nearing six p.m. and neither Santos member is home yet. I take this time to clean up my mess, turn off the TV, and head upstairs. I change into a bikini to catch the last few rays of sun for the evening. I make sure to put on sunscreen before heading downstairs and out into the backyard. The clouds aren't visible, which makes me happy that I can tan.

The water is cool, so I just stay on the pool chair for a while as I soak up the sun. It doesn't take long, though, for the clouds to start to appear and the sun starts to dip in the sky. The temperature gets a little colder, and I know it's about time to head inside. I peek at my phone and see that it's seven thirty. I haven't heard any noises of the screen door opening like they did when Mr. Santos came through them last week.

He must still be at work. I gather my things and don't bother putting on a cover-up as I head back inside. I regret it almost instantly as the AC bites my skin, and I hiss from the sudden cold. As I walk past the kitchen, I halt my steps as I near Mr. Santos' room. The door is ajar again, and my heart races.

He's home. I keep quiet as I try to tiptoe past his door, but that's when I see *him* through the crack of the door. My eyes widen at the sight. He's heading into the bathroom at the far end of the bedroom, and he's *naked*.

His back muscles are prominent, and his wide shoulders make me squeeze my thighs, but worse of all… his thighs are like tree trunks. My eyes linger on his ass, and then I gaze along his body, wondering what it'd be like to climb him. Crawl to him. Wrap my body against him like a koala.

I blink away those thoughts and start to make my way out of his sight before I trip and make a loud noise as my phone drops. Horrified, I pick it up and run down the hall and up the stairs as fast as I can. My ears are pounding and my heart is racing like a horse before I slam the door shut.

I hear a muffled noise, and I know it's Mr. Santos trying to find the reason for the loud noise. But I don't show myself. I can't. I'm too embarrassed. He could've caught me *looking* at him!

I hide in my bedroom before I start to smell food wafting up through the house, and my stomach growls. I have to make my appearance sometime and I'll have to face him eventually.

After last night and then *this*, I don't know how I'll last. I change into reasonable clothes that aren't a skimpy bikini before heading downstairs to face him.

Mr. Santos.

Chapter Eight

ARLO

I GET a text back from Rosie on the way home from work. It's not something I was expecting, and it makes me curious about what she's possibly wanting. I already know she's sneaking off to see some boy, but this is different.

She's asking if she can talk to me about a trip she wants to go on. It's important, and she *has* to go, apparently. I tell her that she can come home tonight and talk, but she leaves me on read.

I don't let that annoy me as I finally get home, shed the work clothes, and head for the shower. On the way to the bathroom, I hear the sound of something clattering right outside my bedroom door and then the sound of running and noise upstairs. That's when I notice I left the door open.

"Shit!" I scramble to get a towel and wrap it around my waist before heading to the hall. Was Clementine home this whole time? I didn't bother to check the backyard, I was too focused on Rosalía's text to do anything but strip and shower the day away.

"Clementine?" I call out into the hallway, but I don't hear anything. She must be in her bedroom.

After a minute of no response, I return to the bedroom and

finish my shower before making dinner and that's when Clementine appears in the kitchen. I'm sipping on a beer before we lock eyes.

"It smells really good," she mumbles before taking a seat near the island.

I give her a half smile before heading back to the stove where the pan of shrimp is.

"I just made enough for myself. I didn't know you were home," I lie.

"Oh," she squeaks out. "I can make myself something, sorry. That was rude of me to assume you made something for me." The sound of her stool scraping against the hardwood floor fills my ears.

I turn around. "I'm kidding, *Girasol*," I say. I press my lips together after saying that fucking nickname. Her cheeks have a hint of mauve to them, and I'm not sure if it's her blushing or just a sunburn.

"Oh," she says again.

"*Siéntate*," I tell her, and she obeys, sitting back down. I prepare a plate of shrimp tacos for her, before placing them on the table. She grabs hers, and she licks her lips.

"This looks amazing, Mr. Santos," she smiles broadly.

"Another *Mamá Santos* recipe," I smile back.

"You mentioned you have a lot of her recipes to try out. I'm excited to try this one."

I nod, and my heart warms a little at her words.

"*Comé*," I say without another word, and she nods.

I watch her slowly as she picks up a taco and takes a big bite into it. The juices of the shrimp and salsa I added shine on her lips, and I lick my own at the sight. Her eyes flick up to mine, and I keep my stare. I know it's fucking stupid to be doing it, and I can just imagine Frankie slapping the back of my head.

But I don't care. She seems to not care either. And that's

73

when she licks her lips, slowly and deliberately, before taking another bite while looking at me. It feels like the world has stopped spinning, and it's just us in this room. I've got tunnel vision, and it's her.

She chews the bite before swallowing and lifting her fingers to her lips. She licks them one by one until she twirls her tongue along her index finger. I imagine she's twirling her tongue along the tip of my cock, and I clench my jaw.

It suddenly feels hot in here, and I cough, breaking myself out of this trance. She smiles mischievously, and that's when I know she did that on fucking purpose.

I should be throwing her over my lap and spanking her a few times for doing that, but I hold myself back.

"That's yummy, Mr. Santos," she finally speaks up. I nod and take a bite of my own taco before washing it down with a Corona. That's when I forgot I never offered her one. I go to the fridge and grab one, popping the top with my bare hands and handing it to her. She watches for a moment, as if transfixed by me opening the bottle, before she smiles and grasps it, our hands barely grazing each other. It feels like a spark of electricity coursing through my body from that slight touch, yet I'm craving more.

"Thank you."

"*De nada*," I reply before sitting back down. The rest of the dinner doesn't go much further than what she just did. We finish our plates and I put them in the sink. She goes there as I wipe down the stove, and I see her start to clean them.

"You don't have to, Clementine," I start. She shakes her head and continues to wash them.

How can something so mundane look so fucking hot? I want to press myself against her back and make her beg me to fuck her right there. My hands are starting to hurt from how hard I'm scrubbing the stove, and I stop myself.

"I don't mind. I did it the first night," she says from the sink. That's when I whip my head to her.

"I thought Rosie did it?"

"No, she snuck out, remember?" She turns to look at me, and she giggles. I can't help but laugh too. She's contagious.

"You didn't have to."

"It wasn't a big deal, Mr. Santos. It's the least I can do for letting me stay here."

"A friend of Rosie's is always welcome here," I tell her before I finish the last scrub and start working on organizing the island from any mess. Once I'm done with that, she's done with the dishes as well. She's drying her hands on a hand towel as I head to the sink to clean the rag and my hands. Her neck cranes up to look at me as I do this, and I try not to focus on her stare. My eyes are fixed on my hands scrubbing under the running water.

"Mr. Santos," she whispers, so softly I almost miss it.

"Hmm?" I ask, finally shutting off the water and looking down at her. That's when I see her brown eyes sparkling with something. I can't decipher it, though, so I lean over and grab the hand towel to dry myself.

"I just wanted to apologize for last night. It wasn't appropriate of me," she starts. I watch her as she nibbles on her lips and then fidgets with her hands. That's when I see her fingers go to her sides and latch onto her skin. I shake my head at her apology.

"It's okay, Clementine. Really."

"No, it wasn't," she says almost too loudly, like she needs me to listen more clearly. So I let her finish. She takes a deep breath. "It won't happen again. I was drunk, and I said things that shouldn't have been said. I'm sorry if it made you uncomfortable."

We stare at each other for a few beats before I place my hands on her shoulder like I would when comforting my daughter. "Clementine, it's okay. I'm not mad, and thank you for apologizing. Next time I won't go near the door when you come home after a party."

Her lips part into a smile as she hears the implied joke. I rub her shoulders for a moment, reveling in her soft skin, and that's when it starts to become less like a comforting touch and more of a massage. My palms rub a little more into her shoulders, and she takes a deep breath as if she's enjoying it before she gasps and takes a step back.

Fuck, I messed up.

"Sorry," I blurt.

She shakes her head. "No, Mr. Santos. It's my fault, *lo siento.* Thank you for dinner."

"Of course, *Girasol,*" I say before she slips around me and heads to the hallway.

"*Buenas noches,* Mr. Santos," she calls out, and before I can respond, I hear her steps retreat from the first floor.

I lean back on the kitchen counter and sigh, wishing I never did that. Wishing I stopped feeding into these desires that shouldn't even exist. She apologized to me for what she said that night, and I massaged her shoulders. Who the fuck does that?

She's making it very clear that what she did was a mistake and that I have to stop these fantasies.

My mind won't allow it, though. It's consumed by her blonde hair, whispered hums, and the prettiest freckles.

FRANKIE IS WHISTLING as he heads toward me on the renovation site. I'm guiding a few trucks to where they need to go before I turn to where he is. He's got his hands on his hips as he watches me.

"What?" I ask, raising a brow.

"Nothing, *cabrón*."

"You're looking at me like I did something wrong," I quip.

Frankie doesn't respond as he walks closer, and I cross my arms over my chest. He wipes his upper lip with the pad of his thumb. "You did *nothing,* and I know it."

"Are you talking about something in code that I should interpret?"

He finally laughs and slaps my shoulder, causing me to almost lose balance, and I try to regain it as quickly. I gesture for the makeshift rest area a few yards away. It's just a picnic table that's got benches attached. We sit down across from each other.

"You know what I'm talking about, *herman*o. *Como esta tu nueva novia?*" He wiggles his brows and has a shit-eating grin plastered on his face.

A very punchable-looking face.

"Frankie," I bite. "*Cállate, carajo.*"

"What? You have that look on your face I know all too well. It means you're keeping secrets, and you never keep secrets from Frankie."

"Stop talking about yourself in third person. You know I hate it."

Frankie rolls his eyes. "Come on, what's the update? Or did your terrible dad jokes come into play and cause her to move out already?"

"No," I finally give in. "I'm keeping my space. It's a respectable thing to do. Rosie, on the other hand…"

Frankie shakes his head and pulls his palms to both ears. "No! I don't want to hear anything about Rosita.*"*

"Frankie," I say, laughing. "I don't know how to talk to her about the whole sneaking out. She never did this in high school, and she's about to be a senior in college. I shouldn't be this concerned, but–"

"But she's your Rosita," Frankie adds.

"Exactly. She even asked about a trip? It seems like a bigger thing than she's letting on. I thought she was planning to get a job."

"*Dios*, she's probably going with him, right?"

"She's an adult," I smile, but it's not real.

We're silent for a moment, and all we can hear around us are the men working and yelling out orders. Frankie is chewing on his cheek before he finally catches my gaze.

"You need to go out and get a date or get laid," he blurts out of the blue.

"Jesus, Frankie." I laugh. "I'm going to start limiting my time seeing you. This is all you talk about recently."

He pulls his hands up in front of him. "It's not my fault you're having these conflicting feelings and not doing anything about it. I haven't heard about a one-night stand in a while."

Frankie isn't wrong–it's been a while since I've had a one-night stand. Maybe it wouldn't hurt. It'd take my mind off *things* that I really shouldn't be focusing on.

"Okay, fine."

"*Bueno! Quieres ir al bar esta noche?*"

"Sure, why not," I respond almost too quickly. Frankie doesn't seem to notice, and he smiles again before standing up.

"I'll see you around 7? And tell Rosita her *tío* misses her if you see her later and not sneaking off with that boy."

I groan and bury my face in my hands. I really do need to talk to Rosie about this–establish some rules or boundaries. That's what normal parents do, right? I don't want things to go unnoticed, and then something happens to her. I don't want to ever be in the position where I regret not coming to her sooner.

Frankie is already heading back to the house, and I stand up from the picnic table and make my way over there as well.

I can go to the bar tonight. I *will*.

No one's gonna change my mind. Not myself and definitely not someone under my roof. *Nope.*

IN DESPERATE RUIN

THE BAR IS loud and pretty crowded. The music is pumping throughout the place. Frankie and I are already down a few beers. We've been catching up with other random topics before he starts to attempt the whole "get Arlo laid tonight" operation.

"What about that one?" Frankie asks, aiming his beer bottle toward a group of women who are giggling. Two are brunette, one blonde.

"Which one?" I ask, taking a sip of my beer.

"The brunette with the teal top. She looks nice."

I give him a look, and he cracks up, hanging his head back as he laughs. "You're a dick," I say.

"What? You can't tell me she's *not* attractive."

I don't argue, because I can't. He's right, she's attractive.

"And now they're starting to catch on to our stares," I slap his chest, and he laughs, waving at them. "What the fuck are you doing?"

"Calling them over! Why else are we here? To get drunk and cry about our old people problems? Fuck that."

I sigh and see the ladies talk to each other before they saunt over. They've got drinks in their hands, so we can't offer to get them some.

"Hey," I wave stupidly, and the brunette that Frankie pointed out gives me a long look before she smiles and sits down next to me. The other girls filter into the booth and sit next to Frankie. He looks like he's about to die in heaven, surrounded by these women.

"Harper," the brunette says as she gets closer. I give her a kind smile.

"Arlo, nice to meet you."

She gives me a once over before flickering her gaze to her friends, who just giggle. She doesn't seem too much younger than Frankie and I. Maybe early or mid-thirties. Her blue top accentuates her breasts and curves well.

"I like your name, want to buy me another drink?" She leans closer, and her perfume fills my senses.

"Sure," I nod before I turn to Frankie, who is already being caressed by two women. Damn, he works fast.

We wave a waiter over and order a few more drinks for the table, and they bring it back quickly. The women are energetic as they clink their glasses, and we start asking them questions. Apparently, they're just visiting for a week, here for a wedding of a college friend.

The brunette next to me, Harper, keeps ogling me whenever I look at her, and I know what's probably on her mind for what she plans to do tonight. I know I should be flattered and *want* to go along with it. Take her home, have sex, and then watch her leave in a rush in the morning. A routine I know too well from my newly single days. But I don't know if that's something I truly want right now.

"Arlo?" Frankie calls out, and I look at him as he wiggles his brows and starts to scoot out of the booth with the two women he's been chatting it up with.

"*Mande*?" I ask, raising a brow and watching him closely.

"We're gonna head to the bar for more drinks and dance. Wanna join?"

"I'm good," I give him a tight smile, and he looks at me and then Harper before giving me a small dance before the girls giggle and pull him along to the bar.

"He's got my friends really excited," Harper giggles.

"That's Frankie. He's the life of the party."

"And what are you?" she asks, leaning in closer and staring at my lips.

Everything in me says to continue this teasing, flirting, whatever it's called. It'll lead to the inevitable.

"Not the life of the party," I admit, giving her a sorry look.

She smiles and moves her body even closer, her hand traveling from her lap to mine, and I stiffen.

"I can make you feel like the life of the party. I've got some–"

"As tempting as that sounds, I'd like to make it on time to work tomorrow," I cut her off.

"Well then, what do you want to do?" She eyes me.

Fuck, I don't even know how to answer that. I look at the bar for a split second and see Frankie taking back shots with the girls, and they're clapping and jumping with him. He yells and pumps his fists in the air.

"We can head to my place," I finally say, and she nods, smiling.

"Lead the way, Arlo," she purrs before we get out of the booth.

I throw one last look at Frankie, who finally sees me, and he whoops before I head out of the bar with Harper. The hot summer air is stuffy as we make it to my truck. I open the door for her, she hops in and we make our way to the house.

It's not until we're pulling up in the driveway that I see a light on upstairs. It's not Rosie's room.

"You have someone living here?" Harper asks as she steps out of the car.

"Yeah, my daughter," I say cooly. I don't need to specify that it's Clementine.

She stops in her tracks as we make our way to the front door. I spin around and see her with widened eyes.

"A daughter?"

She seems to hesitate a little, and I knew this would be an issue. It always is the moment those words slip out with one-night stands. They assume my daughter is a toddler or something that needs tending to.

"She's twenty-one," I say almost too harshly. I don't know

why I'm getting so frustrated by this conversation when Rosie isn't even home.

Harper keeps her stance and looks up at the house before looking back at me. "Is she home?"

"She might be," I shrug. "Look, Harper, if you don't want to come inside, you don't have to."

Before I hope for the best, she shakes her head and takes a step closer. "That doesn't bother me. Just a one-time thing, right?" She smiles as she gets a foot away and gives me a wink.

"Y-yeah, a one-time thing," I mumble.

We head to the front door, and I make sure to keep my steps loud, and I close the door forcibly. If Clementine really is home, I need her to hear that I'm not alone, so she stays upstairs.

The last thing I need is her coming down while I'm mid-fucking a stranger. I don't need that horror-stricken face etched into my memory.

"Nice house," Harper calls behind me.

"Thanks, I fixed it up myself," I say as we head down the hallway toward my bedroom. The house is quiet, and the first floor is dark.

Harper hums before I open the bedroom door and let her go in first.

"I like it." She winks as she heads to the bed and sits down.

She's pretty, but she's in no comparison to–fuck, I have to stop thinking of a certain someone. Here I am, ready to fuck a stranger. I can't be thinking of someone else.

I can't.

"Something wrong?" she asks, patting the space next to her on the bed.

"No, not at all," I lie, before closing the door and locking it for good measure.

"Well then, come on," she giggles before waving me over. I nod and head toward her before she pulls me by my wrists to the bed. She's quick with the make-out session before she's stripping her clothes and pulling mine off.

I try to center my thoughts on pleasure and this stranger, but I can't help but think of pretty freckles and brown eyes.

It's horrible, I know. But I can't help it.

I'm deeply, utterly fucked.

Chapter Nine

CLEMENTINE

HE HAD SOMEONE OVER, and he fucking knew I was home.

I know I shouldn't be pissed, but I am. I heard them all *fucking* night. I knew I should've joined Rosa when she invited me out last night, but I wanted to call my mom as she and Declan started their day. It was a good talk, but then I heard the slam of his car door and a woman's voice outside my window. I even creeped out into the hallway and heard them talking before their voices faded.

Then the headboard slamming against the wall and practically shaking the whole damn house kept me up. I wanted to text Rosa out of spite and complain to her, but that wouldn't do me any good. Why would she want to know who her dad was fucking?

It also didn't help that while I couldn't sleep, the sound of the front door slamming shut woke me up around six a.m. I'm still tossing in the bed, trying to go back to sleep, but it's useless.

I groan and get up, knowing I'll have to just suffer and try to nap later. I get up to get ready for the day and put my hair up in a ponytail before I head downstairs. It's quiet, so I assume it must've been Mr. Santos slamming the door this morning with the woman. I pad my way into the kitchen before I jump and take a step back.

Mr. Santos is pouring creamer into his coffee, and he looks disheveled. But not in the 'just had the best sex of my life last night' way. He looks up and catches my gaze before he doesn't say anything and continues to prepare his coffee.

So he's grumpy, that's obvious. I take a deep breath before heading to the cabinet and pull a glass out to fill with water. The kitchen is silent save for my noises bustling around the place. I finally place the glass down harsher than normal on the island, and Mr. Santos eyes me closely before he takes a sip of his coffee.

"Good morning to you, too," he grumbles.

This pushes me over the edge. I turn to face him and place a hand on my hip.

"Excuse me?"

He watches me for a moment before he places his coffee down and fixes the collar on his shirt. His very *fitted* shirt that shows off his muscles. He's wearing jeans today, and they're just as fitted. I almost drool at the sight, but I have to remain pissed.

"I said good morning, *Girasol*," he repeats.

"Stop calling me that," I bite. A hint of a smile edges his lips before he returns to the stone stare.

"Sleep well? You're usually not up this early."

I let out a haughty laugh before shaking my head. "*Someone* kept me up throughout the night. And then someone slammed the door, waking me up when I finally managed to drift off."

His stone-cold expression melts for a second at my words. "Shit, sorry, *Girasol*. I didn't mean to wake you up."

"Hmm," is all I can say in response. He pulls the mug again back up to his lips as he eyes me.

"I'm sorry too about last night. Frankie had this great idea to—"

"I don't want to hear about it, Mr. Santos." I say quickly, spinning back around and heading for the freezer. I pull out Eggos that I'm suddenly craving. I pop two in the toaster and lean over the counter, staring at the metal reflection. I have slight bags under my eyes, and I want to scream at the person who gave me these.

"It won't happen again," he says almost too quietly. I turn to look at him, and I see his eyes flick to my face and he's got a pretty convincing apology written on his face.

"Okay," I answer softly.

The Eggos pop out of the toaster, and I grab a plate and drop them onto it before heading to the pantry for syrup. I pour a hefty amount and then make my way to the island. I don't sit down, though. I want to finish this breakfast and then head back upstairs as quickly as I can.

"I'll be at work until five, but then I can make dinner. Rosie should be home," he says as he finishes his coffee, heads to the sink, and starts cleaning it. I watch him for a moment, mesmerized by the flexing of his muscles in such a mundane task. I gulp the dryness in my throat before starting on the Eggos in front of me. I fold them like a taco before biting into one. The syrup spills from the ends and onto my chin. I quickly lick it up.

"Okay, sounds good," I reply.

He just grunts in response before he dries his hands and heads to the edge of the island where I'm standing. I have to crane my neck to look up at him, and there's mirth in his eyes.

"Again, I'm sorry. Won't happen—"

"It's *fine*," I snap.

His eyes darken, and he licks his lips before nodding and backing up. "*Llamame si necesitas algo.*"

"*Claro,*" I call out as he makes his way to the hallway. I hear the sound of something hitting the floor before the door creaks open and the jingle of keys. The door slams, and I'm left alone in this big house.

I look around and notice that there's a lunch box on the far counter that he forgot.

"Shit."

I run to grab it and head for the front door. I whip it open, but before I can catch him, I see his truck already driving away.

I head back inside and put his lunchbox in the fridge before finishing my food and heading back upstairs. I grab my phone and send him a text to remind him about it.

Once I see the bed, I hop back in and beg for a nap to come.

I SMOOTH my dress to make sure there aren't remaining wrinkles from being stuffed in the suitcase. Before I can even knock on the door, though, it swings wide open. Rosa smiles widely before ushering me inside.

"*Rapido!* We're pre-gaming before we head to the pool."

As I head inside the apartment, I notice that it's just Rosa and Garrett. He's pouring liquor into red solo cups before looking up and giving me a small smile.

Garrett isn't so bad. He treats Rosa well, so I don't hate him. But I reminded him the last time I saw him that if he ever breaks her heart, I'll do him worse. Even though it felt like an empty threat at the time, I know he took it to heart.

I'd do anything for my best friend. And I know she'd do the same for me.

"Hey, Clementine! Wanna drink?" he asks, lifting a cup my way as I get closer to the small kitchen island. The apartment isn't big, but the kitchen takes up the majority of the main area. The living room has a loveseat couch and a big TV. That's about it.

"Yeah, but I can make my own," I offer.

Before he can protest with the drink in his hand, I grab a cup from the packaging on the table and start pouring tequila and then some cranberry juice. I know I should trust Garrett, but it's out of habit to want to either watch someone make my drink or just do it myself.

My hands shake a little as I finish pouring the juice, and I take a quick breath to steady myself as I cap the bottle. Rosa leans over the counter and is wiggling her brows when I catch her gaze.

"Garrett said his good friends will be there! Some are taking summer classes too, so you might see them."

I take a sip of my drink, and my lips pucker at the slight over-pour of tequila. "Great," I cough out. Garrett laughs as I try to recover.

"*Con cuidado,* Clem!"

I wave my hand in the air and shake my head. "I'm all good, wrong pipe."

Garrett walks to the living room and picks up his phone, texting away. Rosa looks at me once more before doing a small dance as she comes closer to me. She eyes me up and down and gives me a look.

"What?" I sigh.

"You're not wearing that to the pool," she concludes, pulling me quickly down the hall to a bedroom. I stand in the middle of the room as Rosa starts shuffling through a duffle bag I presume is hers. She pulls out a cute, *very see-through*, bikini cover-up. It's basically like a net in the shape of a dress. Or one of those beach bags that are just rope-weaved very poorly.

I was definitely going to turn heads with that one, and not the good kind. Of any sort.

"I can't wear that," I spit out harsher than I mean.

Rosa raises a brow before dropping it to the ground. "*Okay*, sassy. I'm just trying to help you!"

"With what?" I'm not sure why I'm biting back at my best friend. Like a flip of a switch. One thing I know for sure, the

Santos family sure knows how to push my buttons without even realizing it. Maybe I'm still pissed at her dad for last night and then being all grumpy this morning.

I sigh and give her a half-hearted smile. "I like my cover-up." I look down at the teal dress that hits my thighs just right and flows out nicely. I've got a white bikini on, so the straps show and compliment my tan skin.

"Okay, fine," Rosa pouts. She steps closer and reaches for my cheeks. I stare at her brown eyes for a moment as she assesses me for whatever reason.

"What?" I smile.

She leans in and kisses my forehead. She does that a lot when she's nearing tipsy. "I love you, Clem. I just want you to be happy like I am with Garrett."

I playfully roll my eyes. "I'm happy, Rosa."

"I know, but...."

My brow raises, and she's silent for a moment. "But, what?"

She squeezes my cheeks again before dropping her hands. "I don't know. I guess I just feel bad."

"About what?"

Rosa walks to the messy bed and sits down before huffing a breath and looking up. "That you're not going to have a fun summer. It's the *last* summer before we graduate, Clem. I want you to have fun... I *need* you to. Especially with our Greece plans wrecked! You deserve it. I feel bad that you're stuck in a house you're not familiar with."

My steps are soft as I get close to my best friend, and I lay my hands on her shoulders. I bend my knees a little to get closer in height to her. "Rosa, don't worry about me. *Por favor.* You don't have to look out for me."

"But–"

I shake my head. "No! No buts. I can handle my own, and I don't need you feeling bad about me. It's not your fault you found Garrett. I like him for you."

89

"Really?" Her eyes widen with her sheepish smile.

"Yes." I nod. "Plus, I totally gave him the best friend talk of "if you ever hurt her, I will hurt you'."

"You didn't!" She laughs.

"Totally did. He peed his pants, I'm pretty sure. I can be convincing."

Rosa doesn't say anything, but her smile stays plastered on her face, and her eyes are gentle. They remind me of her father's. When his gentle eyes looked at me in the rearview mirror before he dropped us off at the pool party the other day.

I clear my throat before dropping my hands from her shoulders and stepping back. "I think this dress is fine," I finally say.

"Give me a twirl," Rosa exclaims, and I do as she says. The dress floats with the movement and then settles against my thighs, but when I look at Rosa, she's got a weird expression on her face.

"What? Everything okay?" I ask, pinching my brows.

Her gaze is locked on my lower half. "Are you hurting yourself again?"

It feels like all the air escaped in the room and I'm clawing my way to breathe *anything* my lungs can grasp. My hands instantly go to the sides of the dress, and I press the fabric closer to my body.

"It's just a habit, Rosa," I whisper. She stands and is harsh when she grabs my hands, locking them together with one of hers before she uses her vacant hand to lift my dress ever so slightly.

"Those are new, though," she murmurs. I want to break free from her grasp, but she's strong. She doesn't pull the dress any further up to the point where I'm morbidly uncomfortable.

"Don't worry about it," I hiss. She snaps her head up to me, and her brown eyes are fiery. Like there are flames beneath the brown and golden colors in her iris. She's pissed.

"*Me prometiste!*"

This time I *do* pull my wrists out of her grasp before I stumble back. "Rosalía! This is nothing."

"But you promised you'd tell me if you started again. I noticed you constantly scratching your legs last week, but I didn't think anything of it! *'It's just nerves,'* you told me. But this is bad, Clem."

"No, it's no—"

"They're turning into fucking scabs, Clementine! How long have you been harming yourself like this? This is different than just a bad habit." Her voice is loud and rattles in my brain like no other. I take a deep breath and step back. Her eyes widen, and she reaches her hand out to me but I don't let her close the distance.

I want to tell her that it's never going to go away and that this habit will be stuck with me for the rest of my life. Words of my therapist come to the forefront of my mind when she debunks that myth, but I don't want to listen. My mind is warped into a dead-set principle. That I'll always live like this and never get better.

"Well?!" Rosa screams this time, and I jump in place.

"Don't scream at me like that," I whisper.

Her hands go to her hips, and she scoffs before her face fills with even more worry. "I'm sorry, *nena*. I care about you. You promised you'd tell me when it got *this* bad. It's one thing to constantly scratch an itch, but it's different when you're physically harming yourself over and over again to the point there are scabs and faint scars."

"I'm just—" I have to find a lie and quick. I look around the room frantically, and she's waiting, her foot tapping against the floor. "You're right, it's a lot right now. I'm stressed about school and about the trip being canceled."

"Is that it? Because remember April?"

I stare at my best friend and attempt to swallow the wad of cotton in my mouth. April 14th is the date she's talking about.

The night I was at the library writing a paper that was more than half a grade for a class and left way past midnight. I was walking back to our dorm when I bumped into Nathan.

None of my therapy sessions or coping skills could've prepared me for the day I'd bump into him again. I went for almost a whole school year, ignoring and dodging him at every opportunity.

Until April 14th.

He was drunk, *go figure*, and wanted to talk. But he really didn't want to *talk*. There was a lot of yelling, and I had to physically push him off me to run back to the dorm.

That was when I went back to my secondary method of self-harm: digging my nails into my skin until it punctured and bled. It was better than my primary method of using scissors, a razor, or anything sharp I could get my hands on to relieve me of the memories of the assault.

Rosa woke up to find the bloody toilet paper in the trash I forgot to flush when I cleaned the wounds. I lied and told her I missed the deadline for the paper and would get docked a whole grade letter.

It was enough of a lie for Rosa to believe me and think it was all stress-induced methods of self-harm and not ptsd induced. I spoke to my therapist, and she encouraged me to finally tell Rosa the truth about what happened a year prior. But I couldn't. The shame was too much, and I didn't want the pity.

No one ever sees a rape victim the same, especially if it's a close friend.

"Clem?" Rosa's voice is softer now as she breaks my thoughts. I glance at her before I blink back the tears that were attempting to surface.

"April was different. *This* is different. I promise. It's just circumstantial stress."

"*Prométeme?*"

I nod. "Promise."

Rosa is silent as she studies me. She finally smiles before closing the distance and pulling me in for a hug. "I know you're kind of trapped here for the summer, but please let your mom and Declan know what's going on. That might help ease the stress of it all."

"Sure," I whisper as I wrap my arms around her. We rock our bodies for a little before there's a knock at the door that makes us separate.

Garrett pokes his head in the doorway, and he looks between the two of us. "Everything okay? I heard some... things."

Rosa nods, and I smile. "We're perfect, right?"

"*Perfecto*," I answer before I follow her out of the bedroom and back into the kitchen.

"The guys are at the party already setting up a keg and a table for flip cup," Garrett calls behind him as he starts grabbing bags from the kitchen counter.

"Yay!" Rosa claps her hands.

We help Garrett carry some of the bags, and I notice mine has some seltzers in it. I grab my beach bag before we leave the apartment and head to the pool.

But I catch Rosa looking at me every now and again, making sure I'm okay.

I'm not sure if I am, but I'm doing my best.

Chapter Ten

CLEMENTINE

THE POOL IS ALREADY FILLING up with college students, and I can feel my blood pressure spike. Rosa, Garrett, and I have been here for two hours already with some of Garrett's friends. We've gone through the majority of our seltzers and beers before we waited for the pool to fill up more to break into the keg.

The sun was scorching us to the point where even sunscreen didn't seem to do much. I've applied it twice since being out here. I refused to return to the Santos home looking like a lobster.

My solo cup is starting to empty, the remnants of the seltzer I poured swirling the bottom as I stare at it in my hands. Rosa's laugh can be heard across the pool, and I look up momentarily.

That's when my eyes lock with the one person I didn't want to deal with today. Nathan. His blonde hair looks even more light under the harsh rays of the sun. He's got a tan, and he seems even more muscular than the time I bumped into him last April.

He hasn't noticed me yet, so I get up from the pool chair and head to Rosa and Garrett. I feel pathetic to even do so, but I'm buying myself time. My chest is already constricting by the sight of him.

"Hey! You wanna play beer pong?" Rosa asks as I near the table she's in front of. Garrett's talking to one of his friends, and I look back briefly at Nathan, who is still oblivious to me.

How can he look so calm? It angers me to the core that he can be so nonchalant about everything.

"Clem?" Rosa nudges me, and I snap my gaze back to her and nod.

"Yeah, I'm so down only if we're on the same team."

"Uh, duh!" Rosa laughs as she starts to assemble the cups. I take position next to her, and Garrett finally zones in on us.

"Woah! Clementine and Rosalía challenging someone to beer pong?!" he exclaims with a smile.

"If you're okay with losing, get to the other side of the table, baby," Rosa teases as she pours water into the cups from a pitcher.

We've always played beer pong this way to keep things as sanitary as we can. We hate having to drink beer from the actual cups with ping-pong balls that touch every surface. No, thank you.

"You're on," Garrett chuckles before looking around the pool for a teammate. His friends are already off to the side setting up the keg, so he looks across the pool. My eyes widen as I see where his gaze lands.

No, no, no. Please, *no*.

"Hey!" Garrett calls out to the other side of the pool where a few guys, and Nathan, are hanging out setting up their stuff. They all turn to look, and that's when Nathan catches my eyes.

There's a curl to his lips that I can spot a mile away as he nods to Garrett and heads our way. My heart thrums against my chest to the point I'm sure it's going to break some ribs. It feels like my airway is constricted, and I take a few deep breaths to maintain composure. Rosa doesn't notice any of this, and I'm glad. I don't need her freaking out on me and asking what's going on.

I can do this. I can handle him.

"Garrett Lock, how are you, man?" Nathan asks as he makes it to the table, brings Garrett into a side hug, and slaps his back. I watch the exchange before they make it to the end of the table, and Nathan flickers his blue eyes to me.

My stomach somersaults at the sight and I want to leave the party, go *anywhere*. But I have to persevere. I have to be strong. I can do it... Right?

THE FIRST GAME of beer pong is tense and pretty quiet, save for the noise around the pool of all the other partygoers. Rosa can feel the tension and even whispers if everything is okay. I nod every time and gulp down any fears or trepidations.

My silence should be an answer in itself, but Nathan's glare doesn't help at all. Garrett and he seem to be buddy-buddy the more we play the game and drink. I sip my drink, though, instead of chugging anytime they get a ball in our cups. I even find myself hovering my palm over the opening of my cup anytime I set it down.

I don't even think my heart rate has calmed down at all since seeing him. It feels like my body is stuck in survival mode; the fight or flight senses taking over. I try to recall all the coping methods my therapist taught me to complete in public. I can't really do the five senses grounding technique right now without people questioning what I'm doing.

Deep breathing seems to be the only thing I can do at the moment, but even then, it doesn't help. We carry on for one more game before I have to call it quits.

"Are you sure?" Rosa asks, brows scrunched and her face laced with worry. I nod.

"Positive, just need to get some water. Play without me!" I urge before stepping away from the table.

I make a beeline to the chair with my bag, and I rifle through it before I find my phone and make my way to the doors that lead to the inside of the apartment complex, where the bathrooms and a water fountain are.

The AC is cool in here, and I let that envelope me, and I can already feel my heartbeat slow. My phone is hot even with it being in a bag, so it's slow to open. I see a text from Mom with a picture attachment that won't load.

Another is from Mr. Santos, but it's not even a text. It's a reaction to the text I sent him this morning letting him know he left his lunchbox at the house. All he did was 'thumbs up' it. I roll my eyes before clicking my phone off and heading for the water fountain. As I'm leaning down to take a sip, I hear the sound of the door opening behind me and some steps.

Without even knowing who's behind me, I get a bad feeling. My stomach drops and the hairs on the back of my neck stand up. I look up and wipe my mouth from the dripping water and see Nathan playing with his sunglasses in his hands. He looks up, and he gives me a smirk.

"Didn't think you'd be here this summer."

I take a step back from the fountain, and even after drinking enough to be hydrated, my throat feels like it's closing in on itself, and it feels super dry.

"Yeah, I'm here," I croak out.

"Hmm," he murmurs as he takes a step forward. He's shirtless, and his muscles flex as he raises his sunglasses to put on top of his head. His height is a solid six-foot, but he seems a little wider with muscle. Bigger shoulders, bigger arms, and it brings a sense of fright to my core. What I once thought was cute, being so much shorter than him, makes me want to throw up with the disadvantage I have under him.

I gulp as I try to think of something to say. The tension is thick, and it's not hard to miss the way his eyes glaze over my body. He's so obvious about it, and it makes me want to hurl.

"Why are you here?" he asks slowly, inching forward. I back up and find myself hitting a wall. I exhale loudly from the impact, and his lips curl.

"Study abroad was canceled. Can't go back home." I'm not sure why I'm giving him a reason, but the words spill out.

"Pity," he mocks.

His blue eyes stay on mine and it feels like my worst nightmares. I close my own briefly and take a deep breath. That's when I jolt from the touch of his finger dragging down my bare arm. My lips quiver, and I open my eyes.

"I have to–" I stutter out, but he moves his finger to my chin.

As much as he pretends to do it in a comforting way, it invades every part of me. I want to slap his hand away, but I'm too weak. I'm too stunned and can't move.

"You have to what? I saw you looking at me from across the pool. You were practically eye-fucking me from where you were, Clementine. Did you miss me, is that it? Didn't seem like it the last few months, so why now? Huh?" With each sentence, he inches closer and closer to the point where we're chest to chest.

My erratic heart is bursting through my ribcage, and if I don't leave soon, I'll for sure have a heart attack.

"I need to go," I say more firmly.

"But we're having fun," he teases, lifting his finger from my chin to my bottom lip and lightly gliding over it.

"No," I whisper in the softest voice.

"We were so good until you–" he stops himself as he glides his finger over my lip again. This time I whip my head to the side, and a noise that sounds like an angrier grunt leaves his lips. Without a fight, he uses his whole hand to grab my chin and forces me to look up at him. We're practically nose to nose, and his blue eyes flame with something I can't decipher.

Anger? Annoyance?

"Let me go," I say as loud as I can, but it still comes out as a measly whisper.

"You're enjoying it. Admit it. Like all those times you claimed you didn't," he bites back. I hitch my breath, and my hands ball into fists, and my nails dig into my palm. I keep digging until the pain is all I can feel in the moment.

Not him, not his touch, nothing. Just the pain of hurting myself. His grip tightens and brings me back to reality.

I hate him. I hate him. I hate him.

A tear slips down my cheek, and I curse myself for showing weakness. It's not a good look, and I wish I was stronger than this. I've been battling this shit for a year, and yet I still react this way. I'm hopeless.

"Don't you fucking cry," he spits as his grasp on my chin tightens to the point where it *hurts*. Sweat drips down my back. His grip has my cheeks smashed together, and my next few words come out barely coherent.

"You're hurting me."

"You like it," he smirks.

Before I can answer, the sound of the door opens, and Nathan's hold on my chin softens, as does his face. The footsteps are loud as they clack up to us.

"Clementine? Nathan? What are you guys doing here?" Rosa's voice fills the room, and I breathe a breath of fresh air as Nathan steps back.

"Just catching up," Nathan smiles like a goody-two-shoes. But it doesn't look like Rosa buys it. She glances at me, and I try to maintain composure. Her dark brows scrunch for a moment before Nathan takes another step back.

"I'll see you later, Clementine. It was nice catching up. Let's do this again." He winks at me before turning on his heel and heading out. Rosa walks up to me, and I hold back the tears that are threatening to flood out.

"You okay? It looked intense."

Every molecule in my body is screaming at me to tell her the truth. *Anything.* She needs to know at least something about Nathan and I's relationship. But I kept it under wraps for so long and so well that it didn't come out publicly as some big blowout. She only knew that it was tense, and I didn't want to be near him or anyone anymore. Hence the whole dropping out of my sorority deal.

It didn't help that his family had money. Declan swore to fight for me in the courts and use every dime he had when I told him and my mom about what happened. But I couldn't face the scrutiny from Nathan and his friends anymore. He made me feel like an outcast for rumors that weren't true. Rosa seemed to be the only one who believed me, and yet I was the worst friend and never told her what was really going on.

I just wanted it to be over, so I didn't pursue any more legal action. It made me feel weak and unable to fight for myself, but my mom and Declan swore that it was just as strong of a move. I was doing it for myself to keep the peace and not escalate anything else.

What else could it have done, though? My 'reputation' was already ruined, I didn't want to keep up with my college friends except for Rosa, and then I almost changed my major.

Sometimes I think about what my life would be like if I continued to fight him in court. Would he even be at the same college? Would he be in jail? That thought alone makes me happy, but then I remember the route I ended up taking.

I'm not sure if it was the right one. But I don't know if any route would've been good.

"Yeah, I'm okay now," I mumble. Rosa nods and loops her arm around mine before dragging me closer to the door. I stop us, though, before we open it. I take a deep breath and look at my best friend.

Her smile falters as she watches me closely. I can do it. I can tell her.

"What's wrong?" she asks.

And that's when I know I won't ever get over it. Because I can't do this. I need to go.

"I'm sorry, I think I'm coming down with something," I lie. "I came in here to catch my breath, but it doesn't seem to be going away. I might catch a ride back to your house."

"Oh, okay," Rosa responds quietly. "Do you want me to go with you? I can call my dad."

"No, that's not necessary," I press. "I'm just going to call an Uber. But please have fun with Garrett. I'll see you tonight?"

Rosa presses her lips tightly before she smiles. "I'm actually going to stay with him tonight, I hope that's okay. I can go home, though, if you'd like. You just say the words, and I'm there."

I shake my head. "No, Rosa. Absolutely not. You can be with your…is he your boyfriend now?"

A blush creeps on her cheeks. "Not yet, but I think he's going to ask me very soon."

My heart warms for my friend and her relationship. If I can't have any of that, I'm glad Rosa can.

"That makes me happy for you, really," I confess.

Rosa squeezes my arm and smiles. "Thanks, Clem. That means a lot. Text me when you're home, okay?"

I nod, and we walk out to the pool area. I quickly grab my bag before I head to the gates and pull out my phone to order an Uber. I glance back at the party and see there are more games going on, and Nathan is back at the beer pong table with Garrett. Something in me really hopes they don't become friends. That would ruin everything.

My phone buzzes, letting me know that my ride will be here soon.

Guilt wraps around me like a snake, and it squeezes tightly. I need to tell her soon before something bigger happens. The rumors Nathan blabbered about, I can handle. It's other things Nathan might say that I can't handle.

I need to tell Rosa before it's too late.

THE HOUSE IS quiet the moment I get inside and close the door. I take a deep breath and lean my head back on the doorframe.

I let myself have this vulnerable moment as tears cascade down my cheeks and my throat tightens. An almost sob leaves my lips as I try to catch my breath from the sudden emotions.

It's been a while since I've felt like this. April was definitely one of those times, and that's a night I wish I could redo. All those nights I wish I could redo. I wish I never met Nathan.

I wipe my eyes before heading to the kitchen to get some water. But that's when I stop in my tracks before I get too close to the kitchen and hear plates scraping and, finally, voices. It comes to me now that Mr. Santos is home, and that was definitely his truck in the driveway. How could I have missed that?

It wouldn't be a good look coming into the kitchen with glossy eyes, so I wipe them and my cheeks from any remnants of crying before entering.

Mr. Santos isn't alone, and I widen my eyes as I see another tall man with brunette hair, a mustache, and a five o'clock shadow. His brown eyes look at me before he glances at Mr. Santos who's leaning over the island. Mr. Santos glances at me for a moment before the smile on his face slips.

"You okay?" He stands tall and straightens his posture. His friend is quiet as I nod and head to the cabinet to get a glass. The kitchen is quiet as I pad through the area to get a glass of water.

"Clementine," Mr. Santos says in a more firm voice. I turn on my heels and lift the glass to my lips, drinking in big gulps. He watches me for a second before his friend clears his throat.

"I'm Frankie," he says, reaching his hand out. I look at it for more than five seconds before he withdraws with an exhale from his lips. I don't want to seem rude, but my patience is running thin, even toward Mr. Santos' guest.

"Rosa won't be here tonight," I say, a little harsher than necessary, as I place the glass in the sink.

"Figured," Mr. Santos says with a chuckle. His friend, Frankie, laughs as well. I look at them before I glare at them.

Mr. Santos seems to notice, and he crosses his arms over his chest. It feels like we're at a Western Showdown staring at each other.

His friend is glancing between us two before he starts laughing. I glare at him, and Mr. Santos sighs before placing his palms back on the counter and leaning in.

"What's going on, Clementine?"

"Nothing, just needed water," I bite. I can turn on my heels, but his stare keeps my feet planted.

Mr. Santos glances at me again, and this time, it's like he's *looking* at me. His eyes shift from my eyes to my lips and then back to my eyes. "Where were you?"

"The pool," I say quickly.

"What happened?"

"Nothing," I lie.

Frankie whistles, and I shoot him another glare. I don't mean to be so rude to Mr. Santos' friend, but my senses are heightened, and my head is starting to hurt from the crying I did in the Uber and then at the front door.

"You're lying, *Girasol*. Don't make me ask again." His words are sharp, and I inhale a shaky breath.

"Stop pressing," Frankie speaks up finally.

"I've seen that face before," Mr. Santos says defensively.

"What face?" I ask.

"Yeah, what face?" Frankie asks.

"Rosalía would do that in high school whenever a guy broke

her heart and didn't want me to know about it. Glossy eyes, puffy cheeks, and redness all over."

I stay silent as Mr. Santos stares at me dead on. Frankie is silent, too, as he takes in my response.

"Now, I'm not going to ask you again," Mr. Santos lifts himself from the counter and walks very slowly toward me. I don't back up, though. I stand my ground. "What happened there?"

I take a deep breath and contemplate lying again, but he's reading right through me. I can't lie to someone who is so eagerly showing a protective stance. That's how I spilled to my parents. Declan had such a protective nature about it that it flowed out of me much easier than I expected. A lot of tears were included, but nonetheless, I told him.

Tears brim my eyes, and Mr. Santos' brown ones go soft, as do his features. My lips quiver, and I'm not sure if it's because he's Rosa's father and that mine is dead, and Declan isn't here, but I let myself feel as much as I allow. The tears fall down my cheek, and I take a quivering breath.

"Just bumped into someone I really wish I hadn't." I finally let out.

"Did they say something?" Mr. Santos' brows pinch before I see *anger* flash through his eyes. "Did they *do* something?"

Frankie finally speaks up with a much lower voice. "If something happened with that person, let us know. We can take care of it."

"You can't," I whisper. I keep my gaze locked on Mr. Santos' eyes because that's the only thing keeping me stabilized. If I dare to look away, I will crumble.

"Who was it?" Mr. Santos asks, and his jaw clenches.

"I can't," I whisper. He leans in closer and brushes my shoulder for a moment, and as much as I thought I'd jolt from it, I don't. I lean into it and let him rub my shoulder softly.

"Do you want us to take care of it? We will," he asks with a hint of venom in his words. I shake my head.

"Please, no. I just want to forget today ever happened." Another rush of tears falls from my eyes, and the next few seconds feel like slow motion.

Mr. Santos slowly reaches his thumb to my cheeks and wipes each tear away. My heart lurches for his comforting touch, but I don't let myself move closer to him. After he's done, he smiles warmly.

"Okay, *Girasol*. Want anything special for dinner? My treat." He stands tall again, and I crane my neck up to him.

I contemplate my answer for a moment before my stomach growls, and I realize I haven't eaten since this morning. "Pizza would be fine. And maybe those lava cakes?"

He smiles and nods before backing up. His friend catches my stare, and he raises a brow.

"Don't hesitate to let us know if someone bothers you again, okay?" I know he's attempting to ease the tension and make it lighthearted, but his body language says otherwise.

Oddly enough, it's comforting to know that these two burly men would do anything if something happened to me. It doesn't help the feeling of wishing I had that a year ago.

"Thank you," I whisper before turning on my heel and heading down the hall before making my way upstairs to shower and change into comfy clothes.

My cheeks still feel warm from where Mr. Santos' thumb was and I relish in that feeling for the next hour.

Chapter Eleven

ARLO

FRANKIE IS quiet as I take a seat and we wait for the pizza delivery.

My hands are still clenched into fists as I try to slow my breathing before I combust. *Girasol* didn't look okay. But she wouldn't tell us exactly what happened at the pool party.

"*Está bien,* Arlo," Frankie reassures me.

But it doesn't help. My jaw is still clenched tightly and if I clench it any harder I'd break teeth. "*Necesito saber.*"

"No, you don't."

I look at him. "You saw her face, Frankie. *Ay, pinche madre.*"

Frankie gets up and I watch him go to the fridge to pull out some more beers. He cracks them open and heads back toward me, passing me one.

He takes a deep breath before sitting back down and runs his fingers over his mustache. "She'll let you know if she needs your help."

"But–"

"No, Arlo," Frankie warns. "She's a big girl. Probably just

needs some time to cool down from whatever the hell happened over there. Ask her tonight or tomorrow."

I nod, having no idea what might've happened today at the pool, but a million scenarios cross my mind.

And a million of them end with me finding that *cabrón* and sinking my fist into his face. But Frankie's right. I can't make her tell me what's wrong; she just needs time, and I'll give her as much as she needs.

The doorbell rings and I get up, knowing it's the pizza. Frankie is already getting out the paper plates from the pantry by the time I return with the boxes, all too familiar with my home to know where things are placed.

As Frankie continues to set up the table, I head back to the front where the stairs are. I lean against the railing before calling for Clementine.

"Dinner is ready!"

The silence is almost deafening and it worries me a little. Without letting another minute pass, I head upstairs. They creak under each step and once I reach the top, I see the door to the guest room shut. As I make my way to the door, I try to listen for any sounds that she might be bustling around the room. But there's nothing.

I gently knock on the door.

"*Girasol?* The pizza is here. And those lava cakes."

Silence.

"Those lava cakes look damn good, Frankie might eat them all if you don't come out," I joke. I mentally slap myself for attempting to be funny at a time like this, but it seems to do the trick as her door creaks open and she comes into view within the few inches she allows.

Her brown eyes find mine. "I'll be down in a sec, Mr. Santos."

"Everything okay?" I raise a brow.

She opens the door a little more, and I see that she's changed into sweats with an oversized sweater. The clothes almost drown her and she looks damn cute in them.

I clear my throat, pushing those thoughts aside and she runs her hands over her blonde hair before stepping out into the hallway, closing the door behind her. I have to take a step back to allow her room, but we're still inches from touching.

She cranes her neck to look at me and her eyes are sparkling with something. I can't decipher what emotion, but it takes everything in me to not ask her again what's going on. I don't want to act like the overbearing father figure when she can tell me herself if she needs help.

There's more silence as she stares at me and exhales loudly. Her shoulders relax a little and she looks down, her hair covering her face. The next few seconds shock the living hell out of me.

I don't know why I do it, but I do.

My hand carefully holds her chin and lifts her head up to look back at me. She doesn't back away, knock my grip off her–nothing. I brush my thumb over her chin, close to her bottom lip. Her very plump lip that seems to be hypnotizing me at this very second. I can't stop staring at it, even as she licks her lips and her tongue ever so lightly glides over the tip of my thumb. This brings electricity throughout my whole body and down to my cock.

This isn't right, but I can't let her go. And she doesn't stop me.

"Mr. Santos–" she whispers.

"You'll let me know if anyone bothers you, okay, *Girasol*?"

She continues to look at me, her lips curving every way as if she can't decide if she wants to frown or smile.

"I need to *hear* it from your lips," I demand a little louder. My grip on her chin hardens just a little bit and she exhales loudly.

"Yes, sir," she breathes out.

I grind my teeth together at this, and it's like she *knows* how that word affects me with the way her lips curl into the smallest smile.

If she didn't know any better, and if she wasn't a guest in my house... I'd have her over the knee spanking her ass for that.

My thumb continues to brush over her skin in slow motions and it feels like it's just us.

Until it doesn't.

"Arlo!" Frankie's voice can be heard from downstairs and that seems to do the trick in snapping me out of this hypnosis. My hand falls from her chin and she blinks, stepping to the side.

"Wait, Clementine," I say, grabbing her arm before she heads down the stairs. She looks up at me.

"What?"

"I meant what I said," I remind her. Because she needs to know that any friend of Rosie's will get the same kind of protection that I give my own daughter. If anyone wants to fuck with them, then they can gladly deal with me.

She nods before turning and running down the stairs in a speed that's faster than I ever thought possible.

I take a deep breath to steady my thoughts and to be honest, my cock. I have to keep my distance from her.

I have to.

ONCE DINNER IS DONE, Frankie dips and it's just Clementine and I. I called Rosie right after we ate to make sure she's okay. I didn't ask her about Clementine yet; that didn't seem like it was my business.

Now that Clementine and I are alone though, I want to see if I can ask again. It's nearing eight p.m and we're lounging on the couch. She's on the other end of the L-shaped couch, laying down. I'm on the middle cushion, just an arm's length away from her.

If she sat up, her shoulders would be touching my fingertips from where I'm draping my arm over the couch. We watched a random comedy movie about people drunk in Vegas and accidentally getting married. It seemed to be the fix that Clementine needed as she laughed her heart out and even squealed at the cute moments.

She reminded me of Rosie when she and I used to watch movies together. I made sure to pop some popcorn as well and we snacked on it some.

"Can I suggest a show?" Clementine asks as the TV fades to black from the end of the credits we sat through.

"Sure," I mumble, watching as she leans over the couch to grab the remote from the coffee table. Her hair falls over her shoulder and it's the prettiest sight. I hate myself for liking how pretty she looks in every way.

She could wear a trash bag and she'd be the most beautiful woman in the room.

After settling back onto the couch, she surfs the streaming services until she pulls up one I didn't even know I had and searches for a show. She easily finds it and clicks it, but she doesn't press play. I look at her and she gazes over to me.

"Are you okay with this?"

I raise a brow. "Yeah, whatever you want to watch."

"It's cheesy and remember how I told you about those love confessions? This is that show…"

Her hesitancy makes me curious, but I brush it off to the side. I shrug. "I'm fine with that, *Girasol*. Play it."

She nods and clicks the button and the show starts. About five minutes into the show though my questions are answered.

It's not just a cheesy love confessional show. It's a *sexual* one, too, with full nudity. And not just kissing and making out with fade to black scenes. No, the full shebang.

"Oh my god!" Clementine screams in a fit of giggles as the guy on the screen throws the woman on the bed and tears her top off. Buttons go flying and her breasts are on full display.

I clear my throat and shift my body. I look at Clementine and she's covering her mouth as she continues to giggle. She catches my eyes before hers widen and redness washes over her face.

"I swear I thought this would be a tame episode! I'm so sorry, Mr. Santos. I can turn it off." She reaches for the remote, but I shake my head.

"It's fine, it's just sex on screen. It could be worse."

She presses her lips into a firm line as she assesses my tone before I give her a smile to add to the humor of it all. Clementine then laughs loudly before settling back onto the couch.

I reach for the popcorn bowl and start munching on it for distraction. It doesn't help that with the moans on screen that I'm starting to get aroused as well.

Why is this sex scene so fucking long? Just get to it! He's still stripping his clothes off after eating her out. Thankfully, *that* part was shown from the waist up where we could only see her reactions.

It makes me wonder what the hell kind of streaming service allows all this nudity. Did she accidentally search for Regency porn?

I almost choke on a kernel when they scream through their climax. My eyes glaze over to Clementine and she's looking at me before furrowing her brows. I cough through the kernel lodged in my throat.

"Do you need water?" she asks, getting up and running to the kitchen. Before I can tell her no, she comes back with a glass of water. But she's too fast on the hardwood floor and she slips on her socks as she yelps.

It all happens within two seconds. She slips, I drop the popcorn bowl to try to catch her, and the glass of water douses my thighs and crotch before she falls on top of me.

My thighs are drenched and the cold water seeps through the fabric. Her hands are on my knees from where she caught herself and mine are on her arms, gripping her sweater. She looks up in horror and her fingers tighten on my knees. Her face is eye level with my crotch and it does something to me with how briefly she stares at it.

She scrambles to get up and I help her as best as I can before I can assess my own damage.

"Shit, I'm so sorry, Mr. Santos!" She groans before grabbing the pile of napkins on the coffee table and blotting the spill on my thighs. She's quick with her hands and she's doing it in such a hurry that she travels too quickly up my thighs.

She pats the napkins right on my crotch, and I hiss, grabbing her wrists, and her movements stop.

"Clementine, it's okay," I breathe.

"Oh my god. I'm so–"

She backs up and raises her hands in a surrendering position at what she was doing and I shake my head, gathering the napkins and balling them up. I stand up and she's biting her bottom lip before she rests her hands at her sides.

"It's okay," I repeat. The show is still playing in the background and they're finally past the sex scene but after how Clementine just brushed over my cock, that's all I can think about right now.

I try to tame my breathing as I walk around her and head to the kitchen to toss the soaked napkins. I hear her footsteps behind me.

"Are you sure?" Her voice is soft.

"Yes, Clementine, you can go back to your show. It's alright."

She's quiet for a moment and I have to look behind me to make sure she's still there. Her hands are pressed against her sides and her gaze is locked on the ground.

"*Estoy bien, Girasol*," I reassure her.

"Are you mad at me?" She finally looks up at me and her eyes are slightly glossy.

I stare at her in disbelief. "Quite the opposite."

"What does that mean, Mr. Santos?"

I can't tell her that her brushing napkins over my crotch got me thinking of only her, in not so appropriate scenarios. Much like the scenarios we just watched on the TV.

"Forget it," I mumble before making my way to the hallway.

"Mr. Santos!" Her steps are loud as she runs after me and I pause and turn around, but her damn socks got her sliding again as she tries to stop herself from my sudden turn. She collides into my chest and she lets out an *oof* as I catch her elbows. She looks up at me, something shines in her pretty irises that make me question everything. That I'm not so crazy with these thoughts. That those times I thought were just mere moments of either sarcasm or simple flirting was just a fluke.

No, her eyes tell me that she *might* just be thinking the same things I have been.

The inappropriate scenarios and the most *forbidden* kinds of things that we really shouldn't do. We really shouldn't.

But then she swallows.

"Tell me," she whispers, pleading with her eyes.

I shake my head and rub her elbows, my fingers brushing against the soft sweater fabric. "No, *Girasol*."

"You said you're not mad at me, so what are you?"

It's like she's challenging me to finally say it out loud. To finally speak it into existence.

I can't.

"Forget it," I repeat with more tenacity. What I need to do is change out of these soaked jeans. And maybe do something about this erection that is bound to arise with her pleading eyes and words.

"Tell me, please," she whispers. I take a step back and my hands drop from her elbows. She takes a step forward and reaches a hand out to grasp my shirt. Her fingers clench over the fabric and it steals my breath away.

A simple act like this and I'm ready to get on my knees for this woman.

I close my eyes for a moment before opening them and lifting my hands to clasp over hers. I pry her fingers off the fabric of my shirt before holding her hand in mine.

"*Qué me estás haciendo?*" I take a deep breathe before shaking my head. "*Sabes lo que estás haciendo.*"

Her brows pinch and she's the one to shake her head. "No, Mr. Santos. I don't. Tell me."

It's too attractive to see her challenging me in such a way with such little force. Her words are enough to make me confess. It's pitiful to look at it from the outside.

I let out a hefty breath before leaning in close, letting her hand go to hold her cheek. She seems to hold her breath before I lift her chin a little, inches from my face.

It's all or nothing.

"*Me haces pensar en cosas que no son inocentes. Como tu programa de TV.*"

She lets out a small noise for a moment before she blinks a few times. Her eyes bore into mine and my breathing gets heavier.

"You wouldn't be surprised by my thoughts then," she replies. A hint of mauve burns her face.

I drop my hand and straighten my posture before taking a step back. My fists clench in tight balls and my teeth grind together.

It seems as if her confidence is back and she's almost smirking, *chastising* me for what I just confessed. But she looks like she's enjoying it too after what I just said.

"It's late," is all I can muster out before taking another step back and closer to my bedroom door.

"Mr. Santos, it's okay. You said it and I agree." She takes a step closer and I shake my head. As much as I want to dive into this fantasy and temptation, I shouldn't.

"It's not right, *Girasol*. I'll see you in the morning."

And with that I head to the bedroom door and slam it loudly. I feel the weight of it all crash down on me once I'm in the bedroom. I feel like a dick, but also know it was something I couldn't let happen.

What was I thinking? I can't think of those thoughts with her being in the center of them. It's not right and I have to do better. She's a guest in my home and I need to respect that.

But the thought of how we were almost inches apart from ruining ourselves runs through my mind the rest of the night. It takes everything in me not to open that damn door and pull her inside.

I want her desperately.

No, I *need* her desperately.

Chapter Twelve

CLEMENTINE

I'VE GOT to stop before something bad happens.

But Mr. Santos is too *addictive* to stare at, flirt with, and even dream about. And that's what I definitely did the last three nights. I dreamt about his calloused hands wrapping around my body like a red ribbon around a present.

His eyes bore into mine and the way he grunted and pounded into me so effortlessly… It made me wake up in a cold sweat and I had to stop myself from running downstairs to make the dream a reality.

We've been keeping our distance in the house and I haven't seen much of him, even when it came down to dinners with Rosa. He'd make up an excuse that the work day got to him and he'd order in for us. He'd then slip away into his bedroom or leave the house by the time I could make it down the stairs for the food. He'd stay up making noise that sounded like hammering nails coming from the basement.

It briefly came back to me that Rosa said her dad would be trying to convert the basement into a place for her to live after graduation.

Even Rosa was starting to question why her dad was acting

so weird all week. I couldn't tell her what happened. How I practically pushed him to voice what we were doing.

I didn't forget the way his face looked when I tripped that night, grasping his knees and being face to face with his crotch. He looked at me like I was his dirtiest fantasy come to life and he wanted to take me then and there.

I wanted him to, until he pushed me off him and stormed out of the living room.

How long can I go without actually wanting to pursue him? I know it's not right and it's not fair to Rosa. I'm lying to her, my sister. It breaks my heart knowing the wicked thoughts I have are about her *father*.

The well known phrase of 'just one time to get it out of your system' keeps coming to the forefront of my mind. Do we just need to give in to our desires one time and then we can move on?

MR. SANTOS ISN'T HOME when I wake up. It's also getting closer to the beginning of summer school. Classes start in two days, so I soak up as much as I can outside in the pool while Rosa is lounging on a chair. Garrett is on the other chair with a towel over his face.

We bought some pool floats earlier, so that's what I'm currently laying on; a pink flamingo patterned lounge float.

I even wore a new yellow bikini with tiny little sunflowers on it. Rosa asked why I wanted that pattern and I just shrugged.

Thinking of the way Mr. Santos might look at me wearing this though... that's the main reason I bought it. He kept calling me that damn nickname, so might as well own it.

If he wants me to be a sunflower, then I'm his.

The water ripples with the wind and I hear laughter and the slam of two doors near the front of the house. I look up and Rosa does as well, wondering what that is. I can only guess who, though.

It doesn't take them long to head to the backyard. Mr. Santos' friend is pulling the glass door open with a shit eating grin and a handful of packaged meats.

"*A quien quiere comer?* Frankie's dogs are in the house!"

Rosa barks out a laugh and gets up squealing, running toward him as he places the packaged meats on the patio table to wrap his arms around her. He lifts her up and twirls her around before setting her back down.

"Wow, Rosita. You've gotten shorter!"

"Fuck you, Frankie," she slaps his arm.

Garrett is still dead asleep on the lounge chair and I can't help but giggle. That's when I close my mouth the moment I see Mr. Santos slip through the glass doors. My body melts to the float and my jaw drops. It's like I lose total control over every function of my body.

He's *dripping* in sex. He's shirtless, for one. And then that damn golden necklace sits perfectly against his chest to the point where a vision of him on top of me, the gold chain hitting my face, comes into view. I try to brush it away, but it's already too late.

It doesn't help that his swim trunks are shorter than ones I'm used to seeing. His legs are toned and his thighs are thick, hugging the trunks perfectly. And the line of his crotch isn't hard for me to miss. The waistband sits low on his hips, giving me full access to the trail of hair that points in the direction straight to his cock like a devious neon sign. I lick my lips briefly at the thought. His muscles aren't helping with the visual and it feels like I've been dipped in some kind of hypnosis, unable to look away. That's when he finally looks up and catches my eyes.

He smirks.

He fucking smirks.

This only makes me clench my thighs together to relieve some of the heat that's already building up. I need him.

Rosa is clearly out of the loop as she helps Frankie assemble the meats on the patio table and prep the grill. Mr. Santos takes his time walking over to the lounge chairs, his gaze fixed on me. He finally looks away when he heads to Garrett and pulls the towel off his face.

"Woah, dude, what the fu–" Garrett starts, but then stops himself just in time. He jolts up into a sitting position and reaches his hand out to Mr. Santos. "It's nice to meet you, sir."

"*Mija*," Mr. Santos calls out to Rosa who finally looks up. Her smile falls before she curses.

"I forgot to tell you that Garrett was coming over!" She runs to where Garrett is. "*Papá* meet Garrett. Garrett… meet my dad."

Mr. Santos is hesitant for a moment before he finally grabs Garrett's outstretched hand and shakes it. The veins on his hand make me go hot.

Why is everything he's doing making me hot? Is it the sun? I've never felt like this toward anyone. Not even the jackass, Nathan.

I shudder from the thought, trying to get out of that headspace that I know will surely sink its teeth into me. I don't need those memories bursting out now while I'm trying to enjoy the summer air and getting more tan.

Conversations around the lounge chairs get drowned out as I brace myself for the cold water and hop off the float. I stop before my neck hits the water and wade my way through the pool with the float in one arm and then make it up the stairs. Tossing the float to the side of the pool, I cross my arms over my chest. Rosa and Garrett are back at the patio table with Frankie who's cutting open the hot dog package and placing them on the grill.

Rosa's got tongs in her hands, and she looks like she's ready to command Frankie where to put the other meats. Garrett is gnawing on his lips as he finally gives Rosa a kiss on her cheek and heads inside.

Mr. Santos looks up from where he's standing, watching me slowly walk up. He doesn't hesitate to head to the small crate that holds the pool towels. It must be new, I haven't noticed that yet and have always had to bring a towel from indoors.

He takes one out and fluffs it open, waving me over with it.

"It's okay, I can get one—" I start, but he gives me a look.

"*Ven aquí, Girasol,*" he demands and I don't hesitate or argue. Once I'm in front of him, I turn my back and he drapes the towel over my shoulders. I grab the ends of the fabric and hold it tightly before spinning back around.

Craning my neck, I see his brown eyes gliding over my bathing suit choice. The fabric in particular catching his eyes.

"*Girasoles? Para mí?*" he whispers, his finger moving to my chest and that's when my breath halts.

With his broad figure, I'm basically invisible to the patio. His finger is frozen in the air before he looks at me once more, raising a brow.

"Yes," I finally admit. He then moves his finger gently over my chest where the bikini top ties are resting. It's got the fabric pattern on it as well and he plays with it for a moment in between his finger and thumb. He lets out a shaky breath, which only makes matters worse for me. His touch feels like electricity.

He shouldn't be doing this. The way he's reacting toward me in the same way I am toward him. It's wrong and so inappropriate. But it feels almost natural with him.

I have no hesitation, no fear, and no regret.

I want him to touch me more, lay his whole palm on my chest if he must. Something about him makes me comfortable in a way I haven't been in months. It's like my senses are coming alive again and I can *feel*.

My arousal is back at full motion and I'm having sex dreams

about him. I couldn't even watch films with kissing scenes right after the assault. But here I am, even more confident and comfortable in my skin to let Mr. Santos do this.

Every fiber of my being is wanting him to touch me and taste me.

Claim me as his.

Before he can do anything else, we hear a clatter of noise behind us and Mr. Santos whips his body around and I peek around him to see. Rosa is laughing at Frankie while Garrett is holding up tongs with a hot dog between it. I guess he came back outside after all.

Frankie is shaking his head, but he's got a grin plastered on his face.

"*Están bien?*" Mr. Santos calls out and Rosa turns her head toward us and gives a thumbs up before stepping toward Garrett and helping him out with the mess he made. That's when I notice a plate on the ground near his feet and a few hot dogs sitting on the patio.

"Oh my gosh," I say, holding back a laugh. Mr. Santos turns back toward me and raises a brow, giving me a look.

A look I can't quite decipher.

"What?" I giggle.

"He's nice to Rosie, right?"

I clear my throat and nod. "Yes, of course."

He presses his lips into a thin line, nodding a little. "*Bien.* I'd like to think he can handle her heart a little better than that damn hot dog plate."

My lips part. "Wait, what? You're not serious, are you? It was probably an accident."

Just then Mr. Santos' lips curl into a smile before leaning in and winking. He then backs up just as easily before heading to the group. I have to catch my breath for a little before I join them as well.

Grilling is easy going as Mr. Santos and Frankie take over,

making sure no more hotdogs get harmed. Rosa, Garrett, and I are sitting on the patio table playing with a deck of cards attempting to busy ourselves even though we're starving.

"All right, kids!" Frankie yells, placing a huge plate piled high with grilled foods on top the table dodging the spread out cards. "*Comamos!*"

Rosa squeals as she starts passing out paper plates to us and we pile them with our preferred meats. I pass the plate of buns around while Mr. Santos goes inside and comes out with more toppings for our hotdogs and steak. It's like a full ass cookout out here with the spread of meats, toppings, beers, and all.

I bite into a hotdog and the flavors explode in my mouth. I forgot how good grilled food can be, even if it's as simple as hotdogs. Rosa and Garrett are lost in their own conversation as Frankie takes a seat to my right and Mr. Santos takes a seat at the head of the table, to my left. His knee bumps into mine as he scoots closer in his seat. My cheeks burn when our eyes make contact.

For the next half hour, we're stuffing our faces and talking nonsense. Frankie talks about work, but then Mr. Santos shuts him down trying to enjoy his day off. Which then leads to Frankie talking about his workout routine.

It's comical, before I finally understand that he's trying to show a message to Garrett as he flexes his biceps for a moment. I even flick my gaze toward Mr. Santos who is shaking his head while chuckling. When he meets my gaze, he winks.

He *winks* at me in front of everyone. This damn tease.

"Well, I did want to ask you again, *papá*," Rosa starts as she finishes her beer. Garrett looks nervous, shifting in his seat and draping an arm over the back of her chair. I watch them closely, knowing what they're going to ask.

Frankie whistles lowly, but I catch it and give him a look. He shrugs his shoulders enough for me to see before he nudges my elbow and I can't help but smile. He's so easily entertaining and humorous that I can't take anything seriously about him.

"*Mande?*" Mr. Santos asks, leaning back in his chair a little more comfortably. His large hand fondles with the base of his beer bottle, twirling it and causing small scraping noises.

"*Pues*, Garrett and I are wanting to go on that trip, remember?"

His eyes seem to narrow a little as he gazes at his daughter and then Garrett. Garrett looks like he's about to pee his pants or worse. Mr. Santos is intimidating, I get that… but he needs to sit up straight and make it known how much my best friend means to him! That means standing up to her father.

"You are?" Mr. Santos plays dumb.

"*Sí*," Rosa replies.

"And you?" Mr. Santos asks Garrett. His cheeks flame scarlet as he glances between the table, as if to find a scapegoat within Frankie or I, but we don't say anything. I find my own nails scratching against the paper plate in front of me. There's a fly trying to get into the remnants of the pico de gallo on my plate and I keep focused on that.

The air is thick as Garrett takes his time to respond.

"Yes," Garrett finally speaks. "We want to go to LA for a week tops. I want to show her all the places I grew up."

"And she'll meet your parents, then?" Mr. Santos asks matter of factly.

They both nod and that's when I finally see Rosa reaching her hand for Garrett's and they enclose over the table. I smile at that and Frankie makes a little noise beside me. A squeal? If that's even possible coming out of a very tall burly man.

"*No sé*," Mr. Santos says slowly.

"Come on!" Rosa pipes up from her place. "I never get to travel like this. I want to go and meet his family and everywhere that he can show me. We've never been. You know LA or New York will be my future–"

Before she can finish her sentence, Mr. Santos sighs. It's like the air has been cut and it's frigid. "I thought you were going to stay here after graduation? What's this plan for LA or New York?"

Rosa hangs her head. "I told you this so many times. I don't *know* what I want to do after graduation but I want options."

"*Ay, mija. Tienes todas las opciones aquí.*"

"In this small town? No, I'd love to know what else is out there. It'd be good for me," Rosa retorts.

Frankie shifts in his chair and it looks like he's trying to insert himself but treads lightly. We're all treading lightly right now. I don't think Rosa was expecting this much push back from her dad. She made it seem like he wouldn't care where she went after graduation. I knew that he was planning to renovate the basement for her, but I guess that was just something to always have for her to come back to?

It was all confusing for me to wrap my head around as they begin to bicker in Spanish. It's much too fast for me to decipher and even Frankie is letting out a deep breath and shaking his head, taking a sip of his beer. Garrett is clueless, not knowing any of the Spanish that was said beforehand, so he's completely out of the loop now.

"*Basta!*" Mr. Santos finally yells, causing a shift with Rosa. Her lips quiver and she looks at Garrett.

"See? Told you he'd be like this."

I want Rosa to look at me so I can comfort her in any way that I can, but she doesn't. She keeps her body shifted towards Garrett who is now rubbing her back. I look at Mr. Santos.

His jaw clenches and without another word the chair scrapes under him and he's standing. He looks at Rosa once more before flicking his eyes at Frankie and then me last. No words come out and he's quick to head to the glass doors and slide them open before stepping inside the house and slamming it shut harshly.

I let out a deep breath I didn't even know I was holding

during the encounter. Frankie places both palms on the table before scraping his own chair. Instead of going inside after Mr. Santos though, he heads for the grill and seems to start cleaning it.

Rosa is still quiet, and I see her shoulders shake. Fuck, she's crying. I instantly get to her side and give her a hug, and she leans into it. Garrett gives me reassuring eyes.

"It's going to be okay." I rub her back.

"He's never going to change his mind. Might as well just sneak out for that trip too. Doesn't seem like he noticed all the other times."

Frankie whistles again, and I give him a look. "He noticed, Rosa. He missed you around the house. *I* missed you around the house. It's not the same without my best friend."

Rosa finally lifts her head and nods. "I guess. I can't go in there though. I can't face him right now. Garrett, want to go lay out by the pool again?"

Garrett nods. "Yeah, babe. Let's go."

They both get up and head for the lounge chairs and I glance at Frankie who is scraping the grill with a tool. I walk toward him and cross my arms over my chest.

"Rosa deserves to go on this trip," I say sternly.

"I didn't disagree," Frankie murmurs.

"Then tell *him.*"

His eyes finally flick to mine and they go soft. His brows pinch together before he looks back at the screen door. Finally shrugging, he continues to scrape the grill.

"He's not going to listen to me right now. He's in a headspace."

"What kind of headspace?"

He's silent for a moment before turning his lips into a frown. "Me talking to him won't do us any good."

"Seriously? You're his best friend."

Frankie laughs, shaking his head. "You'd be surprised how

hot headed that man is. You know who might get through to him?"

I raise a brow and he locks eyes with me. His lips turn into a smile before nodding toward me. Is he talking about me?

"Me? What?"

"Try it," he urges. He nods his head toward the screen door. I look at it as if I'm waiting for it to go up in flames or something.

I then look back to where Rosa and Garrett are. They're completely lost in their own world. Frankie continues to urge me with his eyes.

"Okay, fine. Not sure why it has to be me." I throw my hands up in the air.

"*Disfrútalo*," Frankie calls as I head towards the screen door. I give him my best scowl, but he just laughs. I slide the door swiftly before walking in and closing it behind me. The air is cool and I curse myself for leaving the towel on my chair.

I walk through the kitchen, but he's nowhere in sight. My bare feet pad through the hallway. My skin prickles in goosebumps from the AC and even my damn nipples start to pebble from the cold.

Right as I near the hallway I hear his voice. It's like he's talking to someone. I get a little closer to his bedroom door and lean my ear as close as I can.

"You have to tell her," Mr. Santos says sternly. There's a pause before he bellows out laughing, but it's not the kind that would be right after hearing a joke. It's more of a passive, condescending one.

"Uh huh. Right, right," he chuckles. "Like you were around to even attempt to show her the ropes."

Another pause.

"*Si quieres enseñarle, ven aquí. Ella necesita a su madre.*"

There's a longer pause after this and a grunt comes from inside the room. It's evident that Mr. Santos is not happy in there. And that he's talking to Rosa's mom. The one that ran off right after the split.

"No, I'm not going to fucking translate that. If you ever cared about us–" Mr. Santos snaps.

I gasp and then pull my hand over my mouth to keep from making any more noise. There's a sudden stillness in the air around me and I pray that he didn't hear me. He laughs again and I breathe out a sigh of relief.

"You left *us*. Rosalía still needs a mother, you know. Call her. I don't like this idea of her running off with her boyfriend to another state. Reminds me of someone I know too well."

His words cut like venom, but it's not something I can argue against. I'm not sure how I'd feel either if someone I was with ran off with their new partner. I understand that this might be a fear of Mr. Santos with Rosa, but she's not her mom.

Even with my experience of my mom and Declan, it's not the same. I can't provide as much advice to him if I wanted to. She met Declan after my father passed. She didn't run away with Declan. But maybe I can offer the support and listening ear he needs.

There's another grunt before Mr. Santos yells a goodbye and then there's silence. My ears are still pressed up against the door, to the point where all I hear is my own heart pounding. Even to the point where I don't hear his steps until the door rips open and I practically fall into his chest. I grasp for any leverage, that being his chest. His very *bare* chest.

I yelp and try to regain my balance, but his muffled groan and sudden hands on my waist surrounds me.

"*Girasol*? What are you doing here?" I look up and see how his once angry eyes dissipate and resolve to a more calm look.

"I-uh, sorry. I didn't mean to eavesdrop. Frankie wanted me to check on you," I ramble.

He takes a deep breath and that's when I notice my hands are still up on his chest and I glide them off slowly. His hands still stay on my waist and it burns through my skin, causing goosebumps to rise all over.

"How much of that did you hear?" he finally asks.

"For what it's worth, she's not her mom. Rosa is her own person and Garrett has been nothing but sweet to her and me." His eyes soften even more at my confession. "I think that's what's more important."

Hanging his head, his hands travel up my waist until they're on my shoulders. This feels a little less intimate and like he's about to lecture me.

"*Gracias, Girasol. Pero, sabes siquiera?*"

"Know what?" My brows pinch and I'm a little confused if we're still talking about Rosa and Garrett or even her mom.

His palm rubs against my shoulder and that's when more goosebumps rise over my chest and even my neck. His eyes don't miss that and a smile almost takes over his face.

"The effect you have on me, *bebita*. It's torturous. It's turning me into a mad man."

"Mr. Santos," I breathe out, my heart hammering against my whole body.

"We can't keep doing this," he confesses at last.

"But–" I almost whine. I almost want to *beg*. I'm not sure what I want to happen. The thought of just getting it out of our system comes fleeting. It's now or never.

I take my time to place my hands back on his bare chest before *pushing* him backward into the room. He lets out a little *oof* from the sudden movement. His eyes widen before I kick the door closed with my foot.

"They're right outside. What if they come looking for you? Me? Us?" His words are a mile a minute and he's not the same confident man that I was just talking with outside the bedroom.

That's when I finally realize that I'm inside his *bedroom*. The room is dim lit with just a lamp on and it illuminates the inside.

"We don't have to do anything," I reassure him.

That's when I see a switch in his brown eyes. They seem to go darker and my stomach flutters from the gaze he's burning through me. Like he's finally got his confidence back and knows what he wants. I chew on the inside of my cheek, waiting for him to say something.

My heart is beating a mile a minute, my body is no longer cold from the AC, and my thighs are on the precipice of clenching from his stare.

"You don't want me to taste you?" I gasp at his words, but he doesn't stop. "I've been thinking about it–dreaming about it–for days. Since the moment you stepped foot under my roof, *Girasol*."

He moves closer to me, and I back up, finding myself up against the wall. I crane my neck up, and he smirks.

"I want," I breathe out pathetically.

"Want what, *Girasol*? I need to hear you say it. *Dime*."

"I want you to...taste me. But I-I don't know, I'm scared," I finally confess. My words fall flat and my mouth goes dry. I hang my head down, but his finger gently holds my chin and pushes up for me to lock eyes with him.

"What are you scared of, *bebita*?"

I'm silent for a moment. I can't wrap my head around actually being here with Mr. Santos. All of those teasing nights and almost confessions to how we're feeling. My sex dreams. And now him confessing that he's had them *too*. It's a lot to take in. But one thing I'm sure of is that I want to explore more of what I'm feeling for him. Like how I thought back at the pool.

He's making me feel again and I don't want to lose that.

I've missed so much of that part of my life, feeling like I was being held hostage by my own mind. Honestly, I was being held back by my own grief as well. Grief for the girl I was before the assault. I know I won't ever be her again–I'm forever changed. But this man in front of me makes me want to dip my toes back into getting back that power. Therapy helps, sure, but in this regard... I want my power back physically. With my body.

I can't tell him all of that though. "It's just been a while," I lie. "I want you to kiss me though... I really do."

He's quiet as he takes in my words before his smirk turns into a soft smile. "I can do that."

My breath holds as I witness before me, Mr. Santos lifting his hands to cup my cheeks. They're calloused yet gentle and he has to lean down to meet me. I get on my tiptoes to help him out, which causes him to chuckle under his breath.

Before I can back out in fear and utter humiliation, he leans in and kisses me.

It's slow for a moment, allowing me to relish in the feeling. It's nice and it makes me miss how much I've pushed away. How good this feels. How safe and comforting. It also feels fucking good to give in to this lust and attraction for Mr. Santos.

He continues to kiss me gently until he separates and leans back a little to look at me. His lips are shiny and my breathing becomes erratic at this sight. How can a man be this attractive? How is this humanly possible?!

The very thought of his lips being shiny because he was eating me out crosses my mind and I let out an involuntary moan. So soft, but just enough for him to hear.

"*Dios, Girasol.* Don't do that. Please."

"I'm sorry, Mr. Santos."

"Don't call me that," he breathily whines. "Makes me feel old."

"I don't know your name," I push. He grins, rubbing his thumb over my cheek and then my bottom lip. His eyes are locked on his movements, as if he's mesmerizing this moment.

"It's Arlo, *bebita.*"

"Arlo," I whisper. I like the way it sounds rolling off my tongue and it seems like he does too and a moan elicits from his plump lips.

"Fuck."

I decide to push him a little further. "I can call you Arlo. Or I can call you Sir whenever we're alone."

His eyes darken a few shades and heat pools in my belly. I've never wanted someone so much. He moves his hand to cup behind my neck, his hand big enough where his thumb can press against my jaw.

"If we didn't have company over, I'd show you just how much I enjoy hearing that word coming from those pretty lips."

I don't get the chance to answer him because the next horrifying second we hear noise outside the bedroom door. Thankfully, it's just Frankie. And he's *singing*.

But Mr. Santos pulls apart and curses under his breath.

My own breathing is still erratic and I have to take a few deep breaths to calm myself. It's hard when he's right there in front of me. It's like even his pheromones are too much for my body to handle. Every fiber of my being is yearning for him. *Burning* for him.

"Come on," he speaks up and I nod, following him to the door. We both pause though as we get close.

His hands reach out once more for my cheek and he pinches it softly. I give him a small smile and he returns it. It's like we're holding secrets within our smiles, which we kind of are, but it feels euphoric and special.

He opens the door, and I follow right behind him back into the kitchen where Frankie is waiting, leaning against the counter with a grin, beer to his lips, and his legs crossed.

"*Cállate*," Mr. Santos bites once we get close enough.

"*Ay*. Not saying a peep," Frankie says, winking at me. This causes my cheeks to burn, and I can't help but gasp.

"Nothing happened!" I squeak before running to the screen doors.

I don't bother listening to their conversation as I head outside and make my way to my best friend out on the lounge chair.

Chapter Thirteen

CLEMENTINE

ROSA EVENTUALLY MIGRATES to the pool while Garrett sticks to the lounge chair. If I could guess, he's still in the aftershock of Mr. Santos' eruption at the patio table. I try to console him with my best smile, but he just waves me off and places his shirt over his eyes again and leans back to tan some more.

"Come in, *nena*!" Rosa calls out from the water. I oblige and head to the stairs, making my way slowly. The water is a little cooler, it seems, and it takes a little longer for me to get used to it before I'm hip deep and then swimming toward Rosa.

Her dark hair swims around her shoulders and she's got her brown eyes gleaming. "I think we're going to go next week."

"To LA?" I ask.

She nods.

"I want to meet his family and just see that place for myself."

"What about your dad? He seemed pretty upset," I counter.

She rolls her eyes and laughs.

"Clem! Live a little! You've been cooped up all this time in that house, you must be going insane. I know I am and I haven't even been around. I want to get out of this town for a little while. Even if it's for a week!"

I stare at my best friend and try to think of the best response. I want her to be happy and to go on this trip with Garrett. But I'm not sure how her dad will act once he realizes this. Would she even tell him?

And what the hell am I doing? Am I really trying to think of solutions for family matters that aren't my own? Rosa and her dad can deal with this without me. I don't need to intervene or have a say in any of it.

"Then go," I finally reply. Her eyes gleam even more and she giggles, twirling her body in the water.

"You'll cover for me then?"

I bug my eyes out. "Cover for you? What? Your dad kind of knows that you'd sneak out anyways, I think."

"Yeah, but just in case. Maybe you can distract him enough where he forgets I'm not even around."

My body warms at the idea of what kind of *distractions* I could do to her dad. And it's all wrong. I can't think of those scenarios while in front of her.

"I-uh, I'll try," I swallow.

"Great!" She exclaimed before gasping. "You know what we should do right now?"

"What?"

"Play chicken fight!" Before I can protest, she's turning around and whistling at Frankie who is sitting at the patio table on his phone and drinking a beer. He looks up and raises a brow.

"*Sí*, Rosita?"

"Come play chicken fight with us! Garrett! Wanna play?"

Garrett doesn't budge and Rosa gives me a look and I just shrug. "He's most likely passed out already. Your dad can be scary sometimes," I joke.

"Ugh, he always does that for guys I meet!" Rosa wails. "Frankie! *Ven!*"

"*Vale, vale!*" Frankie muses before getting up and stripping from his Hawaiian shirt. He tosses it on the patio table before jogging to the pool and screaming like a crazy man.

"*Ah!*" Rosa and I scream as he cannonballs into the water, causing waves and splashes around us.

"Frankie!" Rosa screams as he resurfaces. He just laughs even more before splashing her. He looks at me and I raise a brow.

"Don't you dare!" I scream, attempting to swim away but Frankie splashes me just in time to get my whole upper body and back of my hair. It's icy on my head and I gasp from the sudden shock.

"That was so mean!" Rosa giggles. I turn to look at them and that's when I notice Mr. Santos coming back outside.

"We just need one more, right?" Frankie asks. Rosa nods and she looks around the pool and then once her eyes land to her dad she waves at him.

"*Papá*, come play chicken fight with us, we need one more." He looks up from the table and his eyes peer at Garrett from behind. He finally nods and makes his way to the pool.

Unlike Frankie, he doesn't cannonball into the water. He instead leans down to sit at the ledge before sinking into the cold water. My eyes are transfixed on his biceps and triceps hard at work in holding his upper body as he does this. He strides toward us, not daring to lock eyes with me. Good, I'm already a puddle for this man.

"Alright, Rosie, get on my shoulders," Mr. Santos calls, patting his shoulders and grinning.

That's when Rosa shakes her head and Mr. Santos looks pained. "Sorry, I love you but I want to keep my winning streak." She pats Frankie's shoulder. "I'm going to stick with him."

Frankie hoots and hollers and they high five. His eyes flicker to me and I want to strangle him as he gives me the quickest smirk.

Oh, that fucker.

I turn to Mr. Santos while Rosa is starting to climb Frankie and they burst into a fit of giggles.

"I guess that means we're a team. I'm terrible at this game, just letting you know. Don't wanna mess up any streak you may have," I tell him. He smiles and looks like he's holding back some laughter.

"I'm fine with that, *beb–*" he stops himself just in time. We both look at Frankie and Rosa who are splashing in the water, still unable to get Rosa on top of Frankie's shoulders.

"Use the stairs!" I giggle. They don't seem to listen though as they somehow turn it into a wrestling match and Rosa has Frankie's head dunked into the water. They're literally five year olds at a water park.

I take a deep breath and clap my hands once. "Alright, I'm not sure how we're going to do this. You're way too tall and I think we might actually have to use the stairs."

Mr. Santos looks back at the stairs before he glances back at me. There's mischief in his eyes that I don't miss.

"I'll pick you up from under."

"Under the water?"

He nods. "Spread your legs, *Girasol*," he teases.

And before I can protest, he's dunking into the water and swimming toward me. His frame within the waves is wiggly and huge and I spread my legs just in time for him to settle in between them and rise. As he starts to stand, his hands firmly grasp my thighs and I squeal at the sensation, my hands instantly going to his messy curls. He surfaces and takes a deep breath before moving a hand to wipe his face. I keep my hands encased in his hair and I pull it gently, causing him to hiss.

"*Basta*, Clementine," he warns. The way he says my name instead of *Girasol* makes me clench my thighs together, which doesn't help at all since I'm just clenching his head. It brings not so appropriate images to mind of me clenching my thighs around his neck as he buries himself deep into my pussy. If he just faced the other way, I'd be getting a dream come to life.

He lightly slaps my thighs and *that* doesn't help either. His palm engulfs my whole thigh and I have to momentarily bring myself back to reality.

Rosa is finally able to get on Frankie's shoulders after they take my advice and use the stairs. They're making their way toward us and Rosa is flexing her biceps just like Frankie did at the table.

"Are you ready to lose?!" she hollers.

"Say goodbye to your winning streak," I tease.

Mr. Santos chuckles, slapping and then squeezing the tops of my thighs again. His fingers brush over to the sides and I tense as his fingertips graze over my scars. My fingers grab his scalp more tightly, but then I relax once his fingertips smooth over them in a comforting way. It doesn't feel invasive and I want him to keep smoothing his fingers over them.

I look up at the sky and take it all in. I'm way taller than I've ever been and I start to count clouds out of habit. "I'm so tall, Rosa!" I scream, "I can basically touch the sky!"

Rosa laughs and so does Frankie. But Mr. Santos just says, "You can count those clouds now, huh?"

The fact that it's something only he knows and it's now become *our* thing to talk about, I squeeze my thighs gently around him and run my hand softly through his hair. I try to not make it so obvious in front of Frankie and Rosa.

"No fair!" Frankie bickers, pulling me out of my thoughts. Rosa keeps laughing though.

"Dad, your height won't be an advantage. It's all about the person on top! I'm coming for you Clem!"

"Ready, *Girasol*?" Mr. Santos calls out, craning his neck up to me, but it leaves his lips to graze my inner thigh and butterflies swarm my belly. Fuck, he doesn't even know that anything he does has this effect on me.

"Y-yeah," I stutter.

That's when we finally get in front of Rosa and Frankie and we count down before our hands go up. Rosa and I work hard to push the other down, ultimately leaving us in a fit of giggles. We're hard at work while Frankie and Mr. Santos just laugh below us and even start talking about the fucking sports match going on later tonight in Spanish.

They're completely oblivious to the war happening above their heads.

"Come on, Clem. Give up, you know you wanna," Rosa teases with her hands grabbing my wrists.

"Never," I laugh. I twist my arms where her grip loosens and I can free my wrists from her.

That's when Mr. Santos does something that neither of us can predict. It almost happens in slow motion as he lifts one hand to Rosa's stomach and starts *tickling* her. She's blindsided by the sneak attack and squeals before screaming and bending her body back to get away from the tickles.

"Damn it! That's cheating!" But before she can yell at her dad anymore, her body bends back too much for Frankie to balance out and they're both falling into the water. I squeal and clap my hands, clenching my thighs around Mr. Santos neck.

"Ah, *bebita*, please stop doing that." He laughs as his hands rub my thighs.

"We won!" I scream, leaning down and wrapping my arms around his head. My hair falls over us like a curtain and he laughs, twirling us a little in the water. It makes me a little dizzy, so I hold onto him a little tighter. My lips graze his temple before I straighten up and we see Rosa and Frankie surfacing and cursing each other out.

"If you just held onto me!" Rosa shouts.

"You were bending back like the fucking exorcist! I don't even know how you went that bendy!" Frankie quips, splashing her.

This results in them having a splash battle and Mr. Santos walks us over to the ledge of the pool. He spins around so I can slowly get off before I lean down and dip my legs into the water, sitting on the ledge. He settles himself between my thighs and I gawk at him, craning my neck to look for my best friend and his.

"They're too busy fighting," Mr. Santos assures me.

"Too close," I whisper, running a hand through my hair. He lifts a hand as if he wants to touch my face but thinks better of it.

"I can never get too close to you, *bebita*," he whispers as well. His fingers graze my knees before he takes a step back.

"Oh, you're something." I laugh as I kick my feet up and send some water his way. He grins before dodging the splash and heading over to Rosa and Frankie.

Rosa screams as he lunges for her, wrapping his arms around her waist and lifting up. She squeals as he sends them both into the water. Frankie hollers and whoops as they both surface.

I bask in the sun, letting it dry me off as I continue to stare at the odd bunch. It's barely June and I'm so lucky I decided to stay here for the summer.

Mr. Santos catches my gaze for a moment before he's wrestling Frankie into the water. He makes sure to give me a wink though before they go under.

Chapter Fourteen

CLEMENTINE

FRANKIE LEFT for the night and so did Rosa and Garrett. The backyard has been cleaned and the pool stuff organized. Arlo is putting away the last of the condiment bottles into the fridge while I hoist myself up onto the clean kitchen counter.

Next to me is a package of Oreos and a jar of Nutella. I happily dig in, dipping a cookie inside the jar and stuffing it in my mouth.

"Odd combo," Arlo murmurs as he closes the fridge and heads toward me. His brown eyes burn through my skin and I have to swallow the cookie before I choke.

"It's very delicious," I counter.

"Hmm."

"Try it," I offer. Picking up an Oreo and dunking it into the Nutella jar, I lift it for him to take. But instead he closes the distance, putting himself in between my spread thighs. My breath falters for a moment as my thighs meet his bathing suit. He's still bare chested and my eyes briefly go to his golden necklace.

"Gimme," he whispers, leaning in so close he has to place his big palms on the counter, right next to my hips. Fingertips so close to touching my skin, but not quite. It's like I can feel the heat radiating off him though and it's heavenly. I want to drown in this feeling.

I muster the courage to move the cookie to his lips. "Open then."

He obliges and opens his mouth where I can pop the cookie in. But his lips catch my finger as he closes and then he licks his lips, brushing his tongue over my finger in the process.

Flutters in my core rise up and cause heat to spread throughout my body. It feels like someone turned on the heat in the house and a shiver runs down my spine.

He chews for a moment, while maintaining eye contact, and then swallows. He licks his lips once more. "Tasty."

"Told you," I reply with a smile.

He stands in this position for a while, his hands inching closer until fingertips are brushing my skin.

I intake a deep breath and I flutter my eyelashes at him. "Arlo…"

We're silent as we continue to stare at each other and his fingers start to rise a little to eventually climb my thighs. It's like he's trialing how high his fingers can go and how long he can touch me before I stop him.

It's not long until I'm leaning closer and closer, squeezing my thighs together to cage him in.

Then his eyes widen and it's like someone has snapped their fingers in front of his face and pulled him from this hypnosis. He clears his throat, lifts his hands from my thighs, and takes a step back.

"Want to watch a movie?" he simply asks.

I'm stunned watching him. But then I nod and hop off the counter. His height is always shocking to me, so I crane my neck to look at him.

"Sure, let me just change."

He nods and I head upstairs without another word. I change in less than five minutes and I'm back in the living room, seeing that he's got a few blankets on the couch and glasses of water on the coffee table.

Arlo strolls into the living room and he looks at my—his—shirt and then down at his own draped over his body. He's wearing a Metallica shirt as well and I smile. I sit on the couch, pulling a blanket on top of my legs and pat the cushion next to me. I want him close.

He doesn't fight it as he sinks into the cushion next to me, his thighs spreading wide and claiming the space. It doesn't go past me the fact that he's in sweatpants and I can clearly see the outline of his groin. It's also pretty clear that he's not wearing anything underneath which is just cruel.

I lick my lips haphazardly and I hope he doesn't catch it. I'm not being subtle at all and it's getting to a point where I need to be more careful. For my own sake.

Because I know that now since we've had our first kiss, that's just something I won't stop thinking about. I can't stop *feeling* his lips on mine. That memory and feeling is etched not only in my mind but on my skin.

It's the perfect concoction of insanity for the situation I've found myself in: slowly falling for my best friend's dad.

I grab the remote on the coffee table and start looking through the streaming apps on the TV before I settle for one and find a cute romcom. It's about an office romance between two coworkers and fighting for the top position at their firm. Arlo is extra quiet as he watches, his gaze intent on the TV and never wavering.

As the movie gets to the halfway point, I'm completely enthralled in the romance and the storyline that I don't even realize myself curling into the blanket and even curling into the left side of the couch... where Arlo is.

My head falls on his shoulder and I jolt up, catching myself with my hand on the couch in the space between us. He grunts for a moment, and I see his eyes opening.

"Sorry," I whisper.

His eyes turn to me slowly before a small smile fills his face. "S'okay," he mumbles.

"Were you sleeping?" I tease, unable to contain the smile on my own face. He playfully rolls his eyes before leaning his head back on the couch.

"No, I was closing my eyes for a second. It happened to be ten minutes into the movie, I'm surprised you didn't notice earlier."

Now with the movie as background noise and my attention on Arlo I giggle. "Sure, that second was very long. It's okay, I barely noticed. I tend to curl up into a blanket or just lose myself once I'm really into a movie or show."

"Well, feel free to use me as a pillow. I might not last the whole movie, *Girasol*."

My heart picks up at the nickname and my body heats up. His eyes linger on mine for a little longer and his gaze even dips a little to my lips. That's when the memory of our kiss comes tumbling back and I let out a little exhale from my parted lips.

He visibly gulps and I want to throw the blanket off of me and fan my face. It's getting hot in here and I know it's not just the blankets. It's him.

Him. Him. Him.

God, I want him so bad.

"*Ándale*," he finally whispers, nodding his head to his shoulder, and a smile curls on my lips.

"Okay."

And with that, I brush the blanket a little off me so I can be more comfortable as I lean back on his shoulder, my cheek pressing against his bicep. His muscles seem to flex right under me, and I shiver.

"Cold?" he whispers.

I shake my head. "Far from it, Arlo."

I try to focus back on the movie playing but I can't remember the last few scenes. I can't even focus on the scene in front of us. Are they still talking? What did they just say? It's after a few minutes that I feel him exhale and then he shifts. I feel pressure on the top of my head and that's when I realize what he just did. He kissed the crown of my head.

How can the simplest movements from him be so intimate and so seductive? I move my hands to grasp his forearm and lift my head to look at him. I'm not surprised to see that he's already craning his neck down to look at me. His brown eyes swirl with intensity, and it's like we're able to talk a million thoughts just by looking at each other.

I take a deep breath and lift my hand ever so slightly and graze my fingertips against his jawline. He swallows thickly before he reaches his free hand to grasp my wrist. It's not to stop me though. He moves my fingers closer to his cheek before my whole palm is on his face, caressing him. Arlo leans into it and my insides melt into putty.

This time I take the moment to drag my hand down from his cheek, his hand still encapsulated around my wrist, down to his neck and then his collarbone where the fabric of his shirt starts.

"Clementine," he warns with a harsh whisper.

"Arlo," I mumble, my eyes focused on where my hand is. His fingers tighten around my wrist before he takes a deep breath.

"What are you thinking, *Girasol*?"

I'm quiet for a moment, wondering if I should just say it. I want to kiss him again so badly. My body is yearning for his lips like a moth drawn to a flame. It'll happen regardless, so why not just push myself toward him now?

What's stopping me? It feels like I'm stuck in this trance and bubble of just him. I feel safe and like I'm not the damaged Clementine that I can't ever get rid of. Sure, I can learn to move past things, but I'm stuck in this skin. In this used body.

But right now, I feel the least of that.

"I want to kiss you again... *please*," I push out in a staggered breath.

That's all it takes for him to exhale a deep breath, nod, and then shift on the couch so the hand I'm leaning on can wrap around my waist. I don't stop him, even though I see his eyes waiting for any ounce of regret or uncertainty. I give him none.

Within moments, he's using his strength as if it's nothing to hoist me from the side of the couch to his legs. The blanket slides off my body just as easily. I squeal in the process and my legs are dropping over his, but my ass is balancing on his thighs and knees. I'm nearly a foot away from his core and it bothers me, as much as I'd hate to admit it.

He adjusts himself on the couch and the movement of his hips make me lose balance and I lean in, clutching his shoulders with my palms. He hisses softly and we're nose to nose.

Our breathing is almost in sync and his hands slowly glide to my waist, his arms long enough where he starts to move them around the curve of my ass and his fingers practically engulf me easily. He takes another deep breath and I feel it all over my body; I respond so well to him. He could blink and I'd feel it.

"You really want to kiss me, *bebita*?" he presses.

I nod.

He's silent for a moment, staring at me with the proximity. My legs are too far from his core to really feel anything, but my thighs still clench... or attempt to. His spread thighs make it very hard to find any relief in this odd position I'm in.

"Say it. I like hearing you say it," he pushes.

Without missing a beat I respond. "I want to kiss you, Arlo."

He groans at that. "Fuck, look at what you're doing to me."

"What am I doing?" I lean my head a little and my nose

brushes against his. I attempt to feign innocence, but he catches on.

Without another word, his hold on my hips tighten and he pulls me closer to him. This movement causes me to slide down the length of his thighs, riding my shorts up in the process. My core is immediately slammed up against his and I moan in the process, which catches me off guard. It was completely involuntary. I notice the feeling underneath me and I can't help but gasp.

He watches me slowly as I realize the bulge underneath me. It's still slowly growing with the movements as I shift to get more comfortable. He hisses under his breath once more and it brings flutters to my insides.

"*That*," he says through grit teeth.

"Oh," I just say, a smile starting to stretch over my face. The fact that we're able to go so slow in this yet ignite fires so easily. At least I'm hoping I ignite something catastrophic inside him as well.

My hands glide to his neck and my fingers twirl along the curls at the base and he mutters a curse word in Spanish.

"Can… Can I move?" I ask sheepishly. His hold is still strong on my waist and I can't move an inch. It's like he's molded his hands to my body and I'm trapped here on his growing erection forever.

I'm not complaining, but the fire in my core wants me to *move*. And I have to release this tension before I go crazy.

"I thought you wanted to kiss me?" he teases.

My core is heating up and my pussy is begging to be used mercilessly and at his disposal. I know we can't go all the way just yet, so dry humping and kissing might be what I'll get tonight. If he lets me.

"I do, Arlo," I whisper before leaning even more into him and his grip on my waist tightens if that's even possible.

"Then kiss me, Clementine. You have control here." Even

though his words are demanding, his tone wavers for a moment as if he's waiting for me to let him take over. But I'm enjoying this right now and being able to have control over our movements.

I waste no time and press my lips to his. It's soft and electric. Warm and comforting. We release for a second before I dive back in, clutching his hair even more and his hands smooth over my waist and then to my hips. I gasp and his hands stop.

"Is that okay?" he whispers between a kiss. I nod and move my hands briefly to grab his wrists and moving them back lower to my thighs and then my ass.

"Like that," I mumble and he concedes before we kiss again.

The fire coursing throughout my body is turning to a boiling point and my pussy is craving some kind of friction. I can practically feel a damn heartbeat down there and I need release.

"Can I move, Sir?" I whisper as we separate our lips. He groans underneath his breath before his fingers press firmly into my ass and I inhale sharply.

"You can do whatever you want with me, *Girasol*."

I kiss him again, and this time I move my hips softly. The brush of my clothed cunt against his erection feels like heaven, even if the movement is slow. I groan softly, and he does something I've never heard.

He growls so lowly while his fingers dig deeper into my plush thighs. And in this moment I hope and pray that his touch is deep enough to mark me. It feels sick to think that after all the hurt I've been through and pain I've inflicted upon my skin that I want *his* marks to remain. I want his touch to *burn* me. Erase all the previous touches from not only Nathan, but the scars I've made myself.

I continue to grind and circle my hips against his erection and I brush against something long and I realize it's a vein. Fuck, if only I knew what it really looked like without these sweatpants.

My breathing becomes erratic as my fingers on his shoulders become tighter and my movements are more rapid. Grinding against his erection brings some relief, but my mind goes to places of wanting to do more. But I'm also terrified. So I stay on this feeling of being on the border of wanting to stay safe and wanting to dip my toes into darker waters.

"So pretty like this, *bebita*." His voice breaks my thoughts and I blink my eyes open not even realizing I had them shut. He kisses me again and I melt into it. My hips circle even more and my shorts ride up in between my thighs to bring more pressure to my clit with the bunched up fabric.

"Oh," I whimper as my clit seems to hit the perfect spot as I grind on him in a different fashion.

"Yeah? Right there?" he whispers, moving his lips to my cheek and then my jawline. His kisses are soft and almost feather-like. I clench my thighs around him and continue to grind him as I chase this relief.

"Please." My voice croaks as I pick up the pace.

"I've got you, baby, take what you need."

His words only ignite the intensity in me to ride him past the point where I can't think of anything else. All I see, hear, feel, smell, and taste is *him*.

I moan as his lips move down to my neck and my hands move from his shoulders to his neck as I continue to find the right balance. Everything tightens inside me and I know I'm very very close.

"Arlo, I'm close!" My words falter as I stumble and my hips fall out of tempo.

"Come for me, *bebita*." His lips are back up to my ear and he nibbles on my earlobe. The feeling is so intimate and it causes me to stutter out incoherent words before everything snaps.

My pussy contracts against nothing and I feel my orgasm come at full force. I press my lips together as I ride through it and his hands smooth up and down my waist and thighs.

"That's it," he breathes in a shaky voice. "I'm so proud of you, *bebita*."

My movements still as I try to calm down from the release. I take a few deep breaths before I lift my head and stare at him. His dark hooded eyes are latched onto mine and his hands become less strict and begin to rub over my thighs in soft motions.

"That was…" I breathe out, my brain complete mush.

"I know," he smiles. I lean my forehead against his and take a deep breath before I lean back. His erection is still very prominent underneath me and I almost feel bad that I got to chase my release and he didn't.

I attempt to slide off him, but his hold tightens. But it's not in a demanding way, he almost pleads with his eyes to have me stay on top of him.

So I do.

I lay my head back on his chest and we stay like this for a while. I almost forget that the movie is still playing in the background. It's not until the credits roll when he makes a noise and I lift my head from his chest.

"Do you need anything? A washcloth? Want me to carry you upstairs?" His sweet words make my heart lurch. I've never had a man so caring after intimacy. I'm not even sure the last time a man even gave me an ounce of attention once we were done fooling around.

And here this man is, making sure I'm okay and offering all of these things after *I* got off on him completely clothed. He didn't really get anything in return.

It makes me wonder if he's this caring after what I just did… how would he be after sex? Would we tangle our naked bodies in his bed while he whispers sweet nothings in my ear and we cuddle til we fall asleep?

God, I hope so.

"*Girasol?*" he asks, bringing me back to the present.

I can only smile and nod. "I'm good, Arlo. But thank you. I don't think I'd be able to stand having you upstairs in the bedroom if you did carry me up there… I'd like to savor this."

"Smart girl, *bebita*," is all he says before I get up off him.

Chapter Fifteen

ARLO

LAST NIGHT WAS MORE than I dreamed of. I couldn't sleep without replaying that scene over and over in my head. I had to finally wrap my hand around my cock before I found relief and eventually sleep.

The chances of us doing that was very slim, yet it did. My emotions are all over the place when I wake up.

Pining for a woman that's the same age as my daughter.

Regret for letting things go that far.

Guilt for allowing it to happen with Rosie's friend.

Fuck, I'm screwed in every sense.

It's not until I'm making my way to the kitchen that I notice she's there. I honestly thought she'd be up and out of the house by now.

My pretty *Girasol* is stirring a spoon in a mug, presumably coffee, with how the place smells. I stare for a moment at her profile as she doesn't hear me.

"*Bueno*," I call out and she spins from the counter to look at me. Her eyes bug out for a moment, like I caught her in an act. It looks absolutely adorable on her.

Stop, stop thinking about her like that. I try to chastise myself. But it's no use, having her under my roof is not helping whatsoever.

"Good morning," she responds with a little pep in her step as she makes her way to the island and plops on a barstool.

I make my own way to the fridge to pull out some leftovers from last night's grill to heat up. It's not hard to feel her eyes on me with every movement. There's a moment after taking the plate out of the microwave where our eyes meet and her cheeks turn bright pink. She attempts to cover her face with the mug as she takes a long sip.

I lean over the island as I take a few bites of the leftover hotdogs cut into bite-sized pieces.

"Any plans today?" she asks softly. I look up from where I'm leaning and she's tapping the side of the mug with her manicured nails.

"Make more progress on the basement... or at least attempt to."

She hums before nodding. "Rosa told me about that. How long will that take?"

Her curious eyes make my chest flutter. I clear my throat before responding, "A few months since I still have to work. I might try to fit in some time in the evening if I really need to. So let me know if it ever gets too loud."

She's quiet for a moment before nodding. Her eyes scan the room before they land back on me. I take a few more bites from the plate as I wait for her to reply.

"What if Rosa moves?"

Her voice is soft, as if treading lightly on the topic. It just makes me feel more guilty for the wall that instantly goes up. I don't want to think about that *what if*. Rosie is staying. I'm building her a place to have as her own.

"She won't," I simply state.

"But what if she does? Rosa said yesterday–"

"*No me importa*, she's staying. She can try to run off with that boy, but she'll end up coming back." I hate how spiteful my words come out but I don't want to think about yesterday.

Well, scratch that. There's a few things I'd *love* to continue to think about from last night. But Rosie and her boyfriend's idea to travel far away isn't one of them. I glance at *Girasol* and she's got her bottom lip sucked into her teeth. Her cheeks are still rosy and it seemed to spread to her neck and chest. I let my eyes travel a little lower to her tank top and where the collar dips right above her breasts.

"Eyes up here, silly," she giggles before I clear my throat again and finish my plate. I don't mean to be so nonverbal with her, but I don't want to talk about my daughter. Especially with her best friend.

"You start school tomorrow, right?" I change the subject. She nods and gets up and heads to the sink. She begins to wash the cup behind me and I have to twist around to look at her. Her shorts are riding up, the bottoms barely covering her ass.

It takes everything in me to not get behind her and press myself against her body. To place my hands right over her ass and squeeze.

"Yep! It's just for four weeks," she explains as she places the mug and spoon on the drying rack. She turns around and leans against the sink, craning her head up to look at me.

"Do you have a way to get there?" That wasn't something I've thought about. I usually took Rosalía around town when we're together and I make sure she uses the Uber app for any other travels.

I've offered to get her a car plenty of times, but she's hesitant about driving. I don't blame her, traffic and the drivers just seem to get crazier as the years go.

Clementine shakes her head. "My stepdad offered to give me enough for Ubers here and there, especially if it's for class."

An idea sparks and I know it's very, very stupid to offer, but I don't stop myself.

"What time is your class?"

She gives me a look before speaking. "8 a.m. until 1 p.m."

"I'll drive you in the morning," I tell her.

There's a moment of silence as she takes in my offer and then she shakes her head no. "Arlo, I can't let you drive me every morning! You've got work and–"

"It's no trouble, it's not too far out of the way from my current worksite. We might have to pick up Frankie though this week... he needs to get his car fixed and take it to the shop tomorrow."

"Seriously, my stepdad said to just use Uber," she fights.

I shake my head. "It's not trouble at all, Clementine. I'll take you in the mornings and then you can Uber home."

Home. It feels weird in this context now that we've done some things. Very minimal things, but the feeling still stands.

"I can let him know and he'll reimburse you for gas!"

This bubbles laughter from my chest. "No, no. Don't make him pay me. I've yet to use the paycheck you gave me when you first moved in."

Her hands come together at her midsection before she smiles sheepishly. She reaches a hand to brush a strand of hair behind her ear and I swallow a thick feeling in my throat.

"Okay," she finally concedes. I let out a deep breath I didn't know I was holding.

"Great," I smile.

We're quiet for a moment as we both stay in our spots, staring at each other. That's until we hear the front door unlock and open. Clementine jumps before heading far away from me. We hear footsteps climbing the stairs rapidly and I know I have to talk to Rosie before she leaves again. I turn to see Clementine trying to busy herself by brushing imaginary crumbs off the island counter.

"I'll be right back," I announce before I give her one final look and head down the hall. My steps are loud as I climb the stairs and Rosie's door is ajar.

I knock on it for a few moments before I peek my head in. She's sitting on her bed staring at her phone before looking up. Her once smiley expression turns sour. I don't blame her.

"*Bueno, puedo entrar?*"

She nods before shifting on the bed and I enter, heading to sit next to her. The bed sinks with my weight and I rub my palms over my jeans.

"*Escuchame, por favor,*" I start with a nervous tone. I'm not sure why I'm nervous to talk to my damn daughter. The phone call with her mother comes to the forefront of my mind and it becomes evident that I'm allowing the trauma from her leaving to seep into the current relationship I have with Rosalía.

"I'm listening," she states, not looking at me. She continues to look at her phone but the screen is black. She just stares at her reflection.

"*Mira*, Rosie, I was wrong to lash out like that yesterday, *lo siento.*"

"Is that all?" Her words are like a knife and I try to keep my composure from breaking. I deserve her harsh words, I really do.

She finally whips her head to me and narrows her eyes. "*Escucha. Solo estoy tratando de cuirdate.*"

"*Es en serio?*" she laughs with a shake of her head. She takes a deep breath and stands from the bed, tossing her phone on the mattress. She paces the space in front of me before planting her hands on her hips and staring daggers at me.

"*Qué?*" I ask, hoping she can let me in her thoughts. I want to be better. That's why I want to renovate the basement for her. everything I ever do is for *her*. Does she not realize this?

"Saying you're sorry isn't going to take back what happened. I'm going there regardless of what you say, you know that right? You don't control my life."

I'm shocked at her sudden words and the choice of them. "Rosalía," I start with more bite to my tone.

Her eyes widen as if she realized what she just said, but she doesn't back down. She takes a deep breath before taking a step closer and keeping her glare. "You have to realize that I'm an adult. I'm not five anymore. I'm not eighteen. I'm almost a college graduate. I can make safe decisions for myself."

"But moving states away when I thought you'd stay here?"

There's pause before she huffs her breath and curses under her breath. "*Papá*! Are you even listening to yourself? *You* made that plan! Not me! I only agreed initially because that's what I thought I really wanted. I don't even know anymore, but having the opportunity to travel and experience the places I really want to explore will be good for me. My soul is calling for more and I want to listen to it."

"With a boy," I add. My hands move from my thighs to lace together. I take a deep breath and she does too.

"I'm not doing this for him," she replies. "I'm not mom." Her voice turns softer as she takes another step and at my side. She sits and wraps her arms around my arm before nuzzling her head on my shoulder. I lean into it and take a deep breath, oddly remembering how she smelled as a baby.

The memories coming rushing back and a knot lodges itself in my throat and in my chest. It feels like a huge weight is being pressed onto me.

"You're not her, you're right," I agree.

"*Te amo, papá*. I'm not going anywhere, but I deserve to see the world. Right?"

"As trips, yes. But to *move* and live in another state? I can't protect you that far away." I swallow a thick wad of cotton that's stuck in my throat. She rubs her hands over my arms and squeezes tightly.

"That's over a year away, though. I still have senior year, and then I'll have to apply for jobs. It's just a *what if*."

"You made it sound definite." I try to remind her. She laughs before I pull my arm out of her grasp and wrap it around her shoulders, pulling her into my chest. She giggles as I squeeze tightly. She squirms underneath me before finally accepting my bear hug. I breathe her in before kissing the top of her head.

"You grew up too fast, *mijita. Demasiado rápido.*"

Rosita is quiet before she wiggles in my arms and I let her go. She looks at me before smiling. "I worked hard, *papá*. This trip will be good for me. I really like him, but I know to take it slow. I never thought about him when thinking about LA or New York. *He* actually suggested for me to take a trip to feel things out if I really wanted to go."

"Yeah?" I ask, raising a brow. She nods. "What does he want to do after graduation?"

She shrugs. "He doesn't know yet, either. But that's the point of growing up and graduating. Right? We don't know and *that's okay.*"

Her words seem too sophisticated at this moment. Look at my own daughter lecturing me. Back in my day we had to know what we wanted to do. Even after high school if you didn't plan to go to college, you had to know your life direction. A sense of pride washes over me for her; she's not letting those older ways control her.

"When did you get to be this smart and independent?" I joke, pulling her in again and giving her head another kiss. She laughs before wrapping her arms around me and squeezing hard.

"You taught me to be that way, *recuerdas*?"

I did.

"Go on then," I tell her finally. "But make sure to let me know if things don't go right. I'll be on the next flight."

"I know. That's why I love you, *papá. Gracias.*"

We stay like this for a moment before we break off and I do feel a little better with our conversation. I'm not entirely satisfied with the conclusion of her still going on that trip with a boy I just met, but she's right with what she said.

She knows how to make smart decisions because I raised her that way. It pulls at my chest, the thought of it all. *Mi preciosa nena.*

Chapter Sixteen

ARLO

I'M GRABBING the car keys as Clementine follows behind me through the house. Rosie is with Garrett and I made sure to have her text me if she needed me. But I'm trying my best to also not have to need *her*. It's not always fun seeing your child grow up and no longer be around you as much.

She was like a built-in best friend when she was younger. We went everywhere. With her mom too, but that was before the separation.

"You said this place has the best burgers and pizza?" Clementine calls behind me as I pull the front door open, making sure she goes first. She gives me a small smile.

"Yep, I'm surprised you and Rosie have never been."

She shakes her head as I lock the door and we both walk the small pathway to the driveway. I head to the passenger door and open it for her and she's got that cute, sheepish look on her face again.

It's not *not* like me to do these things. It's second nature. Holding doors, walking on the side of the street, scooting chairs in, ya da ya da. I try to keep it up with Rosie, but lately she's been beating me to it before I can even open the damn door for her.

"Thanks." She situates herself as I shut the door and make my way around the front of the truck. The cabin is filled with Clementine's sweet perfume and it invades my senses.

I take in a deep breath of it before turning the truck on and buckling my own seat belt. I glance over at her and she's got her hands clasped together over her thighs. Her bare thighs that are slowly showing me more and more of themselves as the dress rides up.

It's a pretty pale yellow with tiny details of flowers that I can't quite make out from this distance, but it's beautiful on her. For some reason the dress seems to only accentuate her body more and is the perfect compliment against her freckles.

"Frankie will join us?" she speaks up, breaking me from my thoughts. I nod before backing the truck out of the driveway and putting it in drive.

The route to *Porter's Place* is only ten minutes, so we skip the small talk and mainly listen to music. Clementine has control over the music and she plays country songs mixed in with some pop. I don't really mind since that means I can listen to her sing along.

Once we're parked, I tell her to wait as she reaches for the door handle. I hop out of the truck and head to her door before pulling it open. She's got that face again, of whimsical wonder that makes me want to either kiss her or drive to a nearby alley and devour her.

"What?" she asks softly.

"Nothing, I like this color on you," I say dumbly. I don't know why my head has become complete nonsense around this woman, but I want to stay like this for a while.

Her cheeks grow a light mauve and then crimson as she unbuckles and hops down. I close the door and lock the truck before we make our way into the restaurant. We find Frankie already sitting in a booth to the right, so we head there.

"Where's Rosita?" Frankie calls as Clementine slides in first and I follow. My big frame almost swallows the damn booth and her thighs are pressed against mine, but I kind of like it.

"*Con su novio.*" I roll my eyes playfully. I told Rosalía that we'd go to dinner, but she already had plans with Garrett.

Frankie clicks his tongue against his teeth before he eyes Clementine. I raise a brow, feeling a sense of possessiveness for some reason. I lean in a little closer to her, my bicep hitting her shoulder. She lets a soft squeak as she looks up from her phone before looking at us both.

"How are you handling *Casa de Santos*?" Frankie jokes.

"Better than I expected," she laughs. She looks up at me before quickly averting to Frankie. "I really like the pool. That's the definite perk to it all."

"Not this old man?" Frankie leans over and slaps my shoulder before I narrow my eyes at him.

"*Cállate, pendejo,*" I spit. But Clementine just giggles and it makes my heart skip a damn beat.

Before we can continue this playful fight, a waitress comes over and takes our drink orders. Frankie and I opt for beer while Clementine gets some fruity cocktail the waitress recommended.

"So, what do you guys exactly do again?" Clementine asks, tapping her nails against the hardwood table.

Frankie clears his throat. "We're contractors that renovate houses is the easy answer."

"And dealing with rich pricks," I add, "is a bonus."

She looks at us before she laughs and we join her. "I'm guessing you deal with a lot then?"

We both nod. "Our current client is really sweet, but she demands a lot in such a short time frame. That's the main reason I come home so late some nights," I explain.

"I just thought you guys were out at the bars," she jokes.

Frankie raises a brow and looks at me and then back at her. "You're funny. I like you."

She smiles brightly and it seems to liven this restaurant. The waitress comes back with our drinks and passes them around. Frankie and I order our usual before I ask Clementine what she'd like.

"I'm not sure what's best here, Arlo, so you pick for me!" Her eyes brighten and she nudges me with her shoulder. I catch Frankie's smirk with how she said my name in front of him. I swallow and nod before spewing off the same order I got to the waitress. She nods and leaves us.

The table is quiet as we take sips of our drinks. The perspiration on the glasses begin to sweat down to the bottom of the glasses and onto the table. I spin the base of the beer glass around it, creating an even bigger mess.

"You know, the whole table's gonna be full of water at this point if you continue that," Clementine teases.

"He's such a child at heart, don't mind him," Frankie adds.

I look at them both before grunting. "Teaming up on me, are you?"

Clementine places her hand on my arm for a moment as she shakes her head and giggles. "Never!"

Frankie winks at me as she keeps her hand on me before the food comes faster than we anticipated.

The rest of the dinner goes by quickly as we're engulfed in the delicious burgers and drinks. Frankie tells me more about his summer plans and a trip he plans to take to visit his folks down in Louisiana and then visiting a mutual friend of ours in New York. Even though we try to not talk so much about work, it's become second nature for us. We even started to drift a little into talking about the next project we had planned for this summer with another client before Clementine cleared her throat. But it wasn't in a rude way, more of a *hey, I'm here and I have no idea what you guys are talking about.*

"Sorry, *Girasol*," I say, brushing my hands from any crumbs. We stack our empty plates together to make it easier for the waitress before Frankie gets up to pay for the check. I fought him for a few seconds before he shook his head and got up to beat me to the register.

I look at Clementine and she's nibbling on her lip as she checks her phone to pass time. I lean in and even rest my hand on the table, cornering her into the booth. She looks up and her eyes widen with curiosity.

"What are you doing tonight?" I try to ask nonchalantly.

"Nothing, just getting my things ready for tomorrow," she says slowly. Her eyes trail down and I catch it. The way her eyes move from mine, to my lips, to my neck where the golden necklace hangs.

"Eyes up here, silly," I say, repeating what she told me this morning. Her cheeks grow rosy from the catch.

"Sorry," she mumbles softly. "Did you have plans for tonight?" she adds.

I shake my head before scooting a little closer and entrapping her even more into the booth. She cranes her neck even more to look up at me. Her eyes sparkle with something that I can't quite decipher.

"This is me trying to figure out if we could make plans for us," I whisper. She has to lean in a little to hear me. She licks her lips before I do the same.

"What do you want us to do?" Her words are starting to go shaky with nerves and I know her mind is going elsewhere than actual plans out in town. I grin mischievously, knowing I've got her with the effect I wanted.

"We can think of that once we're home."

She takes a deep breath before nodding, her face getting even more red. Her freckles are all I can stare at though besides her pretty eyes. I subconsciously lift my hand to brush a fallen strand of blonde hair back behind her ear. She hitches her breath before I lean my lips down to the shell of her ear.

"You'd like that wouldn't you?"

"Like what?" Her words come out in desperate pants.

I lean my body a little closer and her hand comes up, grasping my chest. I don't even care if Frankie comes back to the table and finds us like this. I expected him to flirt with the waitress or hostess though, so that gives me time with my *Girasol*.

"You'd like to come home and find something to do with me. A rerun of last night, perhaps?" When her breath gets caught in her throat I know I've got her. "Yeah?"

"M-maybe," she whispers.

I finally pull back, popping the bubble we were just in.

"Let's go then, *Girasol*." I smirk before separating our bodies and sliding out of the booth. She follows suit before she smooths her hands over the skirt of her dress and follows me closely. We make our way to Frankie and we head out of the restaurant to say our goodbyes before we split off.

The drive home is criminal when all I can think about is wanting her hands all over me.

Chapter Seventeen

CLEMENTINE

THE MOMENT ARLO shuts off the engine of the truck, I'm all over him. Literally.

"*Dios, bebita.* You really want a rerun of last night, huh?" His voice is strained and I'm glad I'm not the only one in this predicament. My core is on fire and I want not just a rerun of last night... Perhaps more.

I nod, unbuckling my seatbelt and practically jumping on top of him just in time as he starts to push his seat back to accommodate me. His hands are instantly on my waist once I'm past the center console. My legs are easily wrapped on either side of him and our breaths are rushed and loud.

My hands travel to his chest and shoulders before settling behind his neck. The curls on the back of his head are soft and my fingers play with them. His legs are spread wide even in this small cabin space it lightens up my core even more with how it makes me stretched out for him.

His dark brown eyes engulf me in his atmosphere. I let my eyes graze over the crook of his nose, slight hyperpigmentation on his cheeks, and the curve of his lips, before landing on the golden chain I've come to realize I really like on him.

The grip on my waist moves to the curves of my ass and squeezes softly, eliciting a soft moan from my throat.

"*Tan bonita, Girasol,*" he whispers as I lean in a little more, transfixed by the way his lips move.

"*Quiero besarte, por favor,*" I plead, watching the way his lips curve into a devilish smile. He simply nods before pulling me closer and my dress rides up even more.

His erection is evident as my core brushes right over and we both hiss from the sudden contact. I close my eyes for a moment as I take in this moment. I try to push away all *those* thoughts I've been able to push to the back of my mind for so long.

But they won't ever go away and I hate it.

"*Qué paso*? Where did you go?" His words are soft, but they're also demanding in a way.

I shrug and take a deep breath. I don't want to ruin this moment with him. He's perfect and I'm not.

As I'm deep in contemplation, his hand lifts to move a strand of hair behind my ear. His touch is very soft and I feel safe with him. I feel safe in his arms like this despite being in his driveway where anyone can see.

"Nothing, let me kiss you," I say with a smile. He doesn't hesitate as he nods and pulls me even closer with his other hand and my fingers grasp at his hair strands more.

I lean in and our lips touch, igniting a fire inside me instantly. This feeling is something I'd never get tired of. His hold on me tightens and my hips move of their own volition as they start to circle and grind against his erection. Even though he's wearing jeans, the bump is just enough friction for me to enjoy it.

"*Qué preciosa, tan bonita nena,*" he mumbles through the kiss. My hips move faster and my breathing grows quicker. I have to separate for a moment to catch my breath and his dark eyes are on mine instantly.

"Arlo," I whisper pathetically. "I need you."

"What's that?" He looks over my whole face before a smile fills his expression.

I grind my hips a little deeper onto his erection and he growls lowly. "I *want* you," I pant.

"Here? I was hoping my bedroom, *bebita*." His hands tighten on my hips to stop my movements. I whimper from the loss of getting to my peak. "I want to get on my knees for you and worship you. How can I if I'm in this position? I'm limited here. I don't want any limitations when I finally have you."

There are instant flutters in my stomach from his words and I bite my lip. I nod, speechless. What he just said is exactly what I want. What I need for this.

I promised myself after the assault that the next time I'm in bed with someone it will be with a person I can completely trust and feel entirely safe with.

Arlo Santos is that man.

"*Vamos*," he says and I wholeheartedly agree with a single nod. I hop off his lap as best as I can and he unlocks his door, pushing it open. I get out of the truck and he follows suit, locking it behind him.

We're practically like teenagers running to the house, his hand never leaving the back of my waist as we open the front door. We don't even stop to take our shoes off or anything, we head straight to his bedroom.

My heart continues to pump erratically as we get closer and closer to his bedroom like a ticking bomb. His body almost engulfs the doorframe as he pushes it open. He looks behind him and our eyes lock. He pauses for a moment, waiting for me to say something.

He gives me space and time to decide. To make a choice.

And that's more than I'll ever want from him. The ability to make a choice in this moment.

"I'm sure, Arlo," I say as vocally as I can. As powerfully as I can.

I want this. I want him.

"*Ven, bebita.*" He grabs my hand. It practically disappears into his palm as we enter his bedroom and shut the door.

The room is dark, so we're stumbling together and I let out a giggle when I feel the bed. My palms are out, smoothing over the duvet in big swoops before I climb it. He's right behind me making noises before there's a sound of a click and the lamp turns on.

His shoulders are broad as he flexes his chest and I can't keep my eyes off of him. He's beautiful and I can't believe I'm here in his bedroom. The elephant in the room of him being my best friend's dad seems to fly out of the window.

That's the least of my worries right now.

"H-how do you want to do this?" I'm not sure why I'm even asking but I'm not sure what his preferences are. Does he want me on the bedspread like a starfish? Does he want me on all fours? I feel so inexperienced at this moment.

I'm not entirely sure what position I'm comfortable with. It's been too long since I've slept with someone and the last time was with Nathan and–

"You tell me. I'm here to pleasure you, not the other way around. I will do whatever you want me to do. I'm here for *you*. Like I said, I will worship you in any form."

This brings a big smile to my face and seems to tame my sporadic heart. I shift my body so I can start slipping off my sandals. He *tsks* and I raise a brow before he moves closer and leans down, running his hand over my right calf before landing on my ankle.

Even just this touch makes my core scream and my panties are drenched. I gulp and watch as his fingers are soft against my skin, unbuckling the small straps on the side of the sandal. Once he's done with my right foot he moves to the other. The sandals drop to the floor.

"Can you take off your shirt?"

He gives me a look of pure wonder before he nods and lifts his shirt, pulling it off seamlessly. His chest flexes with the movement and so do the other muscles. The golden necklace glistens under the soft glow of the lamp.

He's burly and makes my knees weak. With how big his frame is, I'm not sure if I'm ready to see his cock. Would he split me in half? Why does the idea of that excite me?

"Like what you see, *bebita*?" His words are confident, yet don't drip in cockiness. He seems to genuinely ask as well. Like my approval of his body will make his world.

I nod and lick my lips. "I really do, Sir."

That word triggers him as he takes a step forward and leans down, placing his palms on each of my thighs. He continues to lean his face close before his lips are at my ear. I take a breath as I wait for him to say something.

"Say that again and I will take you right now, baby. "

There's no hesitation as I respond, "Take me, please. Please, Sir."

His fingers tighten over my thighs and I let out a soft squeak and he smiles at my reaction. Time seems to stop as his fingers trail ever so softly up, and up, until they play with the skirt of the dress. I don't stop him.

My body wants this so badly and how could I ever deny her? Everything in me is screaming to pull him into me, mold his body against mine. They're thoughts that I haven't had before for someone, or at least I can't remember having for someone.

"I like the way you react to my simplest touch, *bebita*," he whispers as his hands grasp the fabric of the dress and hike it higher up toward my hips.

The room seems cooler and I shiver from the contact against my spread thighs. I bite my lip and try to hold back a moan.

His dark eyes stay on mine as he kneels on the ground, head slowly getting eye-level with my thighs and clothed cunt. My breathing picks up and it feels like it'll burst right out of my ribcage if I don't attempt to calm it.

"*Puedo?*" His question is soft, like a whisper, and I nod as his fingers travel up to the waistband of my panties and hook underneath it, pulling it down until the fabric snags from my weight sitting on it.

"Sorry," I mumble, attempting to lift my thighs for him to continue to pull them down past my ankles.

"Never apologize," he says without a pause. His calloused hands wrap underneath the backs of my knees before pulling me closer to the edge of the bed in one swift movement. A squeal escapes my lips from the sudden motion before he's hiking my calves up on his shoulders.

I have to hold myself up by my elbows as I watch him with wide eyes and a curious mind. I can't remember the last time I had oral performed on me. It's been too long. But my pussy is contracting against nothing and really wanting his mouth on it.

He just stares at my bare pussy, lifting his hooded eyes to glance at me for a moment before he leans down. My eyes are not only transfixed with this movement, but I can't help studying the way his shoulders flex keeping my calves up, the way his biceps move to grasp my thighs, and even the veins in his forearms. If it was possible to come from just *looking* at someone, it would be this moment right here.

"You're already dripping for me, *bebita*. You've been keeping this from me?" His breath fans over my pussy and a whine escapes my lips before I try to shift my hips. The hold on my thighs tightens and he lifts his head before shaking his head. "Don't you dare move, I want you."

My eyes widen. "Really?"

He raises a brow. "Don't sound so surprised, baby. I've been thinking about this moment for far too long. Please don't make a parched man die between your legs before getting a taste."

"O-okay," I stumble out before nodding for him to proceed.

He licks his lips before shifting his weight and leaning in even more before all I can see in front of me is his mass of dark brunette hair and the feel of the golden necklace hitting my inner thigh. The coldness of the metal shocks me but also oddly arouses me more.

Before I can take my next breath, I feel the sudden wetness of his tongue gliding over my pussy before pushing through the lips and hitting my clit. The feeling is overwhelming and I swear I see stars from just this action alone. My hands ball into fists on the duvet and I close my eyes for a moment to relish in this moment.

"So fucking delicious," he speaks up and I finally take a breath. My chest heaves forward from the movement and it just pushes my core against him, thus pushing his tongue even more against my clit. I squirm my hips and his fingers just latch onto more of my flesh. The indentations I can see from here are enough to make me want to beg him to press harder and leave marks.

I want to wake up knowing that he touched me. Is that fucked up?

He beats my thoughts to the punch as I start to slowly spiral into the doubts and memories where my mind always seems to go–his tongue presses harder against my clit before he swirls around it, creating sparks in its wake.

"Oh!" I scream, grabbing the sheets tighter as he lets out a moan. It's guttural and animalistic. Something I didn't even know was capable of coming out of a man's mouth.

And *I* elicited that out of him.

"You like that?"

I nod but realize he's still got his face stuffed in my pussy. "Yes, yes very much. Sir," I add that last bit and a growl rumbles out of him and courses through my body. It makes my legs clench around him and this just sparks even more flutters in my core and makes his fingers grasp onto me tighter.

He slides his tongue even lower, teasing my entrance and I swear I've gone to another world. My hips buck forward and push against his mouth, causing him to chuckle and continue to lap up my pussy.

"Tell me what else you want. I'm here for *you* tonight."

I find myself staring at his bundle of hair as I think of a response. He's so responsive to what I ask for. He waits for me to find an answer and doesn't pressure me into anything. The sudden feeling of emotions floods through me and my eyes get blurry, but I blink the tears away as best as I can.

"I-uh," I start, my voice small. I clear my throat before shaking my head and gaining the strength to ask for what I want. "Can you add a finger? But slowly, it's been a while. Please?"

That's when he finally looks up and locks eyes with me. He winks before nodding and burying his face in between my legs once more and attaching his tongue to my clit once more. One of his hands moves from my thigh and I already miss the feeling before he hikes the other hand higher to my left calf to pull me high up on his shoulder. I'm practically hanging on by a thread in more ways than one.

He lifts his head a little before sucking his cheeks in and then spitting right on my pussy. I gasp at the sight, not knowing this would make me feel so hot. I want to fan myself just from this. God, everything he does is hot. How is that even possible?

There's a feeling of something hard and my whole body stiffens from it and I look at him before he catches my gaze.

"I'll go as slow as you need me to," he says before focusing back on his hand. It feels like his thumb is pressing slowly on my clit while another finger runs over my folds, spreading itself over my juices as lubrication. "So. Fucking. Wet. For. Me." These words come out in desperate pants and I can't believe it's coming from *him*.

"I need it, Arlo," I whine, hoping he doesn't stop what he's doing.

Like a prayer answered, his finger prods my entrance and slowly presses inside, my pussy stretching to accommodate his thickness. I gasp through it and clutch the sheets again.

"Shh, I got you, *bebita*," he says before leaning down and latching his tongue on my pussy and creating even more sensations as his finger starts to push even deeper inside me. I squirm underneath him from the pleasure that's coursing throughout my body.

On instinct my thighs clench around him again as his finger fits to the knuckle and he begins to pull it out slowly. I hiss from the sensation and I can't help but move my hands from the sheets to his hair. My fingers grasp his strands tightly and this brings out a noise from him that vibrates over my clit.

"*Ah*! Please, Arlo," I almost beg. He doesn't stop, proceeding to twirl his tongue over my clit while his finger pumps in and out of me. The wave of release comes to its peak and I know I won't be able to last more than a minute more.

"You're close, I can feel it," he says before picking up the pace with his finger *and* tongue.

"Please, please, please," I mutter in garbled nonsense. My brain feels like it's short-circuited as he continues to finger me before my hips lift from the all-too-much feeling of being on the precipice of my orgasm.

"Come for me. I want to taste you, please," he encourages as I grasp his scalp even harder while the orgasm takes over and feels like the best damn thing. I lay on my back to enjoy it all as his tongue and finger continue to inflict this orgasm.

The pull of arousal and feeling of letting go comes to the forefront of my mind and my body acts on it, breaking me through the invisible barrier of feeling like I'd never do this again. It's freeing and tears spring my eyes for a moment as I breathe through it and try to calm my frantic heart.

His hands move back to my thighs and rub in assuring circles. "You did so good for me. So good, *Girasol*."

I exhale loudly before lifting myself up again and widen my eyes as he lifts the finger that was just in me up to his lips and licks it clean. He catches my eyes for a moment before smiling.

"That was–" I'm not sure how to sum up the millions of feelings I just experienced in the span of seconds.

"You've satiated me in the best way," he says before wiping his mouth and leaning down to kiss each of my thighs before getting up from the floor. I crane my neck to look up at him before I avert my gaze and realize I'm inches away from his cock.

I swallow and then push myself up from my elbows until I'm sitting up. The dress falls back on my thighs before I shift to get on my knees. Even though I'm on the bed, he's still taller in this position. I press my palms against his chest and then drag my fingers upward. He takes a deep breath before he places his hands on my hips. His lips still seem to glisten from eating me out and an idea flickers through my mind.

I lean up to wrap my hands around his neck and pull him in; he obliges as I kiss him, tasting myself. It's something I've never done and I have a feeling it won't be the last.

"Mmm," he whispers, pushing his tongue through my mouth and our teeth almost clash as we kiss deeply. Our hold on each other tightens and it's like I can never get enough of this man.

"I want more," I say as we separate for a moment to breathe. We're back to kissing as he hums and rubs his hands up and down the length of my torso. I pull him even closer and despite him being so big that he can stand his ground, he lets me pull him like a feather so effortlessly.

We fall back on the bed in a fit of giggles, well my own giggles while he grunts and chuckles. He's careful to not squish me as we find our pace of kissing and his knee comes between my legs to steady himself on top. My hands roam from behind his neck to his back muscles, shoulders, arms, and then his chest. Everything ripples underneath me and I want to sink my teeth into every inch of him, not just his lips. The thought alone draws out a moan and he groans before separating the kiss.

"You sure about this though? Like I said, we're going at your pace. If you don't want to continue–"

"I'm sure," I cut him off. I know I have to get over this hurdle sooner or later. And there's no one else I'd rather do this with.

He nods before reaching between us and lifting the skirt of the dress over my hips before I help him pull it over me. He tosses it to the ground and then inhales loudly as he takes in my almost naked form. My black bra is the last piece of clothing on me, but I don't care. I want him to see me completely bare.

I unclasp the bra and take it off, throwing it to the side, not looking where it went. He smiles before I take the lead and run my fingers down his chest to the happy trail of hair that sits right above the waistband of his jeans. He hisses before I start to unbutton his jeans.

"Fuck, *bebita*," he curses under his breath before I've got the waistband pulled down as much as I can on my own. I giggle as the fabric snags against his ass, not wanting to move any lower.

"Help," I say before he chuckles and gets up briefly to pull his jeans off.

"Should've done this earlier, sorry," he mumbles before I shake my head and beckon him with my hands to come back to the bed. But then I remember that he's still got his boxers on.

Jesus, this feels like we're virgins having sex for the first time. It's comical, but I'm enjoying every second of it. It seems like he is too as he realizes it as well and lifts a finger to keep me put before he hooks his finger on the waistband of his boxers and pulls them down.

His cock springs free and my jaw practically splits, unable to get back to normal as I stare. The *length* is astronomical and I can't even think about the girth and whether it'd fit or not.

IN DESPERATE RUIN

There's no doubt that I will struggle to fit him inside me if he can even get to the hilt, that is.

"What?" he asks, a smirk growing on his lips as he takes a step closer to the bed. I clench my legs together and bite my lip.

"I-I've never had someone that *big*," I whisper, unsure how that sounds. Does it make me seem even more naïve and inexperienced?

But he doesn't seem phased by it at all. He's sweet as he continues to smile and hop on the bed. His palms go to my knees and spread them, I don't fight an ounce. He settles between my legs, yet my eyes can't stay off his lower abdomen.

"Like what you see then?"

I nod, words unable to form in my mouth. My mind turns into putty and I can't create coherent thoughts.

His hands start to rub my knees until they move up to grab my hips to pull me closer. His cock bobs and hits my inner thigh. There's pre-cum that's glistening at the tip and I lick my lips.

That's when I finally snap out of the trance and remember the most important thing: protection. Duh, Clem!

"I-uh," I start, feeling heat grow in my cheeks and up to my temples. It feels like my whole face is on fire. "Do you have a condom?"

His eyes widen before he shifts back a little before nodding. "Fuck, *Girasol*, I forgot to ask."

"It's okay," I assure him, lifting myself by the elbows.

I watch as he leans to the bedside table and pulls open the drawer. There's a box of condoms there and he pulls one out. He rips it open and starts to unravel it slowly on his cock.

"I wear them all the time, by the way," he starts to mumble. "And I'm all clear too since we're on that subject of protection and whatnot. I get tested after every partner."

"I trust you," is all I can say at the moment. He pauses before looking down at me and I give him a smile. My heart is pumping erratically again and I hope he doesn't see my nerves.

"Yeah?"

I nod. "I trust you, Arlo. I'm all clear too, and well it's been a while for me. I know it's probably going to hurt, but I'm ready."

It seems like he's about to continue but then he pauses again and I raise a brow. "Are you on anything? Birth control?"

I nod my head and bite my lip. "Yes, but it's the pill."

Even though I want to bare everything to this man, there are just some things I can't share right now. Like how I know I should be on a better birth control alternative like the implant or IUD, but that gives me some sense of trepidation. Usually, rape survivors get on the most effective birth control in fear that an assault would happen again, and there needs to be all of the precautions available. A pill would do for now.

I knew I wouldn't want to be touched by another man for a while, but the idea of allowing someone, even a professional, to put their hands on me in such a way to insert the birth control made me sick to the stomach. Although irrational, it felt like it was just another way to have Nathan 'win'. It's a very fucked up way to think, and I even discussed this with my mom when the time came.

She didn't pressure me into thinking I had to get on it or not. And I loved her for it at that moment, understanding why I was hesitant. I already lost so much autonomy, and it would've added to it. Once I got over the mental hurdle, it became an easier routine to stick to.

"And you're okay with this? I'll make sure to do what I need to, but we need to know the risks even with this condom," he says sternly. I know he's not trying to ruin the mood. He's being responsible.

I mean, he's got a daughter, for fuck's sake. I didn't forget that. I *couldn't* forget that.

"Yes, I am, Arlo. I'm ready, I really am," I say as confidently as I can.

I even reach out to hold his arm before dragging him down

with me, and he lays on top carefully with an *oof* leaving his lips. His hips are all the way down to my knees, so he has to scoot up a little to rest his cock on my stomach. I take a breath as I feel the length of him.

"I'll go slow," he reminds me as he leans down to kiss my cheek, then my neck, and then my lips.

I grasp his face in my hands to extend the kiss as I feel him shift, and I feel something huge prodding my clit and then gliding up and down my lips. I can't help but gasp, and he chuckles in that gruff voice of his.

"Please, Arlo," I whine, moving my hands to his shoulders to hold on to. He lifts a hand to spit in it before he moves it to where our bodies are almost connected, and I hear the sound of him wrapping his hand over his cock. I jolt when I feel his fingers press against my pussy, and I shiver.

"You were so wet and tight for me earlier, I can't wait to get you wrapped around my cock, *bebita*."

His words are rattling against my brain as I feel his tip press against my entrance. I take a deep breath and try to relax as he pushes in. My fingernails dig into his shoulders, and he hisses but doesn't stop me.

"So good for me," he praises. "You're taking me so well. Look at you, taking my cock so well."

The way his words echo around the room makes me feel better and can loosen my muscles as he pushes in more. It feels like he's ripping me in two, but I'm beginning to feel the rush of pleasure that soon overtakes the pain. I knew this would happen regardless of the size of the next partner I'd be with.

I'm just glad it's with Arlo, who is going slowly, inch by inch. We both continue this pace before he leans in to kiss me, and I bite his lip by accident when he moves even further.

"Sorry," I whisper. He shakes his head.

"Never apologize. If it's too much, let me know."

My pussy works on its own accord as it clenches around him,

and he growls. A moan escapes my lips, and he brings a thumb to my clit and slowly rubs it in circles.

"I need you to relax, *bebita*. That'll help me get all the way in, okay?"

I nod before closing my eyes and trying to calm myself. Once he's all the way in, he takes a moment to breathe as well. My legs are already getting sore from how spread out they are around his waist for a prolonged time.

And that's not the only thing that's sore. His cock is penetrating me so deep I swear it's up to my stomach. His chest heaves as he continues to steady his breath, and I lean up to kiss his temple before he shudders.

"Just let me catch my breath, okay? So fucking good *para mi, nena. Tan buena, tan buena. Mi preciosa, Girasol.*" His Spanish praise is tumbling out of his lips before I stop him with a kiss and then a giggle.

"Take your time, Arlo." His head lifts a little to see me. That's when he finally begins to move his hips back to pull out as much as he can before slamming his hips forward and a scream leaves my lips.

"*Ah!* Arlo, so fucking–"

"Yeah, baby? *Te gusta*? My cock filling you up?" he continues to pull out again and then slams into me, my body moving up the bed. The headboard of the bed slams against the wall as well and it fills the room.

My heart is thumping against my chest like a drum and I'm surprised I haven't passed out yet. I wrap my legs around the back of his waist and lock my ankles together. This causes him to be closer to me and pushes his cock deeper into me, hitting my G-spot. It feels so good, but so painful as well.

That's when something happens. Something I can't plan for, ever.

Nothing would have prepared me for the collapse of my world within seconds. It's like my world stops and the room turns to darkness. But it's not just my mind playing tricks on me, the room is instantly flooded with darkness.

"Shit!" Arlo's hips snap into me once more before he halts all movement. But my mind is already going to dark places and it barely passes me the way he mumbles *the light bulb in the lamp burned out.*

No, I don't comprehend those words until it's too late. My mind rattles and suddenly I'm back in that damn frat house where I can't move. My limbs are paralyzed and it's dark but I know who's on top of me.

Nathan.

No, no, no, no, no.

"It's okay, *bebita*," Arlo's words are soft, yet they go through one ear and out the other. He feels like a distant memory.

I can't focus on that. On him.

My eyes squeeze shut and I bring my hands up to my face, taking a deep breath as I realize that my limbs work. I even pinch my cheek for good measure.

But why am I still feeling hands on me? Nathan's hands are traveling up my legs and I shudder, wanting everything to stop.

Bile creeps up into my throat and I swallow to keep it down.

"Get off me," I cry out. "Get *off* me, get off me. GET OFF ME!" I scream, swatting at Nathan and wishing to God that he finally learned his lesson this time.

Because that's what's happening right? I found my way back to his place and he drugged my drink again. And he's finally finishing what he started.

"What?" A voice calls out, but it doesn't sound like Nathan's, it's muffled, yet my mind is too confused to tell the difference.

My palms find a chest and I push *hard*. The person finally slips out of my grasp and I take a big gulp of air.

The darkness surrounds me and I can't find my footing. My palms are out, swatting at the air attempting to find *anything* to grab.

"*Bebita*, what's wrong?" the voice continues to call for me.

"Let me go, let me go," I whine, tears already streaming down my face.

That's when I hear fumbling on the mattress and footsteps.

A light above finally turns on and the ceiling light engulfs the room in brightness and I gasp, looking around the room and feeling like I was snapped out of a trance. A horrible, fucking nightmare trance.

I grasp the sheets, pulling them free from the mattress and yanking them up to cover my body.

My limbs work.

My words aren't slurred.

"Clementine?" Arlo's voice comes to me and I snap my neck to the front of the room where he's standing naked, his hand on the light switch. His face is strained and I break out into a sob.

"I'm sorry." My chest hurts from the crying, yet I can't seem to stop.

"What? Don't be sorry," he calls before making his way to me. I sit up higher on the bed until my back hits the headboard. He takes a seat on the bed and reaches over to me, but I flinch for a moment and his hand hangs in the air. His face fills with hurt.

No, no, no. Fuck, this wasn't supposed to happen.

"This wasn't supposed to happen," I repeat out loud. I wipe my eyes, but the tears keep coming. There's a knot lodged in my throat from the emotions of it all and I sniffle. I feel stupid. "Sorry for ruining everything," I shakily let out.

"Clementine, *qué pasó? Dime*," he presses from where he's sitting. I can tell he wants to comfort me, but my body language won't let him.

I'm putting up a wall and I hate that. I *hate* Nathan and I *hate* that I went into that headspace.

"I don't know what happened," I whisper. I look down at the mattress and Arlo takes a few loud breaths.

"I don't know either… Did I hurt you? Did the lamp scare you? Talk to me, please."

I look up at him through blurry eyes and that's when I *see* him. I don't see Nathan anymore. I don't feel Nathan's long, cold fingers on mine. I don't feel suffocated anymore as I continue to stare at Arlo.

"I have to tell you something," I finally breathe out, knowing it's time.

I have to tell him. I had to eventually. I thought I had more time, but of course, Nathan found a way to ruin it even from afar. He took everything from me and yet here he is, still taking. I'm exhausted. Maybe finally telling people other than my therapist, Mom and Declan will help.

He continues to look at me with a painful look that brings more tears to my eyes. He reaches once more and I let him, the pad of his thumb catching a tear.

"*Dime, por favor. Estoy aquí, Girasol. No voy a ir a ninguna parte.*"

I take a deep breath, ready to tell him.

Chapter Eighteen

ARLO

WHAT THE FUCK JUST HAPPENED?

Clementine's face is splotchy and red and I don't know what to *do*. I'm waiting for her to speak, but she's taking long pauses. It seems like she's finally ready though with the way she nods and parts her lips.

I'm terrified to hear what she has to say.

Get off me.

That's what she screamed. But she didn't seem to know where she was. She didn't even seem to understand that I was still in the room with her. It seemed like she was somewhere else, in her head.

I'm not even sure she knew what was going on with the lamp. Right when I was snapping my hips into her relentlessly, the lightbulb in the lamp burned out and sparked, creating a loud sound. It surely didn't help with the addition of my yelling and the way the room was suddenly clouded in darkness like the snap of a finger.

At first I thought it was just a fear of hers being in the dark, which I wouldn't blame her. With the way the curtains are thick and closed over every window in here, the room gets pitch black with no lamp.

I stare at her intently and hope she can tell me what the hell is going on so I can help her in some way.

Her knees underneath the bed sheets pull into her chest and she takes a few calming breaths, but she looks the least bit calm. I rest my hand on her covered knee and she looks anywhere but me.

It causes a rift in my chest and I want to know what happened to my girl.

"Clementine, you have to tell me what's going on. What happened?"

Her voice is faint and I have to lean in more to really listen. "It happened–It happened almost two years ago."

"What happened?"

She bites her lip and it seems hard enough because it draws the faintest sight of blood and I reach my thumb again to her soft lips to brush it away. A tear escapes her eye once more and she takes a shaky breath.

"Rosalía doesn't know and you have to *promise* me that she never will. Not until I'm ready. Please, Arlo."

Her words are intense and it doesn't help my hammering heart. "You're making me worried, Clementine. *Dime, por favor.*"

"My ex-boyfriend... Nathan." She takes a deep breath and my body stiffens. I try to rack my brain to see if I remember the name from Rosie, but my answers fall short. "We were at a party at his frat house and he, uh, he did something. To me."

I shift a little closer and place my hand again on her knee and she seems to almost relax under the touch, which surprises me considering what she might say next.

With the way things are going, I'm terrified my assumption is correct. A father's worst nightmare.

"He must've slipped something in my drink, that I didn't know at the time," she starts again with even more nerves filtering through her. "Once he got me alone, that's when I couldn't do anything. I couldn't *stop* him. I couldn't *move*. I was so scared, yet he just continued. I was in and out of the whole thing. Like I was drowning and being pulled up and under the waves. And then being pulled to the surface to catch my breath just for the cycle to start all over again. It was dark. *So fucking dark* in that room."

"Jesus, Clementine. Did you tell anyone? Where the fuck is he?" The anger seeps out of me and I grab her knees a little harder, but she doesn't seem to care. She looks almost… broken. I could shake her right now and she wouldn't be phased. Having to repeat that night in her head is what's breaking her, I'm sure.

She shakes her head. "It took me a while to finally tell someone. My mom and Declan know as well as my therapist. She's helped me a lot through what happened and what I was trying to do."

That last point catches me off guard. "What did you try to do?"

Another tear rolls down her puffy cheek and I lift my hand to wipe it before she sniffles. She moves her hands to the bedsheets before slowly lifting it from her body to show me her thighs. The faint scars.

"I found a way to forget about the flashbacks. It worked for a while until it didn't. At first, it was the hard way with razors, the tip of a knife, scissors, and anything that was on hand. Then the scars were too much to hide so I was forced to find another way. Keeping my nails long enough to sink them into my skin in various parts of my body where no one can really see."

She shows me the underside of her arms as well and I finally see *those* faint scars. It doesn't stop there, Clementine continues to show me places on her body that she's harmed herself enough where it would be hidden from other people's view.

Silence fills the room as I take in her words. They never

prepare you how to handle a situation like this. No ounce of remorse or sympathy will ease the pain they've endured. I can only offer as much empathy as she will allow me because this is a feeling that one can really understand or feel unless they've experienced it firsthand.

I can't imagine how *alone* Clementine feels right now.

"Clem–" My words fall short as she sniffles and rubs her hand against her thighs. She shakes her head, her blonde strands flying everywhere.

"Trust me, Arlo. Fighting back in the legal sense was something I contemplated, but didn't follow through. Money can stop a lot of bad people from suffering the consequences of their actions. I just happened to find myself in front of one of those monsters."

"Have you seen him since?"

I'm not only curious for her well-being, but I need to know where that fucker is. If I ever saw him…

"Yes."

It's sharp and echoes in the room. It's like a serrated knife cutting the silence between us.

I run my hand through my hair and I take a deep breath. My chest feels heavier and it almost feels like there's an invisible weight pressing over us in this room. It's taking a toll on her and I want to help so badly, but I don't know how. I feel useless and powerless over something that no one should endure.

"Please stop looking at me like that," she whispers, turning her head to the side and staring at the door.

"I'm sorry, *bebita*. I feel like I should be doing something to help you, but I'm at a loss," I confess.

"Giving me the space to tell you and being here listening is enough," she finally says. "I'm not asking for pity or to look at me in a different way. I've done enough of that on my own. It took my mom and Declan a while to even start smiling around me. It felt like anytime I was around or they heard my voice they'd get stuck in this never-ending trance of feeling sorry for me. I'm kind of over that guilt that takes over anyone once I tell them. I'm over people looking at me like I'm broken like they need to walk on eggshells whenever I'm around. I just want to continue to move on from this in any way I can without the stares and pity from others."

I attempt to give her a small smile, but inside I'm breaking for her. She's so strong, so courageous to be here telling me this. I can't imagine what she's been going through. Not just the rape, but the aftermath of it all. It destroys a person and it's never a linear timeline of when they'll start to feel like themselves again.

Healing is never linear and I understand that.

"Please don't tell Rosalía," she reminds me.

I nod.

"I won't, *bebita*. But what can I do?" I want to be here for her. She looks exhausted after telling me. I want to help her in any way.

"Hold me?" Her voice breaks at this and it feels like her walls are crumbling slowly and I don't hesitate to shift on the bed to her side and pull her into my arms.

Her legs are still kind of tangled in the bedsheets, but she doesn't seem to mind as she lets me continue to pull her in. Her head crashes into my chest and I inhale her scent and kiss the crown of her head. My arms wrap around her tightly and I hold her like this for a moment. Her breathing is staggered and she's trying to show her best face, but I don't want her to try in front of me.

"You can feel what you need to, Clementine," I tell her before kissing her head again. Her body relaxes a little more from her wound-up state.

Her back shudders a little and that's when I realize she's sobbing. I don't say anything though. I rub her back in smooth motions and let her cry it all out. My own eyes brim with tears from it all.

"You're safe with me, *Girasol*," I whisper as I continue to rub her back. She pulls further into my chest and I hold her tighter. I keep repeating this over and over until she's no longer crying.

Until she's no longer hurting for tonight.

Because I know that she must be hurting every day. No matter what you do, think, or try to work on this is just something that will creep up on you out of nowhere. You can prepare yourself to the nines, but one instance can make you crumble and fall down.

Like tonight. I wouldn't wish this on anyone. I want to keep her safe forever.

My heart pulls for her and I grip my fingers over her skin a little harder than necessary, but she doesn't push back. I want her in my arms forever.

"*Estoy a salvo,*" she whispers so softly I almost miss it. I smile and kiss her head again.

"*Estás a salvo,*" I repeat.

Chapter Nineteen

ARLO

CLEMENTINE NAPS for a bit in my arms and I almost fall asleep to the sound of her cute little snoring she makes.

I'm not sure if she dreamt anything at all, but if she did I really hoped it was something good. It's hard to keep rewiring my brain to not feel sorry for her. She doesn't want it and she said it herself that it doesn't help her in her healing.

She's getting dressed in nothing but my shirt before I pull on some sweats. We head out of the bedroom and we find ourselves under the glow of the moon in the kitchen. Her eyes are puffy and so is the rest of her face from the crying, but she's still the most gorgeous woman I've ever laid my eyes on.

"What?" She giggles before heading to the fridge and pulling the door open. The refrigerator light shines and outlines her body like an angel. She pulls out a water bottle before closing it and heading back to the island and plopping on a barstool.

"Nothing, I like just staring at you," I say softly.

There's a rise of redness to her face. She looks like a bright tomato and it's the cutest thing. I make my way to her and she spreads her legs so I can stand in between them. I rest my palms on the island right by her arms, trapping her.

She cranes her neck to look up at me. I smile and lift a hand to rub her chin before dragging my thumb along her plump lip.

"You're going to burn a hole into me if you keep staring," she jokes.

"Fine, I'll look away," I laugh before turning my head to the side and fixing my eyes on the stove across the room. But I hear her laugh before I feel her soft hands on my face and pull me back to look at her.

"Kiss me, Arlo," she whispers and I can't deny her.

I could never deny my girl.

I lean in and kiss her softly. She wraps her hands around my neck, pulling me in for a deeper kiss. This time it's her tongue pushing through my mouth and I moan through it, unable to hold in the way she's making me feel. The way she's making me crazy.

"Fuck, you drive me wild."

She separates our kiss for a moment to smile and giggle. The sweetest sound to my ears. "You say that like it's *not* a bad thing. Wild usually causes disaster."

"It's not, not at all. I want wild with you. You make me desperately want to feel *this* feeling with you," I tell her in between more kisses. My hands move to her waist and pull her a little up, causing her to squeal in my mouth.

We're kissing like we're wild teenagers once more and it excites me. My hands grasp her shirt and a soft whimper falls from her mouth.

"We don't have to do anything, okay? Not unless you really want it. It's your pace, remember?"

"I know, Arlo," she answers. She pulls back a little to look at me. "I'm not broken though, so please don't ever treat me like that. I really wanted this tonight. Wanted *you*. I've done really well despite the things that happened. I just want you to know."

I widen my eyes and curse under my breath. "I'm sorry. I didn't mean for you to think that. I actually think you're quite strong. No, you're more than that. You're a force to be reckoned with. A warrior who's just got a little dent in her armor, right?"

Her eyes seem to sparkle, but that's when I realize it's tears forming. I lean in to kiss her forehead before kissing each cheek. She closes her eyes and I take this moment to kiss each eyelid. It's so intimate, yet it feels so perfect.

"I've never seen it like that," she whispers.

"Well, you've got me now to remind you of that."

She opens her eyes and just stares at me. And I can't read her mind, but her hands squeeze me and I know I hit a nerve.

There's something bubbling under the surface and it's an emotion that's been pushed down for so long in my life that I kind of forgot how it feels.

It's not the same kind of feeling when you love someone platonically. No, this particular feeling creates a ripple in the world. Your heart beats differently. Your literal chemistry gets realigned for this person.

And this is something I'm starting to realize I'm feeling for Clementine. It's frightening, but calming at the same time. It's confusing but also something I'm *so sure* of.

"Is it okay if we just keep it to this for now? I still have to get my things ready for tomorrow. I'm a little nervous, to be honest."

I smile and nod. "Of course, *bebita*. Need me to do anything? I'll be driving you in the morning, don't forget."

She places her hands on my bare chest and she shakes her head. "No, I still can't believe you'll do it. I can't let you. I know I agreed earlier, but I can't let you do that. You've done enough for me."

"It'll never be 'enough,'" I admit. "Don't think of it as something that needs to be enough. I'll always want more of you."

A giggle escapes her lips and it brightens my mood. It brightens the whole damn kitchen for that matter.

"You've got a way with your words, Mr. Santos."

I lean in and kiss her nose. "Don't call me that, please. Not after what we just did. I like it when you call me Arlo."

"And Sir," she reminds me. A groan escapes my own lips.

"And that," I agree.

She smiles and I take a step back so she can hop off the barstool. She keeps a hand on me though and it travels down my chest to my hand. Her fingers lace with mine delicately and I'm blindly walking the path she is. Like a lost puppy.

"Are you going to follow me upstairs?" she giggles, turning to look behind her as I continue to follow her lead.

"You took my hand, *bebita*. Did you want me to?"

She halts and I almost collide with her back. I grab her shoulder with my free hand and her skin is so soft. I want to touch her for all my days if she'd let me.

"That wouldn't be wise. I'd get nothing done," she whispers as she twirls and gets on her tiptoes. We're still holding hands and her fingers tighten.

"That wouldn't," I agree. "*Buenas noches, bebita. Te veo por la mañana.*"

"*Buenas noches*, Arlo," she says before lifting her face to kiss me. I lean in and lock our lips. It's delicate and makes my heart patter against my ribcage wildly.

She gets back on her heels before stepping back and releasing her fingers from mine. I watch her like a lovesick fool as she heads to the staircase and runs up them. I run my fingers against my lips before shaking my head and turning back toward the kitchen.

But even though I know I should be getting ready for bed, I can't. My thoughts are swirling with what happened tonight. The good and the bad.

The good of being able to finally *taste* her. God, she's like the sweetest *dulce*. I want to stuff my face in her all day if I could. Her legs could suffocate me while I'm eating her out and I'd say thank you.

And then my thoughts turn dark. I don't know what I'd ever do if I ever got face-to-face with her perpetrator. Nathan. It starts to boil my blood with the thoughts of knowing he's still in this town.

So close to Clementine. To my girl. To my *girls*. I'm not sure what I'd ever do if he spoke another word to Rosalía, if she knows him. Or Clementine.

I just know that either way, I'd land myself in handcuffs.

Chapter Twenty

CLEMENTINE

THE FIRST DAY of summer school is easier than expected and I'm left with no homework. The pool is calling my name as I leave class and walk down the vast, bright hallway.

My sneakers scuff against the floor and it even squeaks at times when the rubber catches against the tile. I'm almost out of the building when I see a familiar blond head that makes me practically duck into the corner and watch with widened eyes.

Of course, he'd be in the same damn building and *of course*, he'd be taking summer classes as well. Just my fucking luck.

The emotions of last night with Arlo come back in a harsh tidal wave and I take a deep breath, attempting to calm myself.

But before I can try to find an exit route on this side of the building where I am, he takes a turn and is going the opposite direction. I let out a shaky breath and smooth my sweaty hands over my shorts.

Once I'm outside the hot air almost suffocates me and I wince from the harsh rays above. We had some weather reports come in this morning that it would be a hot day today. Hotter than usual.

The AC in the building was loud throughout the class, but I

was thankful that it was a newer building so it would work well. I'm not sure how I'd be able to survive a whole month with this weather we were sure to have if I was stuck in a stuffy classroom for six hours.

But now being outside in this unbearable heat has me clutching my chest in an effort to not breathe in the hot air. I take out my water bottle from the side of my backpack and chug it before making the trek across campus to the bus station which will inevitably take a while. The buses around campus were notorious for being off schedule all the time.

By the time I get to the bus stop the back of my backpack is sticking to me and I feel disgusting and sweaty. I almost want to give up and call Arlo to pick me up, but he's working and I don't want to bother him. Besides, I can't just call him for a ride anytime I need it unless it's an emergency. He's busy and it wouldn't be fair.

Rosa has been in LA with Garrett since last night. I haven't talked to her this morning and I'm not sure what I'd say. I've left her last message read, unsure how to reply. There's some guilt that's still lingering around *that* part of last night.

How can I keep that kind of secret from my best friend? It was quite comical the way it scares me more than telling her what Nathan did to me.

As I wait for the bus, the sun just seems to get brighter and harsher. But within ten minutes the bus comes and takes me as far as it can before I have to walk the rest of the way into the neighborhood of the Santos house.

That's when I see Arlo's truck and I feel silly for not even attempting to text him to see if he was free to pick me up. I'm also curious why he's home at 2 p.m. when he usually gets home later.

I can't wait to find out though as I unlock the door and head inside. But that's when I realize that there's a problem. It's *stuffy* in the house and it feels like there's no airflow. Fuck, it's the AC. It's definitely out.

I kick off my sneakers before heading upstairs and throwing my backpack near the dresser. I peel off the clothes that are practically glued to my body and change into the cute sunflower swimsuit. I catch a glimpse outside and see that even the windows seem to be crying from condensation.

I check my phone for any news updates and that's when I see the headlines. Statewide heatwave. That makes more sense now and why it feels like I'm going crazier the more I'm stuck in this stuffy air. I need AC or the pool before I pass out.

I slip on flip-flops and make my way downstairs without a cover-up, because that's just too many layers in this heat, and find myself almost running through the house to the backyard. Seeing where Arlo might be is the last thing on my mind. Cooling off is my number one priority.

I almost want to strip naked and get in the pool and that's when I step outside and can literally see the wave of heat in the air throughout the backyard.

Fuck it.

My steps are loud as I head to the pool and throw my phone on the lounge chair. I look around the backyard, but the neighborhood is quiet. Everyone's probably at work or trying to stay cool indoors. I'm instantly jealous of those with working AC right now.

Before I can stop myself and gain some sanity back, I'm pulling my bikini bottoms down before untying my top and letting it fall. It feels freeing, something I wouldn't usually do. It's definitely the heat though, making me feel this way.

My senses are all over the place and I don't care; my only thought is to cool down. It's like the sun is boiling my brain and with it, burning my good sense away. I dip my toes in the water and it's slightly cold, but not enough. I grunt under my breath before jumping in. The coldness sweeps over my naked form for a moment before it starts to neutralize and feel like a lukewarm bath.

"Argh!" I scream once I surface, running my hands through my hair and wiping my eyes.

"Clementine?" Arlo's voice calls out and I yelp, swimming closer to the edge of the pool to hide my naked body from his view.

I'm not ashamed to be skinny dipping, but I wasn't expecting to be caught this soon.

"I saw your truck," I say stupidly. Of course, I saw his truck! What is this heat doing to my brain? It's turning it to mush.

He laughs before getting closer to the pool. His hair looks slightly wet and his skin seems darker than normal. Like he's been working under the sun all morning. He most likely has, but I still notice. There's also a line of sweat on his forehead that he swipes clean with the back of his hand.

"It was too hot to work once it came close to lunchtime. Let the guys go home. Figured it would do me some good to start the basement renovations, but I've been trying to fix the damn AC all afternoon."

His words wash over me and I feel fucking goosebumps. I bite my lip and my eyes trail to his broad shoulders and then his chest. His shirt is stuck to him with sweat and it's an odd feeling of arousal I've never felt before. I want him in here with me and I want to lick him, take a bite of him, and just kiss him everywhere.

"You're looking at me like I'm a meal," he laughs. That's when his eyes avert to the ground and notices my bikini. "Are you…?"

I nod and find confidence enough to swim from the ledge so he can see my naked body through the ripples of the water in the pool. He gulps and then clears his throat.

"Join me," I tease. I try to give him my best *fuck me* eyes and it seems to work because he doesn't argue one bit. He just glances around the backyard before nodding.

He's quick to pull his shirt over his head and then unbuckle his belt and pull down his jeans. I bit my lip as he tosses those to the ground and then pulls down his boxers. His cock springs and it looks *delicious*. I don't know what's happening to me right now, but I want him. I need him.

His steps don't seem to be fast enough as he gets to the edge of the pool and sits down before sinking into the water. He dunks in quickly before rising up and running a hand through his dark strands. I swallow the thick feeling in my throat.

I walk toward him until we're inches apart. His eyes travel down to where my breasts are and he licks his lips. Something wild in me sparks and I want to see how far I can push him. How far I can ask him to do things with me in this damn pool. For anyone to hear or see.

"Want a taste?" I ask, bobbing my body up and down so my breasts bounce and splash in the water. He nods like a lost boy and then he kneels down. Arlo doesn't waste time to grab me by the waist and pull me close.

His lips latch to my nipple and I moan, feeling his teeth drag along my skin and then he's sucking slowly. His tongue swirls in perfect harmony and all sensations fill me. I want him inside me. I want him to pin me to the edge of the pool and fuck me until I can't think straight.

I make loud noises again and he murmurs under his breath before he lets my nipple go. He then travels his lips to my other nipple and gives the same attention. My fingers trail his shoulders before grasping his hair.

"Please," I whine, unable to take it anymore. The heat is sticking to my upper body once more, so I lower myself a little until he has to let my breast go. He growls before pulling me harshly against his chest.

I squirm under the pressure and our sticky bodies mold to

one another. His dark eyes travel down my face before he latches his lips onto mine. I wrap my arms around his neck before wrapping my legs around his waist. He takes no time to slide his hands down to my ass and press me tightly to his core.

His stiff cock is right under me and I hiss once it makes contact and I swear he *whimpers*. It's like music to my ears and I want to hear it again. I separate our kiss before looking at him.

"I need you, Arlo. I don't know what's gotten into me, but I need you. Right now."

He's quiet for a moment as his hands press against my back, fingers indenting my skin.

"How do you want me?" he finally asks.

I'm not sure what's come over me or this newfound confidence. It's the heatwave, it has to be. But I don't hesitate to respond. "The stairs. *Now.* I want to sink myself onto you. I need you filling me right now before I pass out from a heat stroke."

"Yeah? You want me to split you open right there on the stairs for everyone to see? My naughty girl," he chuckles. I squeeze my fingers against his scalp and he hisses. I try to stare daggers at him, but it doesn't work.

"Yes, Arlo. Now take me to the stairs." It feels like my heart is up to my throat with this new sense of authority I'm slowly testing out. At first I think it's childish, but his response is anything but.

He's quick to lean his head to the crook of my neck to bite my shoulder and I yelp before he's standing up, his hands still on my ass to keep me positioned to his core. Within seconds we're near the stairs and he sits down on one of the higher steps so our legs will still be in the water, but our torsos won't.

I'm still straddling his waist as he settles into a comfortable position before I kiss him again. He grunts before pulling me even further into his core, causing my pussy to rub against his length. I shudder under the contact.

"*Ay, bebita.* Now, ride my cock like the good girl you are," he whispers with tenacity.

I gasp before nodding and positioning my hands on his shoulders to give myself something to hold onto as I lift myself and he uses one hand to move his cock in the right position. The tip brushes against my clit and it brings shivers down my back.

The sun is still scorching and my lips are starting to dry from dehydration. But I don't care. I need him and I'll do anything to get him.

I lower myself a little until his tip brushes down my folds before teasing my entrance. A moan escapes my lips and he pauses his movements, causing me to look at him with fiery eyes. What's he doing? Why is he stopping? I'm so close to finding this relief.

"What's wrong?" I ask with exasperation in my voice.

"I didn't bring a condom out here. I'm so sorry, baby."

I shake my head, throwing caution to the wind and not thinking logically for a second. I *know* it's very stupid, but I can't help it. Not with him sitting here looking like *this*–getting up to grab a condom is the last thing I want to do.

"Arlo, I appreciate that you care this much. That you want to be as safe as you can be. I'm just very fucking hot from this heat and it's making me want you to fuck me until… I don't know. My brain can't process that far enough with how hot it is. So, *please* just fuck me right now. I can't wait."

He looks at me bewildered and even something *else* flashes across his face. I don't know what, but the way he continues to hold my waist to push me further onto his cock seems to be the answer I'm looking for. I wince from the feeling before his jaw clenches.

"Never felt so good fucking you raw. Just how I fantasized. So fucking tight. I can't do it, *bebita*. You're too good. *Tan buena. No puedo, no puedo*," he mumbles under his breath as I sink inch by painful inch. He's ripping me open once again and it's like last night never happened. I'm so tight that I'm practically suffocating his cock with each inch.

"Just a little more," I say out loud, but it's more so encouragement for myself.

"Yeah, baby," he grunts. "Just a few more inches. You can take it, can't you? You're such a good girl for me. You're doing such a good job for me."

I whine as he bottoms out inside me and I clench around him. His fingers practically grip my hip bones from that movement. It feels like I'm filled to the brim and I don't even know if we'll survive this.

Everything in me wants to keep him inside until he comes. I'm not even sure why this crazy idea crosses my mind. But I want him to fuck me until he can't take it anymore and needs to fill me up. Until I'm leaking with his cum.

"What are you thinking, baby? You're clenching so fucking hard around my cock. Are you thinking naughty things?"

I nod, biting my lip and resting my forehead against his. I move my hips a little in a small circle and we both almost erupt in screams from the sensation. He feels so fucking good without a condom.

I'm reveling in the way he molds perfectly to me. We're in our own little bubble. I don't care if people hear us. I just want *him*.

I circle my hips a little more and he grunts, lifting my hips a little before slamming me back on top of him. I scream before he chuckles.

"Scream my name, *bebita*. I want the world to know that I'm fucking this pretty little pussy." My pussy contracts around him and he growls. "You like that idea, don't you? People hearing your screams while you're riding my cock?"

"Y-yes." I hiccup and circle my hips a little faster. The happy trail of hair that's right above his cock rubs against my clit and for some reason, it brings the best sensations as well. The best stimulation.

"I'm getting close," I whimper as he lifts my body again to slam down on him. We continue this pace before I'm a withering mess in his hands. He has to keep me upright with his arms right under my armpits. His hold is strong on me even as he snaps his hips up to keep driving his cock into me.

He's hitting all the right spots that make my vision go white and my heart is hammering against my chest. My upper body is drenched in sweat, and my wet hair is almost already dried from the sun, but the sweat is causing the strands to stick to my shoulders, my face, and anywhere else it can touch.

One of his hands raises to my cheek and he holds my face, tilting me to look into his eyes. They look so caring and so–

"I want you to look at me when you come, okay, *bebita*? I want you to know who's making you feel this fucking good."

"Yes, daddy," I slip out.

I'm not sure how or *why* that comes out of my mouth but it just does at this moment.

His eyes widen for a moment before he smirks and snaps his hips once more into me. My words are jumbled as another cry leaves my mouth.

"Yeah, you like calling me that?" I nod, biting my lip to hold back another scream. "Fuck, *Girasol*. The things I want to do to you every day. And now calling me that? You want me to fill you up? Fuck, you make me so–"

"Arlo!" I scream as the wave of pleasure washes over me like a tidal wave, no, more like a tsunami, pushing me to the edge and then into another world. I can't stop shaking and he holds me up.

"*Ah!*" I yelp as my orgasm continues to pull me in and out of literal consciousness and he's still snapping his hips into me as well as bouncing me on his cock in fast motions. I can tell he's close too and I wrap my arms around his neck even tighter, resting my forehead against his.

"I'm almost there, baby. Where do you want me?" he grunts, his movements getting even more rapid and sloppy.

A thought crosses my mind and I can't stop it from taking hold of me. I don't even know who it is speaking, but the next words tumble out of me. "Come in me, please, daddy. Fill me up."

"*Dios, bebita.* You don't mean that," he practically moans.

"Fill me up, daddy!" I scream, sloppily brushing my lips along his nose before kissing his lips. This seems to bring him to the edge as he groans and snaps his hips into me two more times before he shakes, his cock stiffening even more and that's when I feel it.

The rush of warmth filling me. It feels so good and I'm not sure why I'm letting it happen. Sane Clementine would've never, but this heatwave has twisted my mind into a feral animal.

I clench around him and he hisses. "Please. Don't do that unless you want us to stay here forever. Have me fill you up 'til you're leaking me."

A whimper escapes my lips from the thought of that.

He laughs before smoothing his hands over my hips before rubbing them against my back. I shiver under his touch and lift my face enough to look him in the eyes. They're still dark as ever, but his face has softened.

"I don't know what came over me," I breathe out.

"Me either," he admits.

We attempt to gather our breathing as we sit still in this position. His cock softens inside me and I know if we don't get up and out of the pool soon, his cum will leak out of me.

His hands continue to rub circles on my back and I lean my head against his chest. My thighs are sore from squeezing so tight around his waist. I don't want to leave.

Not just this position and the pool, but being in his strong arms.

"We should go," he says, breaking my thoughts. I lift my head and run my hand through his now-dry hair. I watch his Adam's apple bob as he swallows.

"If the AC doesn't get fixed by tonight, I don't think we'll be able to stop," I confess.

He laughs.

"Let's go see what I can do then."

And with that, we finally get up from the stairs and head to the container that holds the pool towels. He wraps one around my naked body before he wraps one around his waist. I go pick up our clothes before we head inside.

Chapter Twenty-One

ARLO

ROSALÍA'S FACE twists into a scowl as she sets down her drink.

We're at *Porter's Place* with Frankie and Clementine. Our table is fixed right in the middle of the damn place and I'm having a hard time keeping my hands off Clementine.

It's been exactly two days since Rosalía returned from her trip with Garrett and she hasn't been in the best mood. I've tried to talk to her, but she hasn't been telling me much. Clementine seems to be just as out of the loop as I am.

She hasn't been around the house this week as I'd expect if something were to have happened between her and Garrett, but again, I have no clue what's going on.

The waitress comes around the table, interrupting all my overthinking thoughts as she takes our food orders. We've already got our drinks half gone, so we ask for refills as well. Clementine looks at me when it's her turn to say her order and I have to clear my throat and ignore glances from my damn daughter and best friend as I spew out the order I got for Clementine the last time we were here.

Once the waitress is gone, Frankie whistles before taking a

sip of his beer. I do the same before Rosalía's scowl is back on her face.

"Are you going to hang with Garrett tonight?" Clementine asks, leaning over the table.

She shakes her head and glances around the restaurant. "No, he's busy."

Her answer is curt and I definitely notice. It seems like Frankie and Clementine notice as well with the way their eyes widen a bit.

"What happened, Rosita?" Frankie asks, nudging her with his elbow. She glances at him before letting out a hearty laugh.

But it doesn't reach her eyes.

"*Nada, estoy bien*. Just still tired from the trip, that's all. He said he wanted to have a guys night with his roommate."

"Maybe it's for the best," Clementine chimes in. We all look at her and her cheeks get a slight rosy tint to them. "You've been over there so much, maybe he wanted to just be with his friends, right?"

"I guess." Rosalía sighs before leaning back in her chair. Frankie frowns before leaning to her side and wrapping his arm around her shoulders. She laughs softly before smiling.

"There's our girl! Don't ever let a man dull that smile," Frankie exclaims.

Her smile grows at that and it makes me happy seeing her look a little better. I'd have to ask her later if there really is something going on that she's not telling us.

Maybe Clementine can talk to her.

The food comes in record time and we dive into it eagerly. We leave little to no room for conversation as we stuff our faces. The burgers are delicious and I even steal a slice of pizza from Rosalía's plate before she notices and swats her hand at me.

Frankie hollers before attempting to steal a slice as well. This brings Clementine into a fit of giggles and it's like the sounds of an angel. I find myself leaning my body more to her side, her hair slowly brushing against my arm whenever she swishes her head this way and that in conversation and eating.

It's so stupid, but I really want to brush a strand of hair behind her ear. The feeling is all-consuming and the tips of my fingers itch from the desire to do so.

"Hey, isn't that Nathan and Brian?" Rosalía speaks up, breaking me from my thoughts.

Clementine coughs and I pat her back softly as she regains her breath. I look to where Rosalía is nodding her head and that's when I see them.

My jaw clenches and I keep my palm on the back of Clementine as I watch them walk into the restaurant and the hostess brings them to a booth across the room.

"Who?" Frankie asks, looking as well. I glance down at Clementine to gauge her reaction, but she's not looking that way. She's looking down at the table and her lips are quivering ever so slightly and I catch it.

All I see is red in that moment and I fight the urge to get up and go across the restaurant and deck the guy. Whichever one is Nathan. Or both, I'd deck both the guys. I'm sure Frankie would gladly join.

Rosalía shrugs before returning to her plate. But Frankie seems to notice my clenched fist and the daggers I'm throwing at the guys from here.

"*Estás bien, Arlo?*" he asks, raising a brow. I rip my eyes off the boy before nodding.

"*No es importante,*" I assure him.

But Clementine sniffles a little and I catch it. My hand rubs her back a little more and Rosalía shifts in her seat. She's leaning over and resting her hand on Clementine's hand that's on the table.

Her other hand, I notice, is latched onto her leg. I grit my teeth at the sight. That fucker is making her do this. I want to–

"What's going on, Clementine?" Rosalía asks her, concern etched onto her face.

Clementine is quiet before she takes a deep breath and finally looks up at her. "Nothing! Just feeling a little under the weather."

"Oh no, do you think it was the food?" Rosalía asks.

Frankie shakes his head. "Food poisoning usually takes a few hours."

I give him a look and he shrugs before giving a look of *What? You know it's true.*

"Dad, maybe we should just get the check and then head home," Rosalía speaks up, looking at me. I nod and pat Clementine's back once more before scooting my chair back and standing.

That's when I look toward the hostess stand and see the blond there. He has to be Nathan. He's obviously flirting with the girl, but that's when he seems to sense my staring. He doesn't seem to care, he averts his eyes to the table and they land on my girl.

His eyes widen, brows raise before a smirk crosses his face. I clench my fists at my sides, but before I can say or do anything he's making his way over.

Clementine's whole body stiffens and I glance back at Frankie. His face turns serious as he sees my expression. His eyes move to Nathan's as the boy finally approaches us all.

Rosalia smiles brightly, unaware of what's going on. "Hey, Nathan! It's been a while."

"Just wanted to come by and say hi," he grins, but he's like a wolf in sheep's clothing.

Clementine stays quiet from her place, but Rosalía glances at her finally, and her posture changes. She rolls her shoulders back a little and then her eyes avert to mine for the slightest second.

"We're kind of busy. If you need Garrett, though, he didn't join us." Her words are sweet, but her face says anything but.

Nathan laughs before shaking his head and then eyeing Clementine. "That's fine, just wanted to say hi."

Rosalía nods but doesn't say anything. The table is still quiet and I inch closer to the back of Clementine's chair in a more protective stance.

That's when Nathan notices how close I'm getting to her. But I'm not sure what he's thinking, because he's not even looking at *me*. He's staring at her and with the way her head is hanging low, she's not giving him the time of day. And it seems like that's annoying him.

"Not even going to say hi?" he speaks up, causing a rift in the air. "We got interrupted the last time we were talking."

My brows pinch together as I listen to him. She's still quiet, but her head lifts and she shakes it.

"What? Don't be shy, Clementine." His tone is on the edge of teasing, but I see right through it.

"She's tired. We're about to leave," Rosalía says sternly.

But Nathan doesn't seem to care and it's making my blood boil. "Really? Well, come over soon, Clementine. I saw you're taking classes this summer too? Let me take you home after class."

That's when I snap.

"She's using my truck to drive home."

That's when Clementine's head snaps to me and Frankie smirks at Nathan. Nathan looks annoyed and even rolls his eyes at me. I raise a brow at that.

"I am?" Clementine asks softly and Rosalía nods, surely just playing along with what I'm saying. But I mean it.

If giving her my truck during her summer class will keep this scumbag from going near her after class, then I'll give her the damn keys. I'll walk home after work or hitch a ride from Frankie for all I care.

"Right," Nathan laughs, shaking his head. "Call me, Clementine. I miss you. You miss me too, at least you seemed like it at the pool party."

Before any of us could respond, Nathan turns on his heels and walks back to the booth where his friend is waiting. I let out a deep breath and the table is quiet for a few seconds.

"Jeez, I didn't realize what a fucking tool he is," Rosalía says.

Frankie shakes his head and leans on the table. He looks at Clementine. "Is he bothering you?"

She shakes her head. I grit my teeth.

"Yes, he is." The words slip out of my mouth and the whole table glances up at me. I lift a hand to rest on Clementine's shoulder and she seems to relax a little under the touch. I hold back a smile.

"Is he?!" Rosalía hisses, leaning closer and then snapping her head back to where Nathan retreated. Her eyes turn to slits and her face starts to get red with anger.

"No, no! It's nothing."

"*Clementine*," I say with a bite. Her blonde hair cascades down her shoulders as she looks up at me. Her brown eyes are watery like she's on the precipice of crying. It makes me want to march up to Nathan just at the sight.

"Well, you let me know if he continues to bother you," Rosalía pushes. She finally looks up at me and then her eyes avert to where my hand is on Clementine's shoulder. She studies us for a moment before she pulls her purse into her lap and digs through it.

"Let's go pay and leave them to talk," Frankie suggests and I nod, thankful for the idea. He gets up and I rub my hand on Clementine's shoulder once more before she glances at me as I walk with Frankie to the front of the restaurant. I can practically feel her eyes on the back of my head.

"What was that about?" Frankie asks as we're far enough and

approach the hostess to pay. I pull out my wallet and hand it to the girl before turning to my best friend.

"It's a lot, Frankie. More than I'm willing to admit," I say with a hefty breath. He raises a brow at my response.

The hostess gives me my card back with the receipt and I tip and sign it before we walk back to the table to get the girls.

"I've got your back, man," Frankie mutters quickly and I reach over to slap my hand on his shoulder and pull him into a side hug.

The girls are getting their things before standing up and Clementine seems a little bit better. Her hands are laced together in front of her and that calms my nerves.

Rosalía seems hesitant though and I know it would just be easier for her to know, but it's not my story to tell.

I do think it would be good for Clementine to tell her. Rosalía is her best friend and she needs someone in times like these. I want to be that person for her, but sometimes you just need your best friend to vent to. This also isn't an area I'm well versed in to offer support; Rosalía can provide that woman's point of view that would truly understand Clementine's side of things.

We're silent as we walk out of the restaurant and into the parking lot. Frankie gives Rosalía a hug before saluting me and then the rest of us head to my truck. I open the doors for the girls to hop in and then we're off.

Clementine is sitting in the back and I find myself looking in the rearview mirror more than usual, making sure she's still okay. She's as quiet as a mouse even with Rosalía singing along to the songs on the radio.

Our eyes lock for a moment though and she gives me the faintest smile and that eases my heart just a bit.

Chapter Twenty-Two

ARLO

ONCE WE'RE HOME, Clementine waves us off and tells us she's going to bed before I head to the kitchen with Rosalía. She's not as talkative and I don't think this would be the right time to ask her about her trip or Garrett. I want her to have the space and time to tell me.

"*Buenas noches*," she calls before giving me a kiss on the cheek and I squeeze her tight. She runs up the stairs and I head to my own room to get ready for bed.

It's not until I'm out of the shower and heading back into the bedroom, the towel around my waist that my door creaks open. I narrow my eyes, wondering if Rosalía needed something, but that's when I see a flash of blonde hair and Clementine entering the room. She closes the door quietly and then turns, jumping when she sees me.

"I thought you'd be asleep."

I smirk. "You planned to wake me up or something?"

She hovers near the door until she walks slowly to the bed. She's in blue satin shorts and a tank top. Her nipples are hard and poking through the fabric. I lick my lips at the sight and she smiles.

My feet are quick to get to the edge of the bed where she's sitting. Her head cranes up to look at me before her eyes travel down my torso where the towel sits.

"Like what you see, *Girasol*?"

She nods before scooting up on the bed and beckoning with her eyes. She doesn't have to tell me twice.

"I meant to come downstairs for a glass of water," she rambles, "but then I saw your door and had other ideas." She makes it to the center of the bed and I let the towel slip from my waist. A whine escapes her lips as I lean down to grab her ankles and spread them.

I crawl to the end of the bed before trailing my lips over her calf, thigh, and then her covered cunt.

"You can't get enough of me," I say matter-of-factly. She doesn't argue. She only juts her hips up, causing my mouth to press against her clothed pussy and I groan, closing my eyes for a brief moment.

She smells so sweet and I know she's going to taste just as good. With Rosalía gone for a whole week with Garrett, Clementine and I had many, many times to get intimate. A brief memory of me eating her out on the kitchen island comes to mind. And then even out in the backyard where she laid naked for me on the lounge chair and I made her scream my name for over an hour.

That was my favorite time this week.

"I need you, Arlo," she begs. Her thighs tremble a little as she attempts to squeeze her legs together but my hands are tight around her knees to prevent her from moving. She bucks her hips up again and I nuzzle my nose against her pussy.

"Do you really?" I ask in a teasing tone, leaning my lips towards her inner thigh and catching her flesh in my teeth, nibbling a little. She squirms and tries to keep her cries quiet.

"Y-yes, daddy," she whimpers. Hearing those words fall from her lips brings me to another dimension.

That was never something I liked being called whenever I

was in bed with someone. But the way she says it... it makes me fucking hard. It makes me want to ravish her, spread her open and fuck her and pump my cum into her until she's full of me.

Til she's round and full of my–

She whines again from the pressure my hands have on her thighs. I didn't even realize I was squeezing so hard, I was lost in thought. Thoughts I wasn't prepared to think. It's like she's opening a new Arlo Santos and she doesn't even know it.

"I need you inside me, please, daddy," she whispers again, reaching her hand down to grasp my hair. Her dainty fingers clutch around strands and tug hard. I growl before moving my hands to the waistband of her shorts, pulling them down along with her panties. I shrug them off her ankles and let them fall to the ground somewhere.

"You want me filling you with my cock?" I ask, resting my hands on her hips and then pressing my tongue right on her pussy, pushing through the lips to get to her clit. She slumps her head back on the mattress, mumbling under her breath. "Want to be so fucking full of me you're leaking my cum out of your pussy? Huh? Is that what you want?"

My words tumble out fast and I don't even recognize myself. I've never said those words before. Ever.

She just nods and squeezes her eyes shut, attempting to keep a strong hold on my hair. I press my tongue on her clit again before sliding down her lips and teasing her entrance. Her mewls and the movement of her hips become erratic–she's so wet for me.

"Please, please, please," she begs in between pants.

My own erection is pressed against the mattress attempting to find some kind of relief. But I need to prep her. I'm too big for her if I don't.

I swirl my tongue some more before I prod her entrance with my finger and then insert it slowly. Her cries get a little louder, but she's trying so hard to tame herself.

"You're gonna have to be quiet, *bebita*," I warn. I keep pushing my finger until I'm at the knuckle. Then I work it in and out of her before trying a second finger.

This causes her to twitch and squirm in my arms and her face is so red when I finally look up. She's trying so hard for me.

"You're doing so good for me, *bebita*. Such a good girl, you know that?" I praise her before pushing both fingers in really deep and finding that spongy part that makes her legs shake, her panting increase, and expletives tumble out of her pretty lips.

"I need more, please," she barely lets out.

"You think you're ready for my cock?" I tease her by adding a third finger to the mix and this causes her body to writhe. "*Mi nena preciosa, ¿estás lista para más?*"

She nods her head when I look up and I pull my fingers out before licking them clean. The mattress dips as I get up and finally let myself be pleasured. I wrap my hand around my cock, letting my thumb glide along the shaft and I shudder. Pre-cum leaks out of the tip and it's begging for her sweet pussy.

"Do you have any idea what you do to me, *Girasol*? You make me fucking crazy. *Un hombre loco. Que triste. Te necesito, por favor, bebita.*"

"*Entonces ven*, daddy," she says, lifting her hands to grab me. I fall on the bed, hovering over her and keeping my leg in between hers to keep her spread for me. My cock rests against her thigh, but the tip is brushing against her pussy and it takes everything in me to not cum right here.

"Condom?" I ask in short breaths, already feeling like I'm going to die by her tight pussy. It's the best feeling and I want to experience it over and over again.

She shakes her head at me, and I raise a brow. It makes me wonder if she's having the same revelations as I am. That she's having the same sick thoughts that I am whenever I fuck her raw.

We tried the first few times after the heatwave at the pool to use condoms, but she feels so fucking good with nothing in the way. I have been doing better though with pulling out as early as I can to add to the safety measures.

That day at the pool was a one-time thing where I came inside her, but I've thought about it almost every day since. I want my cum inside her every day if she'd let me. Fill her to the brim. Make it leak down her legs.

"I like feeling all of you, Arlo. *Please*," she smiles.

I pump my hand over my cock a few times before leaning in, my tip sliding down the length of her before resting at her entrance. She wiggles her hips a little to cause the tip to push in a little and I groan.

"*Bebita*, I'm not going to last long."

She's quiet as I push my hips forward, my cock slowly entering her. We both hiss at the feeling and I swear my eyes almost roll to the back of my head. She feels so, so good. I feel like a desperate man chasing this high every day now.

"Please, more, more," she begs as I continue to push into her. Her ankles attempt to wrap around me and lock together to keep me inside her.

"I'll give you more," I say through grit teeth. That's when I lean up to grab the headboard and her waist with my other hand. Her eyes widen before she realizes what I'm doing.

With one harsh movement and snap of my hips, my cock thrusts into her to the hilt. I bottom out in milliseconds and she yelps, slapping a hand over her mouth to keep the noises down from Rosalía upstairs.

We're both quiet as we try to hear if she's awake, but the house is quiet. I grunt and feel her pussy clench around me. Fuck, she's perfect.

"Please *move*." Her voice is small under me and I nod, pulling back and then snapping my hips forward again. I run my hand from her waist to the back of her knee to pull it free of her entangled ankles behind my back. I lift her leg until her knee is to her chest, causing me to go even deeper.

"Fuck!" she whisper screams, clutching her eyes closed from the feeling. I'm so fucking deep that I look down and widen my eyes.

"Jesus, *Girasol*. You see that? I'm right here," I say, moving my hand from the headboard to rest on her lower belly. The feeling of my cock protruding her so deeply to the point I can feel her has my mind going into a fucking frenzy.

"*Mmph*," she squeals through tight lips. Her forehead is starting to get beads of sweat and I huff out an exasperated breath as I stay mesmerized on her lower half.

I snap my hips back and forth, watching the sight before me. The bulge moves incredulously with each snap of my hips.

"Want me to fill you up with my cum, baby?" I pant as my thrusts get quicker. I'm getting closer and closer to my release and I desperately hope she lets me come inside her.

"*Arlo*," she whines, her fists grabbing the bedsheets before attempting to find something else to grab onto. That's when they finally find purchase on the sides of my face. Her hands are warm and she pulls me in to kiss me. Her lips are soft and I want to bask in this feeling for a while. That's when she squeals as my thrusts get deeper and harder.

"Answer me," I demand as our lips separate for a moment.

"Yes, yes, please. Please, daddy, please fill me up."

"Yeah?"

She nods, kissing me again. Her free leg wraps around my waist but I catch the back of the knee to pull it up to her chest so now I've got her folded up. This angle drives me deeper and my cock pulses with the urge to burst.

"Y-yes," she whines. "Fill me up, Sir. Please! I need it. I need you," she almost screams.

I push even deeper and I moan, letting a string of expletives leave my lips. "Fuck, *Girasol*. What am I going to do with you? Fill you with my babies?"

Her pussy clenches around me *hard* and that sparks a newfound interest in me. She's definitely on the same mindset track as me.

"Oh, you like that idea?"

"Yes!" she cries.

"Full of my fucking babies, huh? Fuck, I'd fill you every day then."

With one last snap of my hips I groan and fall on her, but catch my palms on the sides of her head to keep from crushing her. My cock pulses rapidly as it shoots out rope after rope of cum. My legs shake uncontrollably and even my toes fucking curl.

It's got to be one of the best orgasms of my life.

Her thighs are back near my waist and they wrap around me, caging me in. Keeping me inside her for a while longer. My breathing is unsteady and I can feel her rapid heartbeat underneath me.

"So good, so good," she whispers, grasping my hair with her hand and running her fingers through it. I lean toward the touch and let my body relax a little more, slowly lowering more and more on her body until I'm sure almost all of my body weight is on top of her.

I nuzzle my head in the crook of her neck and kiss her skin. Her pussy clenches around me once more and I grunt.

"*Basta*, Clementine. Unless you want me to fuck you even harder and fill you up even more."

She giggles before I lift my hand to look at her. Her eyes seem to brighten more and she looks so happy. It brings a smile to my own face.

"Who said I didn't want that?"

I growl and grab her cheek and chin in one hand. Her face is so tiny in my palm, I can't believe it. I feel her swallow underneath my hold. "Not tonight, *bebita*. Let's get some sleep, okay? We've got all the days for me to fill you. Don't you dare leave this bed though. I don't want one drop leaving you, okay?"

She's silent for a moment before she bites her lip and obediently nods.

"Yes, Sir."

Chapter Twenty-Three

CLEMENTINE

ROSA IS STILL ACTING off a few days after having dinner with her at *Porter's Place*. I've tried to talk with her a little more to ask about Garrett. But as far as I know, she's been with him the last two nights.

Summer school has been flying for me as well. Talks with my mom and Declan have been doing better too as I try to call them more frequently whenever I get the chance. It's nice to just talk to them some nights just as they're waking up for the day.

I think they're in London now. I asked them to get me a simple souvenir from each place and they agreed. I haven't mentioned anything about Arlo yet, I want to keep him a secret a little longer. But my mom has noticed my voice is a little chippier and I stay on the phone longer than I used to.

I've kept my distance from any place that Nathan might be and it's been working so far. Arlo on the other hand has been even busier than ever with his job and then renovating the basement. He's there late every night to the point where I snuck into his room last night and he was out like a rock. I tried to poke him awake and whispered his name as loud as I could, but he didn't move.

It's been crazy to think that we've had sex so much lately. The moment I was able to tell him about the assault, it felt like a weight had been lifted and he's just been more attentive and even more caring in bed. It's like it's made sex even better for me.

He never lets us end an intimate moment without leaving me pleased and satisfied. He puts my needs first and that's honestly all I could ask of someone.

And don't get me started on the fact that we've been doing our best with safety measures, but feeling him raw with no condom is a feeling I never want to lose. I know it's very, very stupid and that there is a high chance that things will happen. But when we're caught up in the moment, I don't want him to pull out. It's like I'm a completely different person when we're both in the same room.

I even have to try to keep my hands off him now whenever we're in the same room with Rosa or Frankie. But he seems to be struggling with the same issue as well.

It's evident in the ways he's dragged me to his bedroom the moment we'd be alone in the kitchen and the house was quiet. It's become the hardest secret to keep down with the way he pounds senselessly into me.

I've spoken to my therapist more lately as well. I was able to catch her up with summer school and also the times I've seen Nathan. She didn't push for more, she let me take control of the conversation which I appreciated. I was able to let her know my hesitancy to tell Rosa about Nathan and she offered some advice. We even tried out a few fake scenarios that might occur so I was at least a bit prepared when the time came.

There was a moment the other day where I even mentioned Arlo. Not who he was, or anything. Just that I took her advice to put myself out there and met someone who has been so supportive and makes me happy.

Because Arlo Santos makes me so fucking happy, it hurts.

· · ·

IT'S Friday and he's off work a little earlier than usual and asked me to go to the grocery store with him since Rosa was going to be with Garrett this evening.

We're walking around the store and it feels oddly satisfying being with him. I even clasped my hand over his for a moment after he got a cart and started rolling it around the place. I couldn't keep my eyes off the way the veins in his arms protruded and the smug look on his face when he caught me.

"We need *cebollas*," he says, nodding to the produce section as he pushes the cart toward the little baskets with onions in it. I nod and head to the little rack with plastic bags to peel off and then I start dropping a pile of onions in it. I twist the plastic and make a secure knot before placing it carefully in the cart. I glance up and our eyes catch.

The way he's looking at me, his eyes slowly gazing down my face to my chest, it makes me grow hot and it's ridiculous.

"Stop!" I yell a little too loudly with a smile.

He smirks. "What? I wasn't doing anything."

I get closer to where he's standing and have to get on my tiptoes to even attempt to get to his eye level. The baseball cap on his head dips low with his movement and I feel his exhale fan the top of my head.

"You know exactly what you're doing. Looking at me like that…"

"Does it make you want to kiss me?" His words are sudden and it takes me off guard.

"Arlo," I whisper, looking around the grocery store. There aren't any people I'd know, but Arlo is a local. I have no idea how many of these people know him. Know that he's definitely older than me and that he has a daughter.

I probably look like his second daughter or something milling about the grocery store with him.

"Am I wrong, *Girasol*?"

I shake my head before moving to the front of the cart to keep my distance. "You're evil, Arlo! Keep your hands to yourself until we get to the truck."

His brow raises and his lips curl. "Deal."

"Plus, I kind of peeked into your mom's recipe book and want to try those *Chile Rellenos*. We've got a few more items to pick out."

His eyes spark and a smile grows on his face. He reaches out for me and easily grasps my arm. It's a light touch and ignites a fire within regardless.

"You did?"

"I hope you're not mad. I just wanted to see if maybe we could cook something together?" I admit. I watch him for a second, but there's just adoration in his eyes.

"Of course, *bebita*. I'd love to."

I smile widely and he squeezes my arm before retracting. "Let's go then," I giggle before starting to walk towards an aisle in search of spices. He gladly follows.

WE FINISH grocery shopping before we get back to the truck and he immediately pulls my upper body over the console to kiss me. It's quick and not enough time for me to register that someone might pass by and catch us in front of the truck.

"Want dessert?" he asks, turning the truck on.

"We've got some frozen foods to put away," I remind him, buckling my seatbelt.

"Well then, *after* putting the food away," he says.

I nod, smiling. "Sure. But I'm picking the place."

He guns the engine and I scream, clutching the seatbelt before he slows down and laughs. I shake my head and laugh as well, pressing the button to roll down the window and let the summer air drift in.

It feels amazing out and I close my eyes briefly as I let the air

IN DESPERATE RUIN

dance around my hair and my face. It smells amazing too and it transports me back to the younger days when I had no responsibilities. Just going to the park with my parents. When my dad was alive.

When Nathan didn't ruin me.

I jolt when I feel Arlo's palm on my thigh. It's warm and it grounds me. I turn to him and smile, enjoying the rest of the drive back home.

THE BELL DINGS as we open the door to the ice cream shop, *Sunnyside Creamery*. I decided to change out of the workout clothes I was in and opted for cute jeans shorts and a flowy tank top.

Arlo is right behind me, his palm lightly touching my lower back as we head into the shop. That's when my eyes glance around the place and land on a brunette and dirty blond.

I stop in my tracks and Arlo nearly runs into me. He lets out a loud *oof* before I whip around with widened eyes. He looks down at me, a smirk filling his face before he sees the shock clear as day on my face.

"What's wrong?"

"Rosa's here," I whisper and I see his eyes slowly glance to the back of me before he clears his throat.

"We're not doing anything wrong, *bebita*. We're just getting ice cream."

"Then move your *hand*," I hiss, taking a step back so his hand on my waist falls. There's a pained expression on his face before he clears it, nodding.

"*Lo siento, Girasol. Vamos,*" he urges as he places his hands on my shoulders and spins me around.

He's steering us toward my best friend and I can start to hear

223

their conversation. She's so into the topic they're discussing that she at first doesn't recognize me. But then she sees our forms pulling up at her table and she lifts her gaze.

That's when a bright smile comes to her face. "Clementine! What are you doing here?" Her eyes go to her father before she looks back at me.

"Getting dessert. Didn't think you'd want any, *mijita*," Arlo says behind me. I try to not squirm too much as I feel the faintest touch of a finger glide up the exposed skin of my back near my neck.

Oh, he's so evil.

"I was actually going to text you guys if you wanted me to bring any home," she laughs before Garrett gives us a wave and barely looks at Arlo. My brows furrow and I try to catch Rosa's eyes to ask what's his deal, but she keeps her eyes on the cup of ice cream in front of her.

"*Esta bien*," Arlo answers before drawing shapes on the back of my neck with his finger. It creates goosebumps all over my body and I take a deep breath, hoping no one notices.

I take a step forward to get out of his grasp and it works, but I swear I hear him growl from it. I know he's going to have his way with me once we're back in the truck, but it entices me even more for some fucked up reason.

"Okay," Rosa smiles before Arlo finally follows me to the line. We take our time looking at the flavors and even trying out some samples.

We finally decided on a cup of mint chocolate chip and then peaches and cream. They were the flavors I liked the most and so he wanted me to have options to eat from. I make sure to wave to Rosa while Arlo pays before we head out.

As we walk around the town eating the ice cream and switching cups whenever I'm ready to take a different bite of the flavors, we talk about the simplest things.

He asks me about school and how it's going. I ask him about any new projects he's excited about. That one surprised me–he has a renovation job in the fall where he'll need to travel about an hour down South where some famous country singer wants to redo their whole home.

It dawned on me at that moment that things were changing and still moving despite feeling like my own world had stopped. My life has felt pretty stagnant this summer with just going to class and being with Arlo and Rosa.

But reality is coming crashing down and I'm about to start senior year in two months. Just two more semesters until I've got my bachelor's degree. It's scary to think that I'll be out in the real world with a piece of paper declaring to big corporations that I'm an adult. A full-fledged adult that is ready to pay bills and live on her own. At least that's what I always assumed once I graduated. I'm not sure anymore now that I have a feeling that Rosa isn't going to choose to stay here after graduation.

She was a secure option for me to have a roommate while living here before figuring out what I wanted to do. I could move back to Maryland while I figure things out, but I don't want to be confined to my mom and Declan's house. They deserve to enjoy their space.

"You're thinking hard over there, *Girasol*," Arlo interrupts my internal dilemma and I suck on the spoon in my mouth. I pull it out with a loud *pop* before sticking it back into the half-eaten ice cream cup.

"Just having a crisis about life after graduation," I mutter.

"Why's that? It should be an exciting feeling," he says, nudging me with his elbow. I crane my neck to look at him and he's smiling.

I shrug. "Some days it feels like I know exactly what I want to do, but then other days I don't know. I almost switched my major and there are times where I'm scared that once I actually get that big degree job that I'll hate it and want to change career paths."

Arlo's quiet for a moment as we continue to walk the loop back toward the parking lot where the truck's parked. He takes a big glob of ice cream and sticks it in his mouth. He mulls over the bite before swallowing.

"You don't have to figure it all out the moment you graduate, Clementine. You've still got time to decide what you want to do. That's the fun of growing up. Change your mind a hundred times, hell, even a thousand or a million. It's your life and you've got the reins."

I laugh half-heartedly. "Yeah? Is that what you did? Change your mind a million times?"

He nods and I stop in my tracks. He stops too and looks at me with a soft expression. "Even speaking with Rosa before her trip, we talked about this. It's natural to change your mind at your age. I changed my mind a million times, *bebita*. There's nothing wrong with that. I wouldn't be finding happiness right now if I didn't choose the choices and make the changes I did when I was younger."

"Finding happiness?" I ask quietly. He nods and I take a step closer.

"Yes, Clementine. I'm finding a lot of happiness lately and I'm holding tightly to it. I'm grateful for the hardships I've had to go through because now I'm where I've always wanted to be."

He doesn't say it, but his eyes do. There's a slight pause in his breathing and I know that I'm part of that. The happiness he's finding.

"I didn't know that," I admit. And how could I? I don't know him. I fell into his lap, practically, just over a month ago. We've been so fast in doing things physically that we never got the chance to sit down, or stand up in this sense, and talk about other things.

It's nice though and I appreciate having this time with him. I feel like I'm really starting to get to know Arlo Santos.

He hasn't just become someone I like to be with in bed or even my best friend's dad. No, Arlo Santos has become more.

I guess I'm finding my happiness too, then. In more ways than one.

"Come on, *volvamos a casa*," he nods towards the street and I smile as we fall into step before we head to the truck. He takes my empty ice cream cup before tossing it in an outside trash can and then opens the door for me.

The drive home is nice and quiet as we keep the windows down. Rosa isn't home yet, so we take the time to hang out in the kitchen before she does.

I miss my best friend and really want to ask her about Garrett and see if she's okay. She looked fine at the ice cream shop, but I want to make sure. She can easily fool someone with a smile, but I know there's something else going on.

Arlo's fixing his lunch for tomorrow as I flip through social media apps on my phone at the island. I'm so focused that I don't even realize he's behind me until I feel his torso brush against my back and I stiffen, goosebumps covering my body in the best way.

His body leans into mine and his lips brush my ear. I notice his arms being placed on either side of me on the island, palms flat on the surface. My eyes are so transfixed on the veins on his hand and traveling up his forearm. I swallow hard.

"I've got an idea," he whispers.

"What is it?" I whisper with a crack in my voice. I can't believe beads of sweat are forming at the base of my neck. My hands are shaky and I'm desperately anticipating what he'd say.

"*Ven*," he says before taking a step back. I turn and hop off the barstool before clasping my hand in his outstretched one.

He pulls us to his bedroom where he's quick to shut the door. My heart is beating out of my chest.

"What did you want to do?" I ask again, finding a place to sit on the corner of the bed. He stalks towards me before leaning down and trapping me with his arms. I have to crane my neck and bend my back a little to see his face clearly.

"A new position I just thought of."

"Position? What do you mean?" My mind is whirling with thoughts of what he might mean, but I come up empty. That's when he smirks and glances at the mattress before it clicks.

Oh, new sex position.

We've been so keen on either missionary, me riding him, or him just plainly eating me out. We've never really tried anything else.

"It'll be fun, I think. We both get to enjoy it."

"What position?" I lick my lips. He leans in closer, his nose brushing against mine.

"Sixty-nine," he mumbles. I gasp and I clench my thighs together instantly.

He immediately notices and smiles before kissing my nose and then lowering his lips to capture my parted lips.

"Arlo," I pant between kisses. He hums, but he's not answering. His hands are quick to wrap around my waist, working to get the tank top off me.

It's like he's on a timer and needs to strip us of our clothes as fast as he can. And he does. I'm naked in seconds and so is he. He gets on the bed and ushers me to climb him. His cock is already standing at full attention and leaking pre-cum. It's a sight to see and I've realized that I've never taken him in my mouth.

It's daunting and fills me with hesitation. I don't think he'd fit. Maybe half of him, but his full length? Not a chance.

I don't really have a horrible gag reflex, but at this point, it doesn't matter with how thick and long he is.

"*Ahora, bebita*," he says with a wave of his hand and I break out of my thoughts before turning around so my back is facing him.

"You sure you don't want to see me? It's my first time doing this with you," I say as my hands smooth over his core and then thighs. His legs jump from the touch and his hips move underneath me. His cock bobs a little and I squeeze my thighs around his waist at the sight.

"No, *bebita*. I want to be eating your pretty pussy when you take me in your mouth, okay?"

I nod and decide to lick my hand to provide a little bit of lubrication as it wraps around the base of his cock. He hisses behind me and his hands are immediately on my waist, tugging me closer to him. I almost fall across the length of his body and my hand squeezes tightly around his cock by accident.

"Shit, I'm sorry!" I whisper-shout, but he just grunts.

"Keep going, *bebita*. I'm not going to take you into my mouth until you do."

With that threat, I gather saliva in my mouth before I let the spit slowly fall out of my lips and onto his cock. His hips jut forward from the feeling and he's cursing under his breath in Spanish from behind me.

I lean forward, my clit brushing against his chest in the best way. His hands are massaging my hips and then the curves of my ass before I feel him kissing my skin.

My hand grips his cock and starts moving up and down before I lean in and wrap my lips around the tip. He moans loudly and it makes me even wetter. My tongue slowly sticks out and swipes along the tip before I put more of his length past my lips. He tastes salty and sweet and just something I've never thought it'd taste like.

I can't even remember the last time I gave a guy oral, but I'm glad this will be my new memory.

"Fuck, keep doing that."

My lips part even more and I try to push more of him in my mouth as my hand continues to pump the rest of his length. Inch by inch, he's slowly in my mouth until he hits the back of my throat. I swirl my tongue underneath his cock, brushing over a few thick veins and it makes me clench my thighs even more.

"I'm going to come soon if you keep doing that," he hisses. His grip on my backside tightens and I know I'm going to bruise tomorrow.

I want him to mark me as his and I can't wait to look at those tomorrow in the mirror.

My hips start to circle from the arousal and I'm getting wetter by the second. He juts his hips into me, causing his length to push past my throat and I almost choke, but I keep him inside. I attempt to even my breathing from being stuffed with him.

"Such a good girl, *bebita*," he praises. "Are you ready for me? I think it's my turn."

I hum out a response and he groans from the vibrations that travel from my throat to his cock. I pull back a little before taking him in my mouth a little more than last time. My jaw is starting to hurt, but I want to get to the point where his whole length is in me.

"*Vente*, come to daddy," he mumbles before pulling me harshly toward him.

His cock slips out of my mouth quickly and I scream as my pussy is immediately in his mouth. His tongue latches onto my clit and I hold back another scream before he's sliding it over my folds and attacking my clit once more.

"Feel so good, daddy!" I scream as low as I can without alerting anyone. We still haven't heard Rosa come in yet, so we're okay for now to make noises. It's like a rush doing this knowing she can be home any minute.

"I didn't say you could stop," he grunts before continuing to suck my clit and running a finger along my entrance. I push my hips toward him before attempting to reach for his cock.

"You're too tall," I whimper, attempting to shift up his body. This causes him to lose grip on my waist and I'm able to make it to his cock.

My lips wrap around his cock and I take him inch by inch again. But I hear him groaning behind me, reaching for my hips again, and pressing his fingers into the supple skin. I squirm under his touch and squeal with a hummed noise as I continue to stuff his cock down my throat.

"Didn't think of this, *bebita*," he grunts. "I'm too selfish, baby, I'm sorry."

And with that, his grip tightens even more and he's pulling me back up toward him, causing another yelp to leave my lips as his cock gets pulled out of my mouth. It's like dangling a carrot in front of a bunny and never being able to get it.

His tongue swirls over my clit before he applies more pressure over my folds and then my entrance. It feels heavenly and I bite my lip to hold back any loud moans. He continues to eat me out before I feel the increasing urge of wanting to release. My thighs squeeze as best as they can in this position, almost suffocating him.

"I'm so close, Arlo! So close!" I pant before I feel the wave of the orgasm reach its peak.

"Come on my mouth. I want to taste you. I want to lick every damn drop," he mutters before speeding up his movements. It brings me over the edge before I scream and my body jolts.

My orgasm hits and I'm shaking, feeling him lapping every drop. But he doesn't stop, he continues until I start to feel another orgasm approach. My eyes practically roll to the back of my head and my hands are attempting to still pleasure him, pumping his cock, but I'm starting to lose focus.

"Come on. Come for me again. I want all of it. Give me everything," he encourages and he starts to add a finger into the mix. The feeling is euphoric and my hips grind back into him, adding so much more friction. I know he can barely breathe with how hard I'm pressing up against him, but I don't care.

"Fuck!" I scream as another orgasm rips through me and gushes out. That's when I realize it's more than that.

"Jesus Christ, *bebita*, like a fucking waterfall. Keep it coming," he moans before continuing to lap me up and pumping his finger in and out of me. I whimper and whine, my thoughts incoherent.

"Daddy, please," I beg, letting his cock go before I try to reach one hand behind me to push him away. The overstimulation is starting to hurt, yet my body is betraying me. It wants another go. It wants to stay under his hold forever.

If he needed five orgasms, or even ten, out of me then I'd oblige.

"One more," he pleads as he continues his movements. I cry out as my vision goes white and I can't think anymore. I just feel Arlo and I let him guide me.

The wave I'm on is never ending and it doesn't take me long to release again. I scream, attempting to scoot up, but his grip on my waist tightens before softening.

"So, so delicious. *Mi favorita dulce*," he moans before doing one last swipe of his tongue and I shudder and whimper. He finally lets me go and I tumble over his lower half.

His cock is still leaking pre-cum and in my hazed-out mind, I want to suck every drop of his too. So I scoot up as much as I can before wrapping my mouth around him. He hisses before I brush my tongue on the underside. I push him deeper and deeper into my mouth.

"Fuck, I'm close," he mumbles.

I bob my head up and down and take him in as best as I can. I add my hand on the base of his cock and squeeze, feeling his whole body shudder. He's getting closer and closer and then he groans, slapping my ass before I feel his cock jolt.

It's sudden, but I feel his orgasm shoot through my throat. I do my best to swallow every drop before letting his cock pop out. I lick my lips and he groans before exhaling loudly.

"Never felt so good," he mumbles. "Come up here." He pats my ass and I nod before twisting until I'm straddling his front side. I lay my head on his chest and look up at him. His hands stay on me, tracing invisible shapes with his fingers.

He looks dazed and I lean up to kiss his cheek before kissing his lips.

"I shouldn't sleep here tonight, Rosa should be back soon," I tell him.

He nods and I see a faint frown fill his face. I lift a hand to press firmly against his lips to put the frown away.

"You're right. Tomorrow night, then? I like it when you sleep here." He swallows.

"I do too," I admit.

We stay cuddled like this for a moment before I finally get up and go to his bathroom to clean myself a little before putting on my clothes. But I leave the tank top and steal another one of his shirts. They're comfier anyway.

He heads to the shower and gives me a kiss before I make my way through the bedroom and do my best to flatten my hair. I open the door and slip out.

"Oof!" A voice screams as I collide with them the moment I'm out in the hallway. My eyes bug out of their sockets as I shut the door behind me and see Rosa brushing her shirt from the collision.

"Rosa?" I ask, my heart rate picking up.

"Clem? I thought you were already upstairs? What are you–"

That's when she seems to finally register where I just came from. Her eyes narrow and then she studies me.

They go from my wild sex hair to my reddened face before settling on my shirt. *Arlo's* shirt.

She's quiet as she continues to stare at me.

"Rosa," I start, tears starting to fill my eyes. I want to tell her everything, but I can't. My mouth is glued shut and she just continues to stare at me.

"Clem?" Her words are a soft whisper. Like dust in the wind.

"I can explain, I swear," I start. But she takes a step back and lifts a hand to stop me.

"I-I don't know–what? Clementine, what can you explain?" Her eyes go dark and they seem to narrow even more, a fine resemblance to Arlo. Her dark brows pinch together as if she's attempting to fit even more puzzle pieces together. But it's clear as day with the way I stepped out of Arlo's bedroom.

"Please," I reach out for her but she takes another step back. A sob is lodged in the back of my throat.

"Where is he?" Her words cut like venom and I part my lips, but no sound comes out. Her next words are harsh. "Clementine!" I jump at her exclamation and my lips quiver.

I still say nothing and she huffs before taking a step forward and pushing me to the side. I want to scream at her to stop, to just let me explain. But she's quick to pound on the door.

It's unlocked, but I don't think she wants to see her father naked right now.

"*Papá! Ven aquí ahora mismo!*" she screams as she continues to pound the door with both fists.

"Rosa!" I scream, attempting to grab her shoulder.

She snaps her neck at me and she's glaring harshly. "No! What the fuck, Clementine?!" She turns back to the door and continues to pound on the door. "*No voy a preguntar dos veces! Ahora!*"

That's when we hear footsteps and then the door opens swiftly. I hitch my breath but let it out slowly as I realize that he's fully clothed in sweats and a shirt.

At first, he looks confused as he sees Rosa with her hands on her hips, but then his eyes flicker to behind her where I'm hiding. I bite my lip and want this nightmare to be over.

"Rosie, it's not what it looks like," he starts, but Rosa doesn't let him finish. She's quick to jab a finger into his chest like a child being scolded. If it wasn't such a serious topic, I'd be giggling. But I'm feeling anything but in a laughing mood.

Especially with the next choice of words she chooses to yell at him. It cracks the Earth and I want it to swallow me whole.

"My best friend?! You fucked my best friend?!"

Chapter Twenty-Four

CLEMENTINE

THE BETRAYAL IS evident on Rosa's face. The way her dark brows scrunch even further together, the way her lips twitch as she backs up and is in between Arlo and me.

I want to reach out to her desperately, but she keeps her hands crossed over her chest. Arlo steps into the hallway, taking a deep breath before running his hand through is still wet hair.

Rosa taps her foot on the hardwood floor before glancing at us both. "Well?"

"Rosita, *escúchame, por favor mira*," Arlo whispers, the pain etched across his face. I stay quiet, unsure how to diffuse the situation. I want to tell her that it's all a mistake and a one time thing.

But that's furthest from the truth. Whatever Arlo and I are doing, it feels like more. And as we keep spending time with each other... I feel things that I've never felt with someone before.

He makes me feel safe like I can really start to feel things for someone again. I always thought I'd be stuck in this trance of being repulsed by the opposite sex after Nathan. And then, as cheesy as it sounds, Arlo came around.

My eyes gaze up to his, and he gives me the smallest smile, so soft that it warms me up inside. As if he's telling me *it's going to be okay; I'm here for you, for us.*

"I have to sit down, or I'm going to pass out," she finally speaks up, shaking her head and turning on her heel to head to the kitchen. Our footsteps are loud behind her, and she plops on a barstool. She brings her head to her hands and rests her elbows on the island countertop.

"*Mija, mira,*" Arlo attempts to call out, but it dies the moment it leaves his lips. Like a whisper in the dead of night.

"Rosa, we didn't mean for it to happen," I say loudly. My hands are shaking, and I lace my fingers together in an attempt to stop them. I even bite my lip to stop myself from crying. Distract myself enough with the slight pain to not cry. To not feel it all.

She finally looks up, and her eyes are glossy. My vision goes blurry, and I want to hug my best friend. She sniffles, and Arlo takes a step closer to the island before she shakes her head.

"How could you?" She looks at Arlo. "Taking advantage of my best friend? When Uncle Frankie told me you seemed to be happier lately, I thought you were slowly dating someone and was waiting for you to tell me. But, Clementine?" Her eyes shift to me.

I gulp and keep my stance, not sure if taking a step closer to her would be better or make it all worse.

"He didn't take advantage of me," I attempt to assure her. It takes everything in me to swallow down the knot lodged in my throat. "We kind of pursued each other at the same time… I know it's not what you want to hear. But we're all adults.."

"That doesn't make it better! He's my fucking dad, Clem!" she shouts. I jump from the sudden rise in her voice, and I blink back tears. She's hurting, and I deserve it all. "How could you do this to me?" She looks at Arlo, eyes narrowing to slits as she takes a deep breath. "How could *you* do this to me? *Dios mio, papá.* Clementine? *En serio?*"

Arlo looks defeated, and it breaks my heart. Cracks my chest wide open, and a tear falls down my cheek without my permission.

"*Esto no es algo que puedas predecir.*" Is all he responds with.

Her eyes continue to look between us. Her body stiffens as I reach out to her, but I think better of it. I brush my hands over my hair and then wipe the cascading tear on my cheek.

"I never wanted to hurt you. I promise."

"But, *how*? How did this happen?" Her voice cracks, and I can't take it anymore. I close the distance, wrap my arms around her shoulders, and pull her into me tightly. She shudders underneath me. More tears are falling down my cheeks, and my throat is closing up from the motions.

"I don't know, I don't know," I tell her truthfully. "It just happened. I can go, Rosa. You don't have to forgive me. I know I don't deserve that."

"Clementine," Arlo says behind me, and I crane my neck a little to look back at him. His eyes are full of concern, pain, and confusion. "It's my fault, but that shouldn't take your only option of housing from you. You've got classes to finish; don't forget that."

He's right. I have to finish this damn summer class. I want to crawl into a hole instead.

I take a deep breath and shake my head. "No, it's okay. I'll call Declan." I rub Rosa's back before she peels herself from me and wipes her eyes.

"No," she finally says. I widen my eyes.

"What?" Arlo asks her.

She takes a deep breath and wipes her nose with the back of her hand. She gives us a small smile, but I know it's just a facade.

"What do you mean 'no?'" I ask.

"Stay. It's not even my house to kick you out," she says

breathily. "I just–I can't be here anymore. I'm sorry. This is too much. My head hurts, and it feels like my chest is about to burst."

We're all silent as we take in her words. What does she mean? Is she on the brink of cursing me out again, because I definitely deserve it.

But she seems calm and collected as she takes a few deep breaths. A little *too* calm and collected. She pushes the barstool back, and we both watch in curiosity as she continues to wipe her tears and try to compose herself.

"*Mija? Qué pasó?*" Arlo's voice comes out in more of a plea.

"I'm the one that will be leaving," Rosa finally says.

"What?" My voice is weak, and it feels like I'm being stretched thin before snapping in half. Like I'm the only one holding onto what's between us.

She nods and finally looks at us to give us a small smile. "I can't do this. I don't know what you guys are doing, but I can't. I just can't. I'm sorry. Clementine, I love you," she looks at me and my heart pounds faster. "But what you did *hurt* me. I can't believe you'd do such a thing."

"Rosa…"

She shakes her head and pulls up a hand to stop me from advancing toward her. "No, Clem. I love you, and that's why I need my space, okay? I want to scream and curse you both out some more, but what will that do? It won't do anything. I need space, and it's not here."

"Where will you go? *Lo siento, mija,*" Arlo finally says from his place.

"It doesn't matter."

"Rosa, please," I beg.

She starts to walk out of the kitchen, but Arlo and I are glued to the floor. I want to call for her again, but nothing comes out.

"I've got some clothes at Garrett's. I'll figure it out. Don't follow me, please," she finally whispers before she starts walking down the hallway and out of the house. The slam of the front door echoes throughout the house, and it feels like a part of me has left with my best friend.

And that's when I break.

Chapter Twenty-Five

CLEMENTINE

ROSA HASN'T ANSWERED any of our texts or calls for three days. We don't know where she is. Garrett already let us know that she's not with him, but he wouldn't elaborate when I asked him if she mentioned anywhere she might've gone. Arlo is worried sick, and I want to scream and cry at the same time.

How can one be happy and sad at the same time?

Happy that I can express myself with someone in this regard, but hurting someone else because of it? It's not fair.

I want to find Rosa. I *have* to find her.

Arlo has been quieter than usual. He locks himself downstairs to work on the basement renovation even throughout the night. Our dinners are almost too silent.

Even Frankie came over tonight and brought us Arlo's favorite burger from *Porter's Place*, but it still didn't make him talk. It got to the point where he excused himself and went to the basement to work some more before holing up in his bedroom.

Frankie is sipping his beer as I study my nails and nibble on my lip. He didn't seem too surprised when Arlo finally told him about us.

If there even is an 'us.' He must've told Frankie that we've been fooling around some. But he didn't seem to care.

"I've never seen him this happy, you know," Frankie speaks up from across the kitchen. I look up from where I'm sitting on the couch. He gives me a warm smile, but my insides twist, and I want to throw up.

"He doesn't seem so happy right now. It's all my fault. I ruined my friendship and–"

Frankie waves his hand, dismissing me. "Nah, he'll be alright. Rosita and him have the tightest bond I've ever seen. *You and Rosita have a tight bond as well. You just all need time and space.*"

"How can you say that?" I ask incredulously. He mustn't know how much we're all hurting.

If I could rewind time and erase everything I did to keep Rosa happy, I would. In a heartbeat.

"Because I know Arlo and Rosita." Frankie moves from the kitchen to the living room, and I scoot over on the couch so he can take the cushion next to me. I pull my legs up to my chest and rest my chin on my knees. Frankie leans back on the couch and laughs a little.

"What's so funny? The world is literally ending, and you're here, *laughing.*"

He looks at me before laughing again. "You guys are so fucking dramatic. I feel like I'm in a telenovela. *Como 'La Rosa de Guadalupe'.* That kind of drama."

My lips part, and I gasp. "Are you kidding me? Do you not see how serious this is? Arlo is in his room moping, and we have no idea where Rosa is! You can't be seriously laughing about *that*. What if something happened to her?"

"She's fine," he finally says before lifting the beer to his lips. He takes a long sip before laughing and shaking his head. I want to slap him.

"What do you mean? How is she fine? We don't know where she is!"

"She called me that night." Frankie drains the rest of the beer before placing it on the coffee table. He rests back on the couch as I stare at him with widened eyes.

"She called you?! And you didn't tell us?"

Frankie laughs again, and I don't hold back. I push his shoulder and stand up from the couch. I'm fuming, and I want to strangle him. He's got the same smug face that Arlo used to wear. They're like brothers. They're annoying like brothers, too.

"I'm in her emergency contacts. If Arlo isn't there for her, then I am," he says almost matter-of-factly.

As if that explains everything.

"Frankie!" I scream, not caring if the whole neighborhood hears. I wave my hands in the air, exhausted and annoyed beyond relief. "You can't just come by and not tell us where she is. We thought the worst. Do you have any idea how sick Arlo has been about the idea that she could be hurt?" I place my palm over my chest, and tears spring to my eyes. "How much it's been hurting me that I can't get a hold of her?"

"You guys will be fine," Frankie waves his hand again, and I am *so* angry that I scream.

"Frankie!" My words bounce off the walls, and it's louder than I expect.

Arlo's bedroom door opens, and I take a step back. Frankie turns his head toward the hallway and that's when Arlo walks in. He's got dark circles under his eyes, and worry stretches over his features.

"What's going on? Are you okay, *Girasol*?" He looks at Frankie. "What happened?"

My chest pulls at him and the nickname for me. I missed hearing it from his lips. It makes me think my Arlo is back.

"Nada." Frankie shrugs.

My annoyance is back for his best friend, and my fists clench tightly at my sides, and I feel like a kettle that's about to explode. "Are you serious right now, Frankie? Tell him!"

Arlo looks between us two and his brows scrunch. "Tell me what?"

"Nothing, it's not a conversation for tonight. You need to rest." Frankie sighs, and I roll my eyes before looking at Arlo.

"He knows where Rosa is," I spit out. I'm staring daggers at his so-called best friend. How could he keep such vital information from Arlo?

Arlo raises a brow and crosses his arms over his chest. My eyes stay on how bulky they are, but I try to avert my gaze. Heat pools in my belly, and I still crave him as much as we've tried to keep our distance. We feel guilty for even looking at each other wrong.

But it's like the more we try to stay apart, the more I'm craving his touch. His sweet touch calms me.

"Frankie?"

Frankie finally pats his knees before standing up. "She asked me to promise her not to tell you guys. She really wants her space, okay?"

"She's my daughter." Arlo steps closer and enters the living room, feet away from Frankie.

"And she's family to me. If she wants me to keep her location safe for now, then I will. Just know that she's *safe*." Frankie puffs his chest at Arlo, but Arlo is bigger and taller. Arlo closes the distance between them, and I get nervous. I don't need them fighting like two angry wolves.

"Is she with Garrett? Is that it?" Arlo asks.

Frankie shakes his head. "She needed space, and it's not in Alabama. I took her to the airport the morning after the fight."

"What?" I finally broke my silence. Arlo looks at me briefly, and I can see the sadness in his eyes. I feel it, too. She took something from both of us. I just want my best friend back.

"Montana," Arlo finally breathes out. But he doesn't look

relieved. He looks even more stressed, and he finally sits on the couch. I take a step forward, and Frankie glances at me before shifting away from the couch and further from Arlo.

Like he wants *me* to be the one comforting Arlo.

"Montana?" I ask out loud. "Isn't that where–"

"Yep," Frankie responds with a nod. He digs his hands into the front pockets of his jeans. "She's going to stay with her mom for a little. I told her to call me when she's ready to come back, and I'll pick her up from the airport."

Arlo leans over and runs a hand through his hair. I catch how his whole body shudders, the way his breathing gets heavier and louder. Like he's trying to catch his breath after running.

"I have to call her. I have to go to her," he says.

"Absolutely not. She needs her space, *pendejo*," Frankie chastises. He then points to me and Arlo. "Look, I don't care that you both found something, but if you want to continue anything, then give Rosalía her space. Put yourself in her shoes. She needs time for the shock to pass and for her to find the best way to forgive you *both*."

"Nothing is going to continue," Arlo says a little too harshly.

Frankie is silent, and my lips part. What?

"Arlo, come on." Frankie half laughs. He looks at me with confusion plastered on his face.

"Arlo?" My voice is weak, and it feels like the room is getting smaller. My hands pull to my chest, and tears well up in my eyes.

He shakes his head before glancing at me. "*Lo siento, Girasol*. Come on, we have to be serious. And realistic. Nothing could come from this. It's better this way. I need Rosalía back here. I can't–"

"And you can have both?" Frankie attempts to say. But Arlo cuts him off with a shake of his head.

"No, I can't have both. I can never have both. It's not for me, I've come to terms with that. I need to call her mother."

I try to argue, but Arlo won't hear any of it. He gets up from the couch before stalking back to his bedroom. Frankie sighs loudly and runs his hands through his hair.

"Fuck, that's not how I thought tonight was going to end."

I snap my neck toward him and stare daggers into his soul. "Really? You thought we'd be celebrating?"

He's quiet as he watches me. I don't know what the hell is going on, but my heart hurts. Everything hurts.

"Look, he really cares about you," Frankie finally says after a few beats.

"Sure, he does," I mumble sarcastically.

I look at him through blurry vision. But I don't say a word. My mouth feels glued shut, and all I want to do is go upstairs, lock myself in the room, and cry my eyes out. I want to call my mom. Ask if I can get a one-way ticket to her and Declan.

"He really does," Frankie continues. "I see the way he looks at you. And the way he talks about you? Never heard him say stuff like that."

"You're really encouraging it?" I finally ask. I drop my head low and stare at the ground.

"What? Is that wrong?" Frankie laughs. This makes me lift my head, and he's not laughing sarcastically. He's truly laughing like he can't believe I'd really ask such a question.

"What?"

Frankie sighs before taking a step toward me. "I've known Arlo all my life. He's my best friend. I love him to death, but sometimes he just doesn't think he can get any good in his life. Rosalía is the best thing that's ever happened to him. But he deserves to also find his person. To continue living the rest of his life happily. And I see it whenever he's around you. It's hard to miss."

I can't say anything, I don't know *what* to say. I'd just continue to deny and deny. But I wonder if he's right. It's hard to see what others see outside the little bubble Arlo, and I kept to ourselves the past few weeks.

The living room is quiet, and we don't even hear Arlo in his room.

My soul yearns for him.

"He said this can't continue. I can't force him to change his mind."

Frankie shakes his head. "He didn't mean that. He likes to say shit in the heat of the moment. He really cares for you. It's hard for him whenever the topic turns to Felicia."

Rosa's mom.

Frankie continues, "I knew it would be a shock to him, and he'd get like this the moment he found out Rosita's with her. Felicia knows how to get under his skin, even from a distance. But sometimes, a girl needs her mom. I think it's a good idea that Rosita is with her."

I can't imagine not wanting to go anywhere else. I just had the brief thought of calling *my* mom. It's not fair to think Rosa shouldn't have that same luxury.

"You're right," I whisper.

Frankie rests his hand on my shoulder. "Go talk to him. He feels like he's lost you both, probably. Show him that he's still got you. Then he can work to get Rosita back, too–even though she's going to come back. But he doesn't think so right now."

I nod, letting the tears fall, and his lips twist into a frown.

"You'll be okay. Everything will be okay." His words are definite, not a question hung up in the air to contemplate. His confidence in this situation gives me some, too.

"Yeah, I really hope so."

He pats my shoulder before he takes a step back and starts gathering his wallet and keys on the kitchen counter. I watch him head to the hallway. He turns his hand and gives me a small smile before heading out.

I take a deep, shaky breath before flexing my fingers from

the tightened fist I had earlier. My steps are soft as I near Arlo's bedroom door. I don't want to bother him, but Frankie's words linger in my head.

The knocks are soft as I wait for him to come to the door. Seconds pass, and I'm about to give up before the doorknob twists and the door opens slowly.

His dark eyes meet mine, and they look a little red in the corners, like he's been crying. It makes my chest crack, and I take a step closer.

"Arlo, you don't have to go through this alone," I whisper. He doesn't move, but he doesn't stop me either. I take another step before I press my palms to his strong chest and then glide them up to caress his cheeks.

I get on my tiptoes and brush my thumbs over his lips. He closes his eyes for a moment, and I move my hands to his neck before I lean in and kiss him. His hands slowly wrap around my waist, and my body tingles everywhere.

I've missed his touch, even though it's only been a few days. A soft sound escapes my mouth when his fingers press into my skin, pulling me closer to his body.

We break the kiss for a moment before he takes a step back, pulling me along with him. Our bodies stumble together as we find our way to the bed.

"Let me in, Arlo," I whisper as he sits on the bed and pulls me into his lap; I press my core on top of his.

He groans, not saying anything. His hands are all over me, and it's like he's trying to memorize my body with each swipe of his fingers.

"I care for you," I continue to whisper as my lips press against his again and his hips jut up into me. "I need you, Arlo. You need me."

"*Girasol*," he finally whispers back. It brings flutters to my core, and I grind my hips into him. His hands travel up my body before they lift my shirt.

"Tell me you need me," I say louder, and his fingers pause. He finally looks at me and I give him another kiss.

"I-I need you," he finally breaks. His hands grasp my hips tightly, and I squirm underneath his touch. A touch I've missed so much.

"You've got me. All of me."

His hands pause on my skin before they squeeze me. He looks at me before leaning his lips toward the crook of my neck, and I lean my head back to give him full access. He leaves a pepper of kisses along the skin, and goosebumps rise in their wake.

"You've got me too, *bebita*," he whispers so softly.

His words sink into me and take residence in my heart and soul. There's no one else that I want permanently in there. And it feels all too quick to come to this realization, but it's true.

"Arlo, *please*," I whimper as his teeth tug at my skin, and I moan loudly.

"You sound so pretty. I've missed you. So, so much."

I circle my hips over his again, and he finally comes to and twists his body until I'm landing on my back on the bed with a bounce. He's quick to pull my shorts and panties off before he's stripping his lower half as well.

There are no words exchanged. Just our breathing and our heartbeats coming in sync the moment he gets on the bed and hovers over me, pressing his chest to mine. I wrap my legs around his waist, and his erection pokes my thigh.

"Please, please," I whine, caging him in with my ankles locked together behind him. He groans before moving his hips into me, and I feel the pre-cum swiping along my skin. I shudder at the contact, and another whine tumbles out of me.

He shifts his hand between our bodies before he's pumping his cock in slow motions. I'm ready for him, but I know the stretch will still be painful with barely any prep. But I can't wait any longer. I need him like I've never needed anyone ever before.

I spit in my hand and join him as I rub my clit and then glide my hand between my folds. My hips buck, and I whimper from the feeling of touching myself.

He grabs my wrist before pinning it above my head with the same hand that was just on his cock.

"I can't wait any longer, *bebita*. Please," he pleads. I nod, and he positions himself before pushing his tip into me. I cry out from the pain and pleasure before he's slowly sinking into me inch by inch.

My thighs tremble and ache as they try to squeeze around his waist. Once he's bottomed out inside me, we take a few seconds to gather ourselves. Our chests move up and down erratically, and I press my palms over his chest. This catches him by surprise as I smooth my right hand over his heart.

"You've got me," I whisper, unsure why I need to repeat it.

He smiles before lifting a hand and wrapping it around my wrist. But he doesn't pull my palm off him. He presses his hand over my palm, encasing them right over his heart, practically reverberating from the erratic heartbeats.

"Arlo," I whisper.

"You feel that? That's what you do to me. It beats for you."

Tears well in my eyes, and a sob cracks through my chest before bubbling up and out of my lips. The tears cascade down my cheeks, but I don't attempt to wipe them. Arlo leans down and presses his lips to each cheek, capturing them. My legs keep their grip around his waist, and my pussy clenches around him.

He groans from the feeling, and I grab his chin with my free hand, pulling him to my lips. I swallow his next few strong groans and words before separating our lips.

"Mine beats for you too, Arlo. I always thought I'd never find this kind of peace. This kind of safety. But I have, with you."

"Clementine," he whispers softly. "You don't mean that."

I grasp his chin harder, and he parts his lips. "I do. I mean every ounce of it. You feel my heart too?" I move our hands that are still on his chest to mine, where my heart is thumping out of my chest. "It's beating for *you*."

"I can't fix what happened, though, as much as I'd like to." He hangs his head low, and I have a feeling it's not just talking about Rosa. I pull him closer and kiss his cheek.

"You can't fix what's already been done. But you can do much more than that. You *are* doing much more than that. And you know it."

He's quiet for a moment before he leans down to kiss me. "I can't heal your scars, baby. Never will be able to. I wish I could, but I'll be here to give you peace." He kisses me again before continuing. "I'll be your peace."

My eyes well up, and I nod. "I'll be your peace, too."

He leans in, and we continue to kiss passionately like never before, and his chest is pressing into mine to the point where I don't care if his weight crushes me.

We don't have to declare more than this, and that's enough for me.

He's enough for me. He always will be.

We separate to take a breath, and he pulls his hips back before driving forward and thrusting his cock into me. A moan leaves my lips, and he kisses me, swallowing another moan and then another as he continues the brutal snap of his hips.

I don't last long, and I come quickly. He soon follows after, and then we both collapse on the bed. I'm full of his release, and he pulls me close into his arms, my head lying on his chest.

His hands rub my bare back, and our legs are tangled together. It feels perfect in this bedroom, and I never want to leave. Never want to leave his arms.

"I want to continue this," he says out of the blue.

I lift my head to look at him. He's got a smile on his face

before he rubs my back a little more. A smile breaks out on my own face, and I lean up to kiss his jaw.

"Yeah?"

He nods. "Everything I said was true, Clementine." He grabs my hand with his free hand and pulls it to his chest, where I feel his heartbeat.

My heart thuds wildly in my own chest. I look up at him, and he's looking at me in a way I've yet to see. Endearing, in awe, and... another word.

In love.

His eyes seem to sparkle, and a flutter of butterflies swarm in my stomach because I feel it, too. In everything we've said and done tonight. I *feel* it coursing through my veins and pouring out of his words. It seems to be something we don't have to verbalize.

I feel so much, and it scares me to the bones. But he meant what he said, and I meant what I said. He brings me peace. Even though I'm terrified of what's to come, he makes me feel safe.

He makes me feel like I can tackle anything I set my mind to. I can overcome anything.

"What are you thinking about?" he asks softly. I rest my head on his chest, where my ear is right over his thudding heart.

"Nothing that's already been said in *here*," I whisper, pressing a palm to his chest near my face. I feel his kiss on the top of my head, and I bury myself in his chest even more.

His hand on my back smooths over in up and down motions. He doesn't say anything back, but he doesn't need to.

I feel and hear his heartbeat pick up with my words, and that's enough confirmation for me.

Chapter Twenty-Six

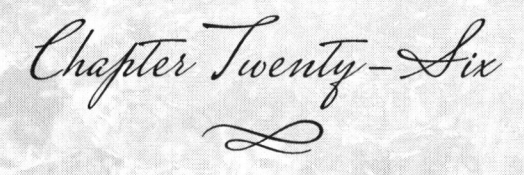

ARLO

IT DOESN'T FEEL like 3 weeks have passed since Rosalía left for her moms. It feels longer.

Clementine is done with summer school and having her here has helped a lot. I don't think I could be getting by without her or Frankie. They make the days go by faster than I expected.

Her birthday was just last week on June 25th, and we went out to a fancier restaurant in town. It was one of my favorite nights, just seeing her so happy to be celebrated. It made me take notes to celebrate more mundane things with her just to see that smile on her face.

Rosalía called me last week to finally tell me where she was. She's been in contact with Frankie the whole time, but I didn't dare tell her that I knew. I tried my best to keep my distance and let her deal with this on her own terms, so I didn't budge.

I didn't text or call until she reached out first. It hurt and it took a while for me to be okay with that. Knowing she was safe was what I cared about most. I haven't spoken to her mother during this whole time and I don't want to. It's not something I want to waste my breath or energy on.

I even started to clean out the damn garage with the help of

Clementine and Frankie. Well, more so Clementine than Frankie. It felt like a huge weight was lifted by doing so.

We spent the weekend looking through old boxes and tossing things that held no more value. We packaged the rest into boxes and stacked them against the wall to make more space in the center area. I wanted to make the garage a space I could hopefully work out of for future projects. The basement is almost halfway done and I can't wait for Rosalía to see it.

I know having her stay here and live in the newly renovated space isn't a guarantee, but I still want to see her reaction. I can't wait to have her in my arms and just have her here.

My hands itch every day to call or text her, but I fight the feeling.

"Arlo!" Clementine's voice is heard throughout the house before she heads out of the sliding door and onto the patio. I'm lounging on a pool chair after working all morning in the basement.

"*Qué pasó, Girasol?*" I call out, hearing her steps get louder as she nears me.

A huge smile is slapped on her face and I shield my eyes from the sun with my hand as I try to look at her.

"Rosa's coming back today!"

"What?" I sit up on the chair and she's jumping up and down.

"She just called me!" The happiness that's pouring out of her is contagious and I get up and smile brightly, unsure what to do with this newfound energy.

I can't help but bend down and pick her up by the waist and holler loudly, twirling her around. She squeals and giggles, her hands wrapping around my neck before I stop us. Her hair is like a curtain around us as she leans her forehead against mine.

"*Besame,*" I say and she doesn't argue. Her lips are on mine in an instant.

We kiss for a few beats before she separates and twirls her

fingers around the curls near my neck. I groan as she pulls the strands tightly, making my cock twitch.

"We should celebrate," she whispers, leaning in to kiss me again.

"Yeah? We don't know what she'll want to talk about though once she's here. We might not have room to celebrate," I try to remind her.

She giggles and I smile at the sight. "She said she's had enough time to think about everything and really wants to come home to talk. She sounded happier than I was expecting. Maybe the space and time apart really was what she needed."

"*Quizá*," I mumble.

I don't want to get my hopes up though. But the look on Clementine's face is too much to say no to.

"Let's celebrate and then maybe get some ice cream?" she says, wrapping her legs around my waist. I squeeze her hips and she squirms before giggling.

It's like music to my ears. I nuzzle my nose against hers.

"Sounds good. Let's go," I say before walking us to the back of the house.

I PICK up Rosalía at the airport and the drive is quiet save for her on her phone tapping the screen. She hugged me once she met me at baggage claim, so I know that the damage isn't permanent.

I've missed her so much though and could barely unwrap my arms when I hugged her. She had to almost pry my grip off her.

We're heading into the kitchen when she looks around the area before settling onto the barstool. I left her luggage by the stairs so I could help her with it later.

Although I assumed she'd just run upstairs to her room, she wanted to get the worst part over. I can't say I blame her.

Clementine comes behind us and she's slow with her steps as she watches Rosalía for a moment.

"Hey," she almost whispers. Her eyes are soft and continue to cast down from Rosalía's stare.

"Hey, *nena*," Rosalía says from the barstool before Clementine takes those final steps to be on the other side of the island. I'm keeping my distance from both, for now, standing on the opposite side of the island.

"How was your trip, *mija*?" I ask, leaning down on the counter. She smiles before glancing at me.

"It was good to see mom. She gave me a lot of perspective. Plus she seems to be doing well there."

Clementine clears her throat. "That's good you saw her. I bet you missed her a lot."

Rosalía nods. "I did. It was a much-needed trip, to be honest. And her partner is nice too. He seems to ground her."

I want to say something, but I'm not sure if this is the most appropriate time. So I just nod and smile.

"Really?" Clementine giggles and it seems to lighten the air around us.

This time Rosalía is the one to laugh and smile. It warms my heart with the sight. "Yeah, I was very shocked. They've been dating for a few years now and just feel comfortable with that. I asked if they'd get married or anything, but that's not an important item on their agenda."

I knew that Felicia wasn't with the same man she left me for. She was flighty and I wasn't surprised with this fact. But to hear that she has been with someone for a few years makes me feel... content.

I've only wanted the best for her, especially as the mother of my child.

"I'm happy for her," I say. Rosalía gives me a warm smile.

"Anyways, I know there's an elephant in the room that we need to talk about. So, let's just get it over with. I've missed you both and Mom really helped me think things through."

Clementine and I seem to both straighten our postures with her words. We're ready to tackle it head-on, together.

"Rosa…" Clementine starts. "I wanted to apologize again, I *never* wanted to hurt you. You have to believe me."

Rosalía waves her off in a friendly manner and smiles. "*Está bien, nena*. Like I said, talking to Mom really helped me. I will say I was very mad at first, but being away has helped a lot."

"Rosie," I start. "I never meant to hurt you. You know that, *verdad*?"

Rosalía nibbles on her lip for a moment before nodding. "Yeah, *papá*, I know. *Pero*, it was hard to deal with at that moment. I just never thought it would happen. I love you both so much, and honestly, that's what matters the most to me."

Clementine lets out a shaky breath and I inch forward, wanting to comfort her. But I stand my ground to not make it any more uncomfortable in front of my daughter. She slowly lifts a finger to wipe a tear that's fallen.

Rosalía notices and makes a sound before shifting to get to the other side of the island. Clementine's shoulders shake and I watch as Rosalía wraps her arms around her shoulders.

"I thought I lost you forever," Clementine sniffles.

"I know. I thought so too, but I'm actually very happy." Rosalía looks up at me while wrapping Clementine tighter in her hold. Her eyes shine brightly and I can tell how happy she actually is. She's not lying.

"Why didn't you tell me? Never mind that. The real question is, are you happy?"

Clementine is quiet for a moment before she shudders and exhales loudly again. She lifts her head and looks at Rosalía before speaking. "Rosa, yes I am. But I do have to tell you something. It's not about this, but it is important."

I widen my eyes at her words. She's finally going to tell Rosalía about Nathan. "Clementine, are you sure? If you need more time, don't force yourself."

Rosalía glances between the two of us and her eyebrows pinch together. "Wait, it's something you know? Is everything okay?"

"Yes, I'm fine. It was a long time ago. But I'm ready now to tell you."

Rosalía separates herself from Clementine, still holding onto her shoulders, before looking at her in the eyes. "You tell me upstairs, okay? I have something to tell you too. I know you've been waiting for me to say something about Garrett."

Clementine nods and I cock my head to the side. Garrett?

"Did something happen with Garrett, *mija*?" I ask, ready to get defensive if I have to.

Rosalía shakes her head and smiles. "*No te preocupes, papá.* I just realized a lot of things for *myself* too while I was gone."

I let out a breath before nodding. "*Bien.* Come here, *mijita.*"

I lift myself off the counter and open my arms. Clementine and Rosalía release their hug. Rosalía walks over to me and lets me engulf her in my arms and chest. Her head pushes deeply into me and I squeeze her tightly. I never want to let her go.

"*Te amo mucho,*" I whisper, kissing her head. She squeezes her arms around my waist tightly as well.

"*Te amo.*"

We stand like that for a moment before she squirms in my hold and starts to giggle when I try to keep her locked in. She finally starts to tickle my sides and I let her go in a heartbeat.

"*Ay*, Rosalía Santos!" I yelp.

She giggles when she backs away. Her cheeks are flushed and she looks like my happy girl again. "What? You didn't want to let me go!"

I roll my eyes playfully before she turns back to Clementine and grabs her hand. Clementine still seems hesitant that Rosalía is good with us. But she just keeps turning her gaze from Clementine to me.

"Seeing you guys happy is just what I want, to be honest. And if it means you two coming together, then I will be fine with that. I can't control the happiness that finds you. I can only reject or embrace it. I choose to embrace it, with all my heart."

Clementine's eyes get watery and I can't lie and say that mine are too. Rosalía's lips tremble and I take a deep breath. She reaches her hand out for me to grab and I do. She pulls both Clementine and me toward her, enveloping us in a three-way hug.

I wrap my other arm around Clementine. I kiss the tops of both of their heads.

"Okay, you're squeezing me!" Clementine screams, attempting to get out of our grasp.

"Oh, you're stuck with us Santos now!" Rosalía squeals, squeezing tighter.

I squeeze my girls tighter as well and they both try to squirm from my tight hold. They're almost breaking with laughter before I loosen the hold.

"Yeah? I'm fine with that," Clementine finally laughs.

Those simple words make my heart leap and the happiest it's ever been. I've got my girls back.

What more can I ask for?

"ARLO, it's been a while. How are you holding up?"

I take a deep breath, pressing the phone closer to my ear. The girls have gone upstairs, presumably to talk about Nathan and Garrett. I wanted to take this time to call Rosalía's mother.

"It's been good. Rosalía is back and seems to be doing better."

Felicia lets out a hearty laugh and it brings me back to years ago. It's been a while since I've last heard her laugh like that. We've become so accustomed to yelling at each other any moment we get on the phone.

"I'm glad she's home safe. I presume she talked with you and… what's her name?"

I pause for a moment, taking a deep breath. "Clementine."

"Ah, yes, her. Sweet name." Her voice isn't laced with malice at all. "Rosalía cares for her a lot."

"Yeah, me too," I confess.

Felicia clears her throat for a moment before speaking. "You know, you deserve to be happy too, right?"

"What do you mean?" I ask, letting my fingers run down my pants before finding a loose seam. I let my fingers roll and tug at the thread.

"You know, Arlo," she says. "You were never really happy. You thought you were. But now, this seems like it, right?"

I'm quiet for a moment as I take in her words. She isn't wrong. I tried to fake being happy for the benefit of our daughter. It hurt more trying to hold on to everything we had than accepting the truth and moving on. I was so bent on not being filed under the 'separated' category with Felicia that I refused to move on in every sense.

"Yeah," I whisper.

"Arlo," she chastises playfully. "You even sound less rude on the phone. You don't sound bitter and like nothing is going right."

"Felicia," I warn, feeling the anger start to boil.

"Hey! I'm not trying to start anything, okay? I'm just telling you what I've been able to observe this summer now that I know what's been going on. She makes you content and that's what matters."

Like mother like daughter. I want to roll my eyes at how alike they are.

"Yeah, I am," I admit. "I just didn't realize it would be with *her*, you know?"

"That's not something you can control, Arlo. I know how much you love to control and have things your way. But you can't do that when it comes to true happiness and… love."

I swallow the thick feeling in my throat. Love. She's right.

"I didn't realize that this could be something that came so easily. Something I didn't have to fight so hard to keep."

Felicia laughs. "Yeah, it's great. I don't have to argue to feel heard. I don't have to–you know what? It's best if we don't continue to compare everything to what we used to have. Because that's just what we had: a *used to* love. It's not the standard, never was."

Her words ring true. It was never the standard, we just tended to put it on the pedestal to compare all future relationships with; whether it was a good or bad comparison.

"So, tell me about him. Rosalía seems to approve of him, so I do too. Are you happy with him?" I ask.

She sighs, happily. "He's the best, Arlo. I never thought I'd connect so easily with someone. He wants the exact same things I do in life. He's got a ranch too and some neighbors that help out whenever he needs it. It's a huge thing here to have a ranch, apparently. I love the quiet around me and the town. I love him. He's a good man."

I smile. "I'm happy for you, really. I'm thankful Rosalía could see such a great example while visiting."

And I mean every word. As much as we try as adults to make our lives perfect, it's almost impossible. We're just kids forced to grow up, really. But at least having some happiness in our lives can show others–or our kids–that it's possible to achieve. The simple things in life bring the most happiness.

My mind goes to *Girasol* and how much I care for her. It's only been a summer, but I'm really finding myself wanting more and more with her. It's a feeling I've never had before. I know it can be considered reckless and that I'm feeling things *too fast* but I don't care.

I feel what I feel. And right now? I really, really care for her. As much as my heart can provide.

"Arlo?" Felicia's voice breaks my thoughts and I clear my throat.

"Yeah?"

"Tell her how you feel, I know you're thinking it. Just because everyone around you is happy, doesn't mean you don't have to be. Hold onto her tightly. Rosalía loves her to death and I'm sure you do too. You just have to confess it."

I swallow again and nod. "*Tienes razòn.*"

After a few more beats, Felicia and I say our goodbyes. And it feels like a weight has been lifted. In more ways than one. I've got my daughter back and I've got a better relationship with her mom.

And now I've got no excuse to tell the woman upstairs how I feel about her.

I *do* deserve happiness. They're all right.

Chapter Twenty-Seven

CLEMENTINE

ROSALÍA PULLS a pillow to her chest as I lay back on the bed, my head bumping into the headboard. I grab a throw pillow and pull it to my stomach and then look at my best friend who's keeping her gaze on the bed.

We talked a little bit more about her trip with her mom and the things she saw. She got to ride horses, feed the cows, and even meet some of the neighbors around. She said there's a famous Montana ranch there that is a few miles away where she was able to spend a day.

It's run by two brothers who remind her a lot of her dad with their determination and strong stature.

It made me really happy knowing how much she was able to do there in Montana and how much closer she seemed to get with her mom.

"So what happened?" She finally breaks the silence. I take a deep breath and squeeze the pillow tighter.

"It was a while ago. With Nathan." My voice cracks a little, but I try to persevere.

"Wait, Nathan? Why didn't you tell me earlier?"

I look at her before giving her a weak smile. "I'm trying to work on that, believe me. Remember how I said I started seeing a therapist? It's because of what he did to me."

Rosalía is silent for a moment before her eyes narrow and her brows pinch. "What did he do?"

Here goes.

"Right before we broke up, we went to that frat party his house was hosting. Remember the rager they had for their frat brother?"

She nods. "Yeah, it was a lot. I can't even remember most of what happened. We split up and just met the next day, remember?"

I nibble on my lip. "That's the thing, Rosa. I barely remember that night. I just remember it in pieces. Separating from you during the party, going to get drinks with Nathan. And then finding myself unable to get him off me."

She's quiet for a minute before her lips part. "Wait, Clementine. What did you just say?"

I press my lips together in a tight line and will myself not to cry. I've mourned for my past self long enough. I want to stop feeling so sorry for the past Clementine and work on my present and future. But it's hard when it comes to my best friend.

"He drugged my drink and then tried to have sex with me. I wasn't in the mood and wasn't for a while. Remember how I told you I thought he was going to leave me because I wasn't letting him just have sex with me whenever he wanted?"

Her hands tighten into fists. "Yeah, but I didn't think he'd be stupid enough to go that route. Are you seriously telling me he forced you to do that? He raped you?"

The word *rape* coming out of my best friend's mouth brings a different shock to me. I'm usually the one who has to say it out loud. But Rosalía does it so effortlessly. With such tenacity and knowing the power it holds. I still feel myself shrink away from the power of that word.

I nod.

She scoots a little closer to me before dropping the pillow and wrapping her arms around me. I try to blink away the tears, but they don't listen. They come falling down and it feels like I'm reliving the moment of telling my mom and Declan again. The night I told Arlo.

I let Rosalía hold me tightly, smoothing her palms over my arms. "I'm so sorry, Clem. If I had known… Fuck, why did you let me be around that guy? I wouldn't have brought you to any of those pool parties. Or anything in the past when he was there."

I shake my head. "It's not your job to protect me, Rosa. Don't change your life decisions based on me."

She lifts her head and her eyes are swimming with worry and questions. "Yeah, but this? This is *different*, Clementine. He's a rapist. He should be… Fuck, I want him locked up. No one hurts my Clementine."

A sob rips through my body and I let it out, as well as the waterfall of tears. Rosalía hugs me harder, rubbing her hands on my back.

"I don't need anyone's pity, Rosa. It happened. I can only learn to move on."

"Yeah, but you shouldn't *have* to. No one should when this happens. And I'm not trying to pity you, *nena*. I want you to get the justice you deserve. Does Declan and your mom know?"

I nod before sniffling. "Yeah, they were the first ones I told. There's no point in going the legal route. We tried. It was a lost cause and I didn't want to ruin myself even more than what was done. Almost switching majors and dropping out of the sorority was my way of being done with it all and giving myself space."

Rosalía pulls away and nods. "I get it. These kinds of things aren't easy to get justice for. He's got money, a lot of it. But Clementine, you shouldn't have to face him every day at pool parties or on campus. You *shouldn't*."

"It's only one more year," I try to joke.

She shakes her head. "That doesn't make it any better. I

guess I'm just trying to see if there's anything else we can do now. What can I do?"

I think for a moment. Because I really don't feel like wasting any more energy on Nathan and what happened.

"I just want my best friend to be here for me when it gets hard."

She rubs my back. "Of course, *nena*. Anything for you." She's quiet for a moment before her eyes sparkle and eyebrows raise. "My dad knows right?"

"Yeah, he does. He was the third person I told. I wanted to tell you, I swear."

"I'm not upset about that! Of course, not," she laughs. "I'm just glad you've been able to tell someone else besides your parents. It's not an easy feat."

"He's been so–" I stop myself. "You probably don't want to hear that. Sorry."

She shrugs before smiling. "I love you both so much. I always wondered if I'd lose you the moment you graduated and found somewhere else to be. I always selfishly wanted you to stay in my life somehow. You're my best friend and I never want to lose you. You mean so much to me, Clementine."

"You've got me, forever," I say softly.

"I know. And now it makes it even better, to be honest. You guys are my favorite people in the world. Besides my mom, of course. But this kind of makes me happy in a weird way knowing I'll have you guys both forever."

My heart swells at her words. Tears brim my eyes and I lean in to hug her. She squeezes me back tightly. "I love you, Rosalía."

"And I love you more, Clementine. Always, *nena*."

I squeeze her once more before we separate.

"Wait, so tell me about Garrett. What's going on?"

Rosalía huffs out a breath before shaking her head and smiling. "We're taking a break."

I gasp. "What?"

"Yeah, I just need space to think. The trip to my mom's was good for reflection. I think we were doing things too fast."

"But you went to LA…" I remind her.

"Yeah, that's where I kind of realized that things wouldn't be long-term. Garrett is sweet and treats me well, but there's just something I can't quite put my finger on."

"Do you love him?" I ask.

She shakes her head. "No. I know it's a little too soon to think so either way, but also it's not. A lot of couples find out they're in love a few months in. And then they go through the trials and tribulations that most relationships go through. But from the get-go they know if they're in love."

I nod. That's what I feel for Arlo. It's been a quick summer, but my feelings for him have only grown and truly solidified into things that I know come down to a bottom line. I love him.

"And that face you're making? That's how I know it's out there and I haven't found him yet."

I look at her and my cheeks burn. "What face?"

"The red cheeks, the distant eyes. You can't stop thinking about him. It's such a tell when you're in love. It's not even infatuation at this point. It's love and I want that."

"Oh," I squeak, attempting to rub my cheeks, but Rosa takes my wrists and pulls them down.

"Don't be self-conscious about it! Own it! Lovesick Clementine is a good look on you and I want to experience that. I saw it in my mom too whenever she talked about her boyfriend. Her lovesick tendencies and the flush in her face."

"It can be overwhelming at times," I confess. My cheeks continue to burn as my mind continues to move to Arlo. How much I care for him.

"But it's a good overwhelming, right?" she asks.

I nod. "It really is. He makes me so happy and the fact that I can trust him with anything."

"If you can trust anyone with such a sacred confession, it's my dad." She smiles. "He does his best. He really does. I've always wanted him to just find his person. If it's my best friend in the whole world? I'm fine with that."

His person. First Frankie and now Rosa are saying these two words.

"You really think I can be his person?" I whisper.

She looks at me for a moment before nodding. "I do, Clem. I wouldn't want anyone else to be."

Tears fall past my cheeks again and she lifts a hand to wipe them away. "I love you, Rosa. And whatever you decide after graduation, I want you to put yourself first. Don't think of me, okay? I'm happy here. Happier than ever."

"I had a lot of time to think about that, actually," she starts. She fidgets in her place before she pulls the pillow to her chest again. "I think I know where I want to go after we graduate."

"Yeah? Where? *Dime*," I ask, smiling. I lean in closer.

She smiles and her eyes brighten. "I kind of want to just pack my bags and go to New York City. Is that crazy? I feel like that place is calling my name. I don't know why, but it's such a strong feeling."

"Do you plan to visit at least before then?" I ask, hoping she's not just going to chase a feeling when she hasn't stepped foot in the city. But I can't judge, I'm practically chasing a very concrete feeling I have for her dad.

"I actually wanted to ask you…" She hesitates. "Would you want to go to New York with me during our winter break? We can book a hotel and stay there all break and go see the neighborhoods before I start apartment hunting."

"What? Are you kidding me?!" I squeal, almost jumping in my place. "Of course, Rosa! Thank you for even thinking of me being the one to join you."

She playfully rolls her eyes. "Who else would I bring?" She laughs. "But yeah, I just want to find myself, you know? I know you come from a different state, but I've been confined to Alabama my whole life. I want more; I want to experience more. I don't want to be tied down to one place. My soul seems happier even just thinking of the possibility of moving elsewhere."

"I get it," I agree. "That's why I went to college in another state. I wanted something new from my hometown. It's not fair to expect you to stay here, Rosa. I want you to find what I found here even if it's states away."

"And you'll obviously visit me as much as you can." She winks.

"Yes, obviously. You're not getting rid of me just yet," I respond with a giggle.

She's quiet for a moment before she reaches for my hand and holds it tightly. "I love you, Clem. I love you so much."

It feels like I've cried so much today, but my body isn't done producing it. Tears well my eyes again and make my vision blurry. "I love you more, Rosa. You deserve this."

"And we still have senior year. We have to make the most of it!"

"We will," I assure her.

She leans in and pulls me in for a hug and we hold each other tightly. I take a deep breath and feel all my worries leave my body. I feel safe in her arms and it makes me so happy.

THE HOUSE IS quiet as I walk downstairs the next day. Rosalía is long gone and texted me that she went to go to a workout class and to talk more with Garrett about her solidified plans.

I see movement in my peripheral vision as I enter the kitchen and see Arlo cleaning the pool. He's scooping up leaves and shaking out the net before scouring the edge for more.

My feet are quick as I head to the sliding back door and make my way outside. I'm in his Metallica shirt and shorts and his eyes glance up basically devouring me once they land on my outfit.

"*Buenos días, Girasol,*" he says loudly before scooping the last bits of leaves. I wave and head to him. He's putting the cleaning equipment back before he heads to me.

I notice that he's wearing white shorts with tiny designs on them. Tiny sunflowers. The fit is amazing on his thick legs and the color contrasts beautifully against his tanned skin.

"Nice shorts," I tease.

He looks down before giving me a playful look. "Rosie left them for me on the kitchen counter. Said it was a gift."

I raise a brow. I didn't hear her last night after I went to bed, but she can be sneaky if she has to. Especially around Arlo, with the amount of times she snuck out.

"*Girasoles,*" I tease. "*Para mí?*"

My words surely bring him back to the time he said the exact phrase when he found out I bought a swimsuit with pretty sunflowers on the print. A smile stretches on his face.

"*Sí, Girasol. Para tí. Mi hermosa flor. Mi flor favorita,*" he coos. He closes the distance between us and wraps his hands around my waist. I get on my tiptoes and curl my arms around his neck. I breathe in his scent and bury my face in his neck.

"Arlo," I whisper, holding on to him tighter.

"*Sí, mi amor?*" His words bring flutters to my core and I lift my head to look at him. Even on my tiptoes and him leaning his head, he's so far away.

"*Besame,*" I plead with pouty lips. He smiles before leaning even more and locking his lips with mine.

"What else?"

"Hmm?" I ask, my heart thudding even harder in my chest.

"Your face is telling me you have something else to tell me." He squeezes my waist and I squirm underneath him.

"I hate how much you can read me," I confess with a half-laugh. I narrow my eyes at him and stick out my tongue.

"No, you love it. It's easier for you to talk to me when I can read these feelings. You don't have to work too hard or force yourself to talk."

"You're right," I sigh. "I don't hate it."

"You love it," he smiles.

I nod. "And something else."

The sun is burning down on us and I'm starting to regret coming out here with a shirt. I should've changed into my bathing suit or something. I can already feel the beads of sweat gather at the nape of my neck.

"*Dime*," he says softly. He's not pushing, he's waiting.

I take a deep breath and move my hands from his neck to his cheeks. I hold him softly and he breathes me in, his eyes closing for a moment before they lock on my face.

"I love you, Arlo."

It comes out easy. Not in a shaky voice, but a steady one. There's no hesitancy.

His jaw clenches for a moment as his eyes search mine. His hands on my waist tighten before loosening.

"*En serio*, Clementine?"

I blink a few tears before he leans down and kisses my cheeks where they fall. "I'm serious, Arlo. I love you so much."

He's silent for a moment, but not out of hesitancy. Because I can *feel* it. He loves me.

He kisses my lips before kissing my nose and then my forehead. "*Te amo más de lo que mi corazón puede contener. Arde por ti. Cada fibra de mi ser te llama.*"

We stare at each other for a long moment before he lifts a hand to my lips and brushes his thumb over it. I shudder under the touch. Goosebumps rise all over my body.

"*Mi hermosa flor. Siempre seré tuyo.*"

"Arlo," I gasp. "Don't say that."

"It's true, Clementine. You know it."

"I love you," I say again, with more intensity. He bends down to grab the backs of my knees before he lifts me up. I squeal from the movement before wrapping my arms around his neck again for balance. My ankles clasp together at his back.

He nuzzles his nose with mine before kissing me.

"*Te amaré por todos mis días*, Clementine."

A tear escapes my eye and I sniffle, kissing him harder. "*Mi persona*."

"Mi *persona*," he adds once we separate.

We stare at each other for a moment before we're back to kissing. It feels like the world has stopped and we're able to be in this moment forever. Just us.

Arlo and Clementine.

I never want to leave it.

Chapter Twenty-Eight

ARLO

ROSALÍA TOLD me about New York City a few days after her coming back from her mom's and it lessened the blow of it all knowing that Clementine would go with her during their winter break. They've already started looking at hotels to book and I gladly offered to pay for it, knowing that it would be the safest place for my girls.

I'm trying to be better at being there for my daughter but not being a helicopter parent. If she wants to travel and move to another city to find herself, I can't stop her. I would only make her resent herself, and resent me if I forced her to stay.

I was very surprised though to hear that *she* was the one that broke things off with Garrett. As much as I wanted to protect my baby from any men in the world, I didn't realize that she'd be the one breaking hearts.

But she didn't see it that way. She chose herself, in her words. And I couldn't be a more proud parent when she told me that.

It's now almost the start of the new school year for Clementine and Rosalía. They've got a week until they have to be back to their new off-campus apartment. It definitely would be hard to adjust back to being alone again in this big house. But with the way I've been able to repair my relationship with Rosalía, she promised to come home more often.

I wasn't particularly anticipating her coming home every weekend, but if she could manage a few weekends in the semester, I'd be happier than ever. Clementine on the other hand has been anticipating the fact that she can stay with me whenever she wants. But I had to remind her that finishing her degree was the most important. If she couldn't come over one night I wouldn't argue against it.

Her parents on the other hand return from their trip this week and plan to visit this weekend. She's been on the phone with her mom and her stepfather more often in the last few weeks and has been hinting at seeing someone.

It felt a little juvenile to keep hinting at things, but I knew she would tell them at her own pace. They seemed very supportive of anything she needed from what I could tell so far.

With her parents visiting this weekend, it's got me a little nervous if I have to be honest. It's new territory of having to figure things out with the relationship I have with their daughter. Rosalía has even had to sit me down one night and tell me to stop freaking out.

Clementine has become one of the most important people in my life, besides Rosalía. I didn't want to mess things up for her by any means.

But Clementine ultimately told me that she wants to keep things steady for now until she's absolutely ready to tell them. And I'm completely fine with that. She wants to hint that she's seeing someone but wants them to respect her privacy until she's ready.

And that's all we could want from them until we're ready. I'd like her to be done with school until we think of any 'what if's'.

"Arlo?" Clementine's voice rings throughout the house and I finish up adjusting the tie around my neck.

"In here, *bebita*," I call out. Her figure pops in the doorframe of the bedroom and I turn to see her. The glow of the sunset peeking through the hallway encases her in the best way, making her look like an angel.

"*Lista*?" I ask, smoothing my hands together before tugging on my suit jacket I laid on the bed. She nods before stepping inside.

Her dress is a pretty yellow, curving at the top of her breasts, hitting her mid-thigh, and straps as thin as sin. Her shoulders are tan and speckled with freckles. She's my Aphrodite.

"You look so handsome," she smiles, closing the distance before placing her palms on my dress shirt.

"You look like an angel," I respond back, wrapping my hands around her waist. The fabric of the dress is soft and I can't help but clench my fingers around it, pulling her closer. The heels she's wearing give her some height, but not nearly enough.

I still have to lean down to kiss her, but I don't mind. Anytime I have to lean down to meet her height, it's like I'm falling for her every time. At least that's what I think in my head, Clementine just calls it a cheesy pick-up line.

"Maybe we can be late?" She moves her hands up until they're brushing over my neck and then my cheeks. I pull back a little to look at her pretty brown eyes.

"They're a pretty strict restaurant that will give away your reservation if you're even five minutes late," I argue.

Her eyes move from mine to my lips and I feel my heart beat faster. It always does with her. I won't ever get used to this feeling.

"Then after," she promises.

"After," I agree with a kiss.

She steps back and takes my head, leading the way out of the house and into the truck. The ride is quick to the restaurant.

We're not really celebrating anything tonight, but I wanted to take her out. Especially before her last year at school started. I wanted her for myself one more night.

The dinner is at a steakhouse with some specialties in seafood. She got a big steak while I opted for some lobster. The night flew by with easy conversation and talking about future plans for when she's back at school.

We decided that we'd take a trip somewhere for her fall break and then she'd go to New York with Rosalía during the winter. Conversation flowed into less serious topics after that as we dived into dessert.

It wasn't until we were back home that we found ourselves back in close parameters and not being able to keep our hands to ourselves.

"*Besame*," she pleads as she's attempting to push my suit jacket off my shoulders. I shimmy out of it and help her loosen my tie before her fingers are quick to undo the buttons in my dress shirt.

"You're quite persistent, *bebita*," I tease, but one look from her wild eyes shut me up. If she wants to lead things, then I'll gladly let her.

"It feels like it's been too long," she confesses.

And she's not wrong about that. We've been so busy the last week we barely had time to enjoy each other's company at night. And with Rosalía back home every night, we didn't want to disrespect her in that regard. I could tell that Clementine still felt guilty about the night we had sex and Rosalía found out and left for 3 weeks.

The wound was still pretty open in that regard, so I didn't argue with it. I actually felt the same way. Thankfully Rosalía is at the new apartment setting up her room, so Clementine and I have the place to ourselves. We think she did that on purpose, though.

"Then come to the bed," I urge, attempting to step away, but she keeps me in place with her hands on my waist.

Her eyes are big and sparkling and she licks her lips. "I can't wait, Arlo. I need you in my mouth."

"What?" I almost laugh, but she's serious. Her hands are instantly on my belt, unbuckling it and unbuttoning my dress pants. I hold back a groan as she pulls down my pants and then my boxers. Her hands are a little cold, so I hiss once they're on my skin.

"Sorry," she pouts. I shake my head and widen my eyes as I see her getting on her knees. Her hair is perfectly curled with a clip to hold back her front pieces. I lay my hand on the crown of her head before moving it to caress her cheek and then her chin. I lift her face a little and she looks up at me with such adoration.

"*Te quiero*," I whisper. She smiles before licking her lips and wrapping one hand around the base of my cock. Her tongue glides along the underside of my cock and I buck my hips forward a little from the sensation. A hiss falls from my lips before she's licking my tip where pre-cum is already leaking.

"Fuck, *bebita*," I groan. Her sounds are muffled as she pushes further onto my cock and attempts to take me whole.

She bobs her head back and forth as well as continues to move her hand that's wrapped around me. The feelings are too much and my grip on the crown of her head tightens. I push her head a *little* more and she starts to gag a little before regaining her breath.

"You gonna take all of me?" I ask, leaning my head back and enjoying her sweet lips. She mumbles something before I push her a little more again and her free hands grip my thighs. But not to push away–to gain more balance.

"Just like that, baby," I groan, my legs starting to shake from the intensity of it. My orgasm is peaking through, ready to burst. She quickens her pace and pushes my cock further into her throat and it's heavenly.

"Fuck!" I yell, pushing my hips even further into her, cutting off her air supply as my cock drives deeper. I look down and see tears falling out of her eyes and her grip on my thigh tightens to the point where they'll be tiny indented bruises. But I love the way she marks me.

I want to mark her in other ways tonight though.

She continues her fast pace, makeup now ruined from how much she's attempting to gather her breathing and tears springing from her eyes. Her hair is damp at the front from her sweat and it's honestly the best fucking sight seeing her in desperate ruin for me.

"*Bebita*, I'm so close, where do you want me?" My words are short as I pant and can't contain it.

She pulls her mouth off me in a loud pop before she stares at me with her doe eyes and smiles. "You choose, sir."

I groan and tightly my fist around her roots, pulling her closer. She squirms before moving her knees to get closer.

"*Ábre*," I command. She opens her mouth and sticks her tongue out like a dog. I pump my cock with my other hand and she keeps her hands resting on my thighs.

"Please," she whines and pleads before I jut my hips and my orgasm approaches fast. Thick ropes of cum burst out of me and I paint her tongue, lips, and even a little on her cheeks and nose.

"*Dios mío*," I pant, my hands still pumping my cock but slower as the last bits of cum drip out.

She licks her lips before bringing her fingers to her face to scoop any remnants on her cheeks and nose before putting them in her mouth. She then leans up and licks the tip of my cock and I hiss and jolt.

"*Calma*," I say through gritted teeth.

Once she's done, she licks her lips one last time before getting up. I help her in the process before grabbing the fabric of her dress and tugging it.

"Off, now," I demand.

"Yes, sir," she giggles before turning for me to help her unzip it. Once it's completely unzipped, the fabric pools at her feet and she steps out. She kicks off her heels and I do the same with my pants and shoes.

Her lace lingerie immediately catches my eye. The way the white fabric clings to her breasts, the curves of her ass, and even has a delicate design that I can't wait to rip.

My thoughts go feral as she heads to the bed and crawls on top, spreading her legs wide. Her palms are flat on the bed while she's got her ass in the air. It gives me the best view and I need her now. I can't wait.

"You wore this for me?" I ask, stalking closer to the bed. I wrap my hand around my cock, pumping it slowly, getting riled up just at the sight of my girl.

She nods, her hair flying back as she whips her head back to look at me. Her brown eyes catch mine and a sly smile stretches across her face.

"Just for you, daddy," she whines, bucking her hips back to give me more access and sight to her already dripping pussy. The clothed lingerie is already looking soaked. This elicits a moan out of me as I grab her and rub my palm over the curve of her ass.

"Just for me," I repeat, completely falling into a dazed and hypnotized state. Even though I've got the high ground, I'm putty in her hands. If she tells me to do something, I will.

She's got all the control here and I don't even know if she realizes it.

Her body pushes back into my hands as she shifts on the bed, leaning her front half even more into the mattress. My hands travel from the curves of her ass until I'm between the thighs. She jolts for a moment before she moans as my fingers brush along her clothed pussy.

"So fucking wet for me, *bebita*. You want to be stuffed? Want me to fuck you until you can't speak?" She moans once more and I slap her ass, causing her to push her lower half more toward me. Her lower half is being brushed against my erection and I fight every molecule of my being not to just push myself into her right now.

"Yes, please," she whines. Her hands go in front of her, grabbing the bedsheet and curling it into her fists.

"Tell me, *bebita*," I command.

"I want you to stuff me, daddy. Fill me until you can't fit anymore. Fill me up, cum in me, *please*," she begs in a high-pitched whine.

"Fuck," I hiss, slapping her ass one more time before grabbing the waistband of her lingerie and pulling hard with both hands. The fabric tears loudly and she just moans even louder, like music to my ears. "You don't even care if I rip this pretty thing? You wore it because you wanted me to destroy it?"

She nods, unable to respond. She's practically melting in my hands as I toss the torn fabric and glide my fingers through her wet folds. My finger brushes her bundle of nerves and she whines, jolting forward, but my left hand is strong on her hip to keep her in place.

"You're not going anywhere, you're going to stay right here. Okay?"

"Y-yes," she pants.

I line my cock with her entrance, swiping my tip along her wet fold and we both stiffen and groan at the contact. I push my tip in slowly, feeling the tightness of her swallow me inch by inch.

"So tight. Always so tight for me. You want to keep me here forever?"

"Forever, Arlo. Please, daddy," she almost shrieks as I push further into her. The feeling is euphoric and my eyes almost roll to the back of my head. Her front half dips even lower into the mattress, only giving me a better angle to sink into her.

Once I'm fully sheathed in her, I rub her hips before leaning over and kissing her back before peppering her with kisses along her shoulder blades, mid back, and then her neck. She shivers from the contact and I can taste the slightest sweat on her body. She's so fucking delicious.

"You ready?" I whisper, leaning even more to bite her ear. This angle of leaning down only pushes me deeper into her, hitting her in the deepest and best places. She whines pathetically and her pussy tightens around my cock.

"Y-yes. I'm ready, please," she begs.

My hold on her hips tightens as I lift myself and pull out slowly before slamming into her at a rapid pace. The whole bed shakes and her body moves up the mattress a few inches from the impact.

She screams as I continue to thrust into her, my grip on her tightening even more. She's going to be painted with not just my bruises tonight.

"So fucking good," I mumble through thrusts as I hit deeper and deeper into her. She mewls loudly, her fists turning white from the grip she has on the bed sheets.

Her moans and sounds get louder and louder the more I continue to thrust into her. My legs are shaking from the release that's soon to approach. Her body stiffens and jolts, letting me know she's getting close. I lean down, pressing my chest to her whole back. I reach one arm around her waist before I settle my hand between her thighs. My thumb finds her clit and I swirl the pad along the nerves.

She screams with the overstimulation as I continue to thrust.

"Yeah? Like that, *bebita*? So fucking good for me. Look at you taking me, you're such a good fucking girl," I mumble as my thumb moves faster and the snap of my hips matches the pace.

"Please, please, please," she stumbles as if she's praying. It's adorable the way she breaks down like this.

"My pretty baby, so fucking cock drunk on me? Is that what you are? Huh? Answer me."

She wails before nodding and pressing her face on the mattress, turning her head to the side to glance at me. Her breathing is uncontrollable as she pants out loud.

"I'm your pretty baby, so drunk on you."

"That's right, *bebita*," I say with a grunt. My hand moves from her clit to give her some relief before moving to her lower belly where the bulge is prominent.

It brings me back to the thought of wanting to mark her in other ways. More permanent ways.

"You feel this?" I ask, pressing my palm against the bulge and feeling the way it moves with every thrust of mine.

She nods and mumbles incoherent words. "S-so good, daddy."

"Yeah? You like calling me daddy?" I ask, stilling my hips for a moment as I rub my palm on her lower belly.

She doesn't respond for a moment so I lean over and grab the underside of her chin to lift her from the bed slightly. She whines from the movement and her palms are attempting to keep her upright.

"Answer me, Clementine," I press.

Her eyes spring with tears and her lips part. She's unable to process a coherent thought and those pretty eyes draw up blank. She just nods.

"I do. Yes, I do."

"Say it," I demand. I pull back my cock and she whimpers from the feeling of losing me.

"I like calling you daddy!" she screams and I snap my hips to connect with her, pushing my cock further into her.

"Don't say things you don't mean. If you wanna call me daddy, then take this cock like a good girl. Let me fill you with my cum. You like that idea? Being so fucking full of me. Of my babies? Make me a daddy again?"

Her lips quiver as she cries out again and nods her head quickly. "Yes, please!"

"Use your words, Clementine," I say as I draw back my hips again and thrust hard into her. The headboard shakes as it slams against the wall and she cries out again.

"Fill me up, Arlo! Fill me up until nothing else can fit. I want it, I want you. Give me your babies," she pleads.

"Come here," I grunt before lifting myself up and dropping her chin. I grab her hips and pull myself out. She cries from the loss before I'm turning her over on her back. She lets me do all the work as she lies flat on her back and her body glistens with sweat.

"I want to see you when I fill you up, okay?" I grab her hips and pull her closer to me, placing her legs over my shoulders as I lean down.

"Y-yes," she whimpers as she moves her hands to my core. Her fingers are like butterflies, slowly touching me and then not. Light as a feather and bringing goosebumps all over my body.

"You make me fucking crazy, Clementine. The things I want to do to you every day," I grunt as I realign my cock with her entrance and waste no time to thrust into her. I'm almost to my peak and I know she's holding back as much as she can.

But I need her to come first. She always needs to come first before me.

"Come on, *bebita*. I want you to come for me. Be a good girl and let go."

My hand goes back to her core and I place the pad of my thumb on her clit before swirling it in soft circles. Her eyes shut tightly and moan after moan spill out of her pretty lips.

Her pussy tightens around me and I know she's very close.

"Arlo!" she screams, whipping her eyes open as I feel the pressure of her orgasm all over me and leaking out. I continue to slam my hips against hers, causing her arousal to drip on her thighs and the bedsheets.

"Come on. One more for me!" My thumb circles faster around her clit and she tenses underneath me. Her lips are quivering, sweat is lining her forehead and her chest is glistening. I lean down and lick a long stripe along her neck and she shakes.

"Arlo, please, I need you," she breathes desperately, "to come, please!"

"Almost there," I assure her as I continue the fast pace and it begins to get sloppy.

Seeing her parted lips gave me an idea.

I move my free hand to her chin and grip it tightly, squishing her lips together as I lean in front of her face.

"*Ábre, ahora,*" I demand. She parts her lips even more under my harsh grip.

I gather saliva in my mouth before letting it slowly drip into hers. It slides on her tongue and she moans loudly.

"Swallow."

Her eyes widen for a moment before she does as I say. Her lips attempt to close, but my grip is still tight around her cheeks. Once she swallows my spit I lean in to kiss her.

My thighs shake as I finish my last few thrusts before my palm flies from her clit to her hand to lace our fingers together.

"Fuck, Clementine. I'm gonna fill you up to the brim. Fuck!" And with that, a rush of arousal comes crashing through and my orgasm hits harshly. Rope after rope of cum fills her walls and she groans from the feeling. I let her legs go, but she wraps them around my back, caging me inside her.

Her sweaty face is bright red and I lean in to kiss her again before rubbing my hand over her skin.

"*Mi flor favorita. Mi amor. Has sido tan buena para mí. Tan buena, tan buena,*" I mumble through more kisses.

"I love you, Arlo," she barely lets out in the faintest whisper.

"I love you more, *bebita. Más que nada en este mundo.*"

Her eyes find mine and we stare at each other for a moment before she smiles. And I do too, because *fuck* her smiles are contagious.

Her happiness is contagious. I never want her to be unhappy. Ever.

Chapter Twenty-Nine

CLEMENTINE

WE'VE GOT the grill going and my parents are on the patio helping Frankie assemble the meat that needs to be cooked.

I can't stop smiling and laughing at the sight. It warms my heart and just having them here with the Santos and Frankie is so nice.

"*Girasol, ayúdame con las bebidas, por favor,*" Arlo calls from the sliding doors. I nod and wave to my mom who looks back at me. She gives me a wink before I head inside. Arlo is in his swim trunks and no shirt. I lick my lips at the sight.

"Where are the drinks?" I ask, noticing there aren't any on the kitchen island. He rounds the counter before curling his finger and nodding his head to the hallway.

"*Ven,*" he calls out before I walk closer and follow him down the hallway. I'm a little confused since I thought we got all the drinks last night and put them in the fridge.

"Where are we going?" I giggle before he stops and takes my hand to lead us to the front of the house, away from the people in the backyard.

"I missed you, *bebita,*" he admits as he pulls me into his arms and smashes his lips against mine. My hands go to his bare chest and wrap around his neck, fingers lacing around the golden necklace.

A moan filters through my lips before he grins and separates from our kiss.

"*Mmm*, I missed you too, Arlo," I giggle.

"Do you think we have a few minutes?" He looks at me with intensity swirling in his eyes. His hands smooth down to my waist, down to the edge of the cover-up dress I'm wearing over my bikini. His calloused hands are on my bare hips before they play with the waistband of my bottoms.

"I don't think so. They'll wonder where the drinks are." I pant as he leans in and attaches his lips to my neck. He licks a long stripe before I buck my hips into his and feel his growing erection practically stab my midsection. "Arlo!"

"Yes, *bebita*? Keep screaming my name and I'll have to take you right here," he groans before kissing my neck some more and lifting his hands more and more until they're under the top of the cover-up and squeezing my breasts. They're sore from last night when he wouldn't stop sucking them and pleasuring me so much.

I probably have hickeys all over my body, to be honest, hence the cover-up that I refuse to take off.

"You have to calm yourself," I laugh, attempting to push his chest but he just squeezes my breasts even more and a moan leaves my lips.

"Just one minute. That's all I need. I want you full of me before we go out there again," he whispers.

I gasp. "In front of my parents?! We promised to keep it low-key until I graduate," I remind him.

Because that's what we discussed the other day. We were to keep things out of the public eye, my parents, until I graduated from Frontier. They didn't need to know who exactly I was dating, but they knew enough. She seemed happy that I was starting to put myself out there.

Even my damn therapist was smiling more than usual when I told her the same. I wanted to come clean about Arlo with my therapist, but I couldn't. I knew she wouldn't judge me and actually walk me through good conversations if needed, but I wanted to keep Arlo a little more to myself before I told the world.

Having Frankie and Rosa know was enough people for me right now.

Arlo's hands running back down to my bottoms brings me out of my thoughts and I moan.

"See? You want me to fuck you until you're screaming my name. Until I'm filling you up and you're leaking me." His dirty words make me think of all the times we've been having sex with no protection and just relying on my birth control.

As much as I loved the idea of him filling me up, I wanted to still be safe in some regard. But I knew that ultimately, we were playing a very dangerous game. But I loved the game when it came to Arlo. I loved the feeling of him inside me and claiming me as his. I wanted more with him, I really did. But he was the one constantly pushing for me to finish my senior year. The next two semesters were going to go by slowly if he kept teasing me like this.

"You're going to be the death of me," I whimper, grabbing his cheeks and pulling his face away from my neck. He pouts before tilting his head and kissing the inside of my hand.

"Fine, I'll control myself, *bebita*."

I smile and get on my tiptoes to kiss him quickly. We hear someone enter the house and we separate immediately before he removes his hands from underneath my cover-up.

"Let's go get those drinks," I remind him before winking and heading back to the kitchen. He's quick to follow behind me and I feel his stare burn through me.

We see Frankie and Rosa laughing as they're picking up more of the food trays we've prepared this morning to grill and have outside. They look up at us and I feel my cheeks start to burn.

"Already?" Frankie laughs with a shake of his head. "You guys can't stay away for more than a few hours, huh?"

"*Calláte, pendejo*," Arlo warns, but there's humor in his tone.

"Come on, Clem," Rosa speaks up, nodding her head to the fridge. The drinks, right.

I head to the fridge and pull out the cases of sodas and beers before heading outside with Rosa. We lay out the trays and drinks on the table before I pull each one out of their case and place it in the cooler next to the table. Frankie returns to the grill but claps his hand and hollers as he sees Declan take over with the tongs.

"You know I bumped into *you know who* last night," Rosa speaks up in a hushed tone next to me.

I raise my brows. "Wait, really? Where?"

She shrugs. "I was looking at luggage at the store before he came into the same aisle."

"The luggage aisle?"

She nods and sighs. "I wanted to punch him the moment I saw him. But I had to remind myself that he didn't know that I knew."

I lift my hand and touch her shoulder, giving her a thankful look. The last thing I need is for him to reach out to me because Rosa threatened him. I just want him out of my life for good. I've got such good things in my life right now, I don't need that ruined by him in any way.

"He told me he's moving," she says with a louder tone. I see Arlo turn his head from the grill to look at us and I give him a reassuring smile before grabbing Rosa's elbow and pulling us closer to the pool.

"What do you mean?"

She leans into me and nods. "He's going to London. Said he was accepted into the study abroad program or something."

"Really?" My heart is thudding harder in my chest and my breathing starts to quicken.

"Really, Clem. He's going to be there for *both* semesters. Won't even be back for graduation. He's got family living there now that wants him to stay there after graduation. Some kind of job is already lined up for him."

Tears start to spring into my eyes and my vision goes blurry. "I can't believe it."

"I know," she says before wrapping my arms around my shoulders. "He's going to be gone. You won't have to deal with him our senior year and after. He's really gone."

A sob breaks out of me and my whole body shudders and it feels like the sky has opened up and given me a warm embrace. Like it's heard all my cries asking for him to go away.

And now he is. It might not be behind bars, but a whole ocean away is enough for me.

"Burgers are ready!" Frankie calls behind us and I sniffle, rubbing my fingers against my eyes to wipe the tears away.

We hear footsteps behind us and we both turn to see Arlo walking up to us. He's got a worried expression on his face as his gaze moves from me to Rosa.

"*Están bien?*"

"*Si*," Rosa says with a happier tone. "I told her something that she'll most likely have to tell you, *lo siento*." She pulls away from me and Arlo notices my tear-stained cheeks.

"What happened?" His voice becomes more stern and I love him for his protective nature over me.

Rosa pats my shoulder before kissing my cheek, heading back to the grill, and starting to talk to my parents. I take this time to close the distance and crane my neck up to Arlo.

"He's gone," I say.

"Who's gone?"

"Nathan." My voice breaks but I try to recover.

"What? *En serio?*" Arlo's hand comes up to brush my cheek with his thumb before brushing under my eyes where tears have started to dry up.

I nod. "Rosa saw him and he said he was moving to London. *For good.*"

A smile breaks his face and I can tell he wants to wrap his arms around me and pick me up. I want him to, but we've got company.

Instead, he steps even closer and brushes my cheek again before looking at me intensely with his eyes. I can read what he's trying to convey.

"I know, Arlo," I whisper.

"*Estoy aquí. Para siempre.*"

His words cut through me and I feel tears fill my vision once more, but I blink them away.

"I love you," I whisper. Without thinking I wrap my arms around his waist and press my face into his chest.

He stiffens for a moment before he relaxes, wraps his arms around me, and holds me tightly. I sniffle into him before I kiss his bare chest and then release him.

His hands stay on my body before he lets them go back to his side. We hear chatter grow behind us, so we take a step away from each other before we head to the table.

My mom gives me a smile before I head to her and give her a big hug. I'll tell her and Declan later tonight about the great news. And then hopefully my senior year of college will fly by as I start my internship and work hard to get straight A's. And I can't forget the trips with Rosa this winter break.

Knowing that I've got Arlo by my side and my best friend to get through the next few months makes me happy. Makes my heart so fucking happy.

I sit down at the table as Frankie passes around the plate of grilled food and we start to assemble our plates. Arlo sits across from me and gives me a wink before I smile brightly.

My mom looks at me for a moment before giving me a bright smile and nudging Declan who looks at me and gives me, matching her demeanor.

I look back at Arlo and feel the sudden rush of heat fill my cheeks and face. I can't believe within one summer I found all of this happiness.

With my best friend, my parents, and now Arlo.

He glances at me as he's passing a plate to my mom and gives me another wink.

My person. I've found him and I'm never letting him go.

Epilogue

ARLO

THIRTEEN MONTHS LATER

"ARLO?" Clementine's voice drags me out of my nap and I glance around the bedroom to see that she's standing by the bathroom.

I raise a brow, lifting from the bed and yawning, stretching my arms over my head as I try to remember what day and year it is. That nap was a good one.

I've been working on another new project with a house owner that's about two hours away. There have been times when I needed to book a motel for the night because of how late Frankie, the guys, and I work to get things done by the deadline the owner gave us.

It's my one day off before we're set to finish in two weeks. I decided to come home since I knew Clementine missed me. Rosalía already left for New York about three weeks ago and I knew how lonely she was getting without her best friend.

We were set to visit her in a few weeks in October and to

visit a friend of mine in Jersey too. Speaking of my friend in Jersey, I see the TV is still on and showing recaps of his training. It's hockey pre-season and he's already doing amazing with the New Jersey Jaguars.

"Yeah, *bebita*?" I call out once I'm getting up from the bed. She's already turned back to the bathroom and is making noise as she goes through the cabinets.

"I need to show you something," she says in a muffled voice as she's turned away from me.

"What is it?" I ask, finally making my way to the bathroom and seeing her on her tiptoes looking through the cabinets. I quirk a brow and let my eyes glance over her beautiful body.

She's got on the prettiest pink dress that I will for sure rip off her in the next few minutes if she'll let me.

Clementine finally turns to me and her cheeks are red and she looks like she's been crying, but she doesn't seem sad.

"*Girasol*?" I ask, stepping closer. That's when her eyes glance to the sink and there's something on it.

A stick.

Something I recognize, but haven't seen in a while.

"Wait, is that?" I whisper and she nods. She picks it up daintily as if it'll break before she steps closer to me and I look down at her.

Her lips are chewed almost raw and I lift a hand to caress her cheek before my other goes to the stick in her hands.

The very visible pink plus sign on there is burning through my vision and there's a feeling of happiness that overtakes me.

"Guess you have your wish," she teases, grabbing my hand that's resting on her cheek before pulling it down to her stomach. My big palm practically engulfs her entire stomach and the idea of it getting bigger with *my* child in it makes me giddy. Like a kid opening presents on Christmas.

"*Girasol*," I whisper.

Her giggle fills the room before her eyes get watery. I rub her stomach in soothing motions before moving the pregnancy test to the counter and pulling her close, leaning down to wrap my hands underneath her knees and pulling her up. She instantly wraps her legs around my waist and I twirl us around the bathroom for a moment before she holds me tightly and presses her lips against mine.

"I love you so much, Arlo. And now..." Her voice breaks as she kisses me again and I feel her tears drip on my cheek. I kiss the tears away before pulling back.

"*Girasol, me has dado más de lo que podría pedir. Te amo, mucho. Para siempre. Por el resto de mi vida, Girasol. Ambos. Mi Girasol y mi bebe.*"

"Our baby," she whispers through tears.

I kiss her and she holds me tightly with the kiss. Her lips part and I dive my tongue in. She whimpers and moans and the happiness of it all goes straight to my cock. I want to dive into her again and again.

I'm not sure I'd want to stop after the first baby. My love for *Girasol* is bountiful and I want all of the babies.

"You're looking at me like you want to devour me and also impregnate me again and again," she says, separating our kiss.

"How did you know?" I tease, kissing her neck and licking a long stripe along her sweet and delicious skin. Her hips move to brush against my waist and I groan.

"Just a hunch," she giggles. "We've gotta find a way to tell Rosa..."

We're quiet for a moment before I nod and kiss her cheeks before her lips. "Let's surprise her. When we visit next month."

She smiles brightly and nods. "Okay. Let's do that."

"Together," I say breathlessly.

"*Juntos,*" she giggles.

Her brown eyes catch mine and she giggles again before I walk us out of the bathroom and into the bedroom. I place her on the bed before I kneel down and place my body in between her spread legs.

I grip her thighs before running my hands up to her stomach. She groans before placing her hands over mine where her womb is.

"*Todo mi mundo*," I whisper. She takes a deep breath and her grip on my hands tightens.

"*Para siempre*," she answers back. I look at her and she's got this adorable expression on her face.

And it's for *me*.

My world. My person. My sunflower and reason my heart beats forevermore.

And now I've got another soul to protect and love. And hopefully more in the future.

That's more than I could ever ask for in this lifetime.

THE END

Coming Soon by G. Elena

IN THE WORLD OF *IN DESPERATE RUIN* COMES A SPINOFF SERIES SET IN NEW YORK CITY:

BLACK SILK CLUB

Velvet Rose

Prequel

(Coming 2024)

Book 1

(To Be Announced)

Book 2

(To Be Announced)

Book 3

(To Be Announced)

Coming Soon by G. Elena

IN THE WORLD OF *IN DESPERATE RUIN* COMES A SPINOFF SERIES SET IN SCORPION'S CREEK, MONTANA:

LAGARTO VERDE RANCHO

Roping the Wind

Book 1

(To Be Announced)

Book 2

(To Be Announced)

Book 3

(To Be Announced)

Also by G. Elena

Illicit Acquiescence

A Forbidden Romance

Thank you

I have to start this by thanking you, the reader. Thank you for giving this forbidden romance a chance. If you're a longtime reader of mine or a new one, thank you for choosing to pick up this book. This was a wild ride while writing and I've never had characters talk to me more than Arlo and Clementine. I did not plan those kinks, by the way, they were screamed at me.

To my beta readers Aaliyah, Arielle, Bria, Cassidy, Cathy, Cyndi, Gia, Jessica, Katie, Lila, and Shelby thank you for all you did when this book was in its roughest form. Your constant encouragements helped me so much in the thick of editing.

To my editor Jenni, there are no words to tell you how grateful I am for you and your friendship. I'm so lucky to have you by my side and I'm so happy you take such great care of my manuscripts.

To my proofreader Cassidy, thank you for polishing up my manuscript to make it as perfect as it can be.

To Brianna, thank you for being my unofficial Spanish editor. You're amazing and I hope we can continue to work together on future books!

To Karla, my Rosalía. Thank you for your friendship, laughter, and memories. You were there to hold my hand in the darkest times of my life and I wouldn't be who I am without you. You mean so much to me and I can't wait to continue manifesting great things for our lives.

To Lizzie, I don't know how I would've finished this book without you. Arlo and Clementine would have been an abandoned manuscript without your daily encouragement and support. You have been so vital to my author career, I'm so thankful for you. Here's to many more amazing PR boxes and book launches.

To my wonderful book friends Bianca, Emily, and Shelby you guys have always been there for me and I'm so honored you chose to stick with me even after I left that writing site. I cherish your friendships so much and the love you've given me with each published novel. I can't wait for the future and for the day we meet and hug.

To Kelsey, thank you for your friendship and being so supportive and excited whenever I ranted about a new book I had in the works. Thank you for being there for my wins and for coming with me to see my books at our local bookstore, I will always remember that.

To Emily, thank you for always being here and being a big support. I can't believe we're nearing our ten year mark of being friends very soon. Love you.

To my childhood friends Adna, Angel, Jed, and Nedim, thank you for always rooting for me with these wild dreams.

To Sandy, thank you for always being here and for your almost two decade friendship. I cherish you so much.

To my parents, thank you for always supporting me. Thank you *mamá* for being so proud of me and telling everyone you meet that your daughter is an author. Thank you dad for always being proud. And thank you both for not reading these books, but still showing support in any way you can. *Los amo*.

To Milo, I hope you're proud of me for publishing my third novel. Love you. Always.

About the Author

G. Elena is the forbidden and dark romance pen name for Grace Elena. Please check out her main author page for Romcoms, small town romances, and contemporary romances. She is a Mexican-American author who loves to write with strong Latinx leads.

You can keep up with her on Instagram (graceelenaauthor) or visit her website at graceelenaauthor.com for more insight to her books. If you'd like to get access to sneak peeks to her future novels before anyone else, join her Facebook Private Group "Grace Elena's Vineyard".

Made in the USA
Coppell, TX
06 May 2024